Still Life
with Elephant

Also by Judy Reene Singer

Horseplay

A NOVEL

Still Life with Elephant

with Elephant

Judy Reene Singer

Broadway Books / New York

BROADWAY

PUBLISHED BY BROADWAY BOOKS

Published in the United States by Broadway Books,
an imprint of The Doubleday Broadway Publishing Group,
a division of Random House, Inc., New York.
www.broadwaybooks.com

BROADWAY BOOKS and its logo, a letter B bisected on the diagonal,
are trademarks of Random House, Inc.

Library of Congress Cataloging-in-Publication Data

Singer, Judy Reene.
Still life with elephant : a novel / Judy Reene Singer. —1st ed.
p.   cm.
1. Self-perception—Fiction. 2. Elephants—Fiction. I. Title.
PS3619.I5724S75 2007
813'.6—dc22
2006037099

ISBN 978-0-7679-2677-5

PRINTED IN THE UNITED STATES OF AMERICA

1   3   5   7   9   10   8   6   4   2

First Edition

Neelie, of this book, wanted a daughter more than anything, while I was twice blessed to have had the best daughters ever. I couldn't imagine my life without them. This book is dedicated to my heart and my soul,

Jamie Elisabeth and Robin Laurie.

Acknowledgments

Always at the top of my list, dearest Jane, Jane Gelfman, my agent, who is always supportive and enthusiastic and funny and *honest*. And to Deb Futter, my editor, whom I love, love, love, because she always GETS IT.

A special thank-you to Bunny Brook and her Wild Animal Sanctuary, who graciously permitted me the opportunity to meet and gladly worship at the feet of the magnificent Fritha. And to Fritha, with her wise, sad eyes and gentle soul and mischievous personality, and who suffered terribly as a baby, a burn victim in a tragic war.

To my beloved friend Richie Chiger, who loves Fritha with his heart and soul and who kindly introduced me to Bunny and Fritha and who patiently took tons of pictures and fed Fritha apples and carrots so that she would pose with me.

Thanks to Dr. Lonnie Kasman, DVM, who helped me with the medical aspects of elephant care.

Thanks to Maria, Laura, and (another) Deb, who listened patiently when I read and agonized.

And forever, to Alex, who is always there for me, and doesn't mind when I wake up in the middle of the night to write stuff down, or look at him with glazed eyes while he is talking to me, because I am really somewhere in Zimbabwe.

Still Life with Elephant

. . . **Chapter One** . . .

⌒───WHEN MATT first mentioned her, two years ago, I thought
he said he was getting a collie. And I thought, Great, I love dogs.

I get like that—a little vacant, listening with half an ear. I hear
a snatch of conversation and convert it into something else. I mis-
understand things. Sometimes I'm not listening at all. I can't help
myself. I have a chronic preoccupation with an inner dialogue that
leaves little room for the outside world. I practically go deaf when I
get nervous. I've been this way for a long time, and maybe that was
some of our problem.

"The frog is woebegone," he would say.

"Frog?" I would ask.

And he would put his hands on his hips and give me that look,
before repeating himself. "I said, I won't be gone for long."

.   .   .

So she called me, my husband's colleague—that's what the collie turned out to be. She called to tell me she was pregnant.

Even though I had a radio blasting—I always keep a radio playing nearby—I heard that well enough. There is no mistaking when
someone tells you that she and your husband are pregnant.

"Neelie?" she started, then continued in musical tones. "I'm so
sorry to be the one to tell you, but Matt couldn't bring himself to do
it and you need to know. Matt and I are pregnant. About three
months now."

Isn't that just too cute? Matt and I are pregnant, the way cou-
ples announce it nowadays. When I was a kid, the wife got pregnant

and the husband got a big pat on the back. Now they are pregnant together. So inclusive. Except for me, of course. Matt's wife.

They had been in love for about a year and a half, she said. Maybe two, she couldn't be sure. Which meant it started just a few months after he told me he was taking in a collie to help him with his lions. Lions. I seem to remember that I heard "lions." Which is not so far-fetched; Matt, after all, is a veterinarian, and he sometimes helps out at a wild-animal sanctuary about ten miles from us.

He was taking in a colleague to help him with his clients.

And his love life. She apparently was taking care of his love life as well.

◦   ◦   ◦

Her name was Holly, and she was a small-animal specialist, and she was recuperating from a divorce, looking to relocate from Colorado, and wanting to join a practice in New York, in the small town where her parents lived. Where we lived. I found all of that out at the welcoming dinner I cooked for her in our home. She looked like she had just breezed in from a day on the Aspen slopes. Blond hair, lean workout body, crisp blue eyes. Big-Sky blue eyes, although I know Big-Sky is really Montana. She mentioned that she liked crafting. I was surprised, because she looked so outdoorsy.

"I'd never take you to do crafting," I said.

"Rafting," Matt said, exchanging glances with her.

"White-water rafting," she said, tossing her blonde, Colorado-outdoor-sun-bleached hair, her Big-Sky eyes now looking vastly amused at me. Of course. Who does white-water crafting? In my defense, I was whipping the cream for a lovely chocolate-cream pie, which is my signature dessert. Which she declined, because she DIDN'T LIKE CHOCOLATE.

I mean, come on.

I guess she wanted to keep that lean, sinewy-cat, predatory figure, because she was certainly still on the prowl. I just didn't know it.

I had a slice of pie, and Matt asked for a *very thin* slice, which he never did, he loves my pie, and maybe I should have sniffed out something suspicious right then and there.

They worked well together. Matt always said that. She just seemed to anticipate what needed to be done next, and had it finished before he asked. She was full of energy and great ideas. She was a good surgeon, she was a good diagnostician, she was good with the clients.

She was very good with Matt.

• • •

I love horses, and that's how Matt and I met. It was ten years ago. I was twenty-eight and had a decent private practice as a therapist with a master's in social work. I owned a horse, though I rarely rode him. I was in one of those stupid circular dilemmas that horsepeople get into. I needed to work to pay for my horse's upkeep, but couldn't ride him much because I was working such long hours to pay for his upkeep. So he was more of a pasture potato.

His name was Mousi, which was short for Maestoso Ariela, which, I must admit, is a weird name for a male horse, but he was a Lipizzaner, and they are named for both their mothers and fathers. It's a very egalitarian way to do things, like the Norwegians, who do it with "sen" and "datter" tacked onto their surnames. No one gets left out that way.

Mousi was colicking. He was sixteen, and he was my whole world, and now he was nipping at his sides and rolling back his upper lip like a wine connoisseur at a tasting. I knew right away it was the sign of a belly ache. My old veterinarian had just retired, and I needed to find someone new. Matt had been practicing in the area for a while, and I had heard from horse friends that he was good and cute. I mean, a good vet and cute. But he was also good and cute. He came out to the barn right away, which is very important for a colic, and quickly got Mousi comfortable. I liked the way he worked. Quiet and sure of himself, gentle with Mousi, and very skillful when he had to pass the nasogastric tube to pump warm water and mineral oil into Mousi's belly.

"I guess he was a quart low," he joked, as Mousi's colic eased. I liked his sense of humor.

When we were finished, I grabbed my wallet to pay him.

He said, "Doodle gate?"

"Is that like Watergate?" I asked. "With cartoons?"

"Watergate?" He gave me a puzzled look. One of those puzzled looks that tip me off that I haven't really heard things right.

"Date," he said. "Do you date?"

"Yes," I said, embarrassed, busying myself with something crucial, like arranging the bills in my wallet in denominational order.

•   •   •

We liked each other right away. I didn't demand much from our relationship, and he was distracted most of the time anyway, busy building the equine part of the practice. I wasn't quite there, he wasn't quite there, and it was a good fit. We fell in love. We got married.

Six years later, he bought the practice out from the retiring senior partner. It was a large practice by now, and getting larger. Things were going great. And then we tried to have children. It didn't happen for us, and we even went to a fertility specialist, who tested everything from the hair inside our nostrils to the carpeting in our bedroom. After several long months, we found ourselves sitting in his office, facing him at his desk, while he sat with our papers in front of him, a potentate holding court, handing out the grave pronouncement of infertility. Matt had sperm clowns, he announced. I immediately pictured Matt's testicles hosting a kind of Comedy Central, and giggled a little. Matt and the fertility doctor both looked at me. There is nothing funny about a low sperm count.

But I guess those clowns came through when he needed them.

•   •   •

After Holly and I spoke, I hung up the phone. Actually, I didn't hang up, I just put the phone down on the kitchen table and walked away from it, walked out of the house and straight to the barn, like one of the zombie people in _Dawn of the Dead_. Grace, my Boston terrier, followed, looking worried.

I tacked up Mousi and walked him around the ring, and asked him if he thought Matt was going to come home that night. Mousi is pretty wise for a horse. How do you start a divorce? I asked him. Because there was no question now, that was what I was going to do. How will I get through it? How do I wake up every morning knowing Matt is gone? And what happens afterward? Do I move to Colorado and break up someone else's marriage, sort of like a reciprocal trade agreement?

I rode Mousi around the riding ring on a loose rein and continued to talk to him. Horses are terrific to talk to, because you don't have to strain to listen for answers. They never lie. Mousi just listened, flicking his white ears back and forth like semaphores, and I knew he was being very sympathetic.

We had a long conversation.

How many times had I invited Holly over for dinner? I asked Mousi. Dozens! How many times had I sent my best Tupperware containers to the office, filled with extra food for her, because the poor thing never had time to cook? Dozens! How many times did we include her in our plans because Matt said she was lonely? How many times had I helped Matt pick out just the right Christmas, birthday, thank-you-for-working-late gift? Ha! And all the while, I told Mousi, all the while, behind my back—all the while—she and Matt—well—

Those collies, you can never trust them.

⁓‌‌‌‌‌ "**S**o—HE didn't come home last night?" Alana asked me. She is my dearest, closest friend, and I had called her early the following morning.

I was holding my breath to stop the hiccupping that was the result of too much crying, which was how I had spent the whole night.

"Nooo," I answered, releasing a cascade of pent-up hiccups. "He never came home."

"What a bastard!" she proclaimed. "You'd think he would have done the right thing and called you himself."

"The right thing would have been not to screw her."

"What a snake," she said. "And a coward," she added. "You'll never be able to dust his chicken."

"Dust his chicken?"

"Trust him again," she said.

"The thing is"—I hiccupped—"I trusted her, too. She came into my home. She ate my food." Hiccup. "I even trusted her with my mother's secret recipe for fruit stollen." Hiccup, hiccup.

"I would think you'd be more upset that you trusted her with Matt," Alana said dryly.

"Well, I trusted Matt first, of course," I said. "I trusted him to uphold his end of our marriage. If I trusted him, I shouldn't have to worry about trusting anyone who's with him." I then excused myself to grab my third box of tissues in twenty-four hours.

"So now what?" Alana asked when I got back to the phone.

I didn't know.

I kept thinking about when I finally did get pregnant. Last year. It was after four in-vitros. And it wound up being ectopic. I went through an emergency operation and lost an ovary and a fallopian tube, after which the surgeon came in, and said very matter-of-factly, "Sorry, but we lost your ovary and a tube," like, Oops, where did I put those damn things, anyway?

I thought how very ectopic this all was getting now. So ectopic that now Matt's baby was in someone else's uterus.

"You want me to come over and spend a few days?" Alana asked.

"No," I said, "you have your own family to worry about. And I need to be by myself."

"You should have someone around you," she said. "You should be able to walk a shoe in some gum."

I didn't ask her what she meant. I reheard it later in my head: she had said, Talk it through with someone.

I spent the next three days alone with my stack of CDs, playing mostly stuff by *Black Sabbath*. I was angry. Sad. Angry. Sad. Furious. I didn't do my usual morning jelly-donut-and-coffee run, which I even managed to do two years ago after I had broken my right leg. At the time, I just used my left leg for both pedals, on a manual-shift truck, because I have to have my jelly donuts.

Matt didn't call. And I wasn't about to call him. What would I say? "How exciting that you're finally able to start a family! Need help picking out names?"

Matt didn't e-mail, write, telegraph, send up a smoke signal, or in any way let me know that he was sorry or repentant or still alive. It was as though he had disappeared into a black hole. Or maybe I had. Because it felt like I had just stepped off the curb and fallen into a deep abyss of disbelief and misery. Was he still going to work? With *her*? Like it just was any regular, ordinary day, except that he was just coming home to a different person at night?

I hoped she was puking ten times a day and gaining weight like a brood mare.

It was Thursday, three days after Holly's phone call, when I finally heard from Matt. "I didn't know she was going to do that," he said, by way of apology.

"Do what?" I asked. "Get pregnant or call me?"

"Actually, both," he said. "I was horrified when she told me. I just couldn't face you."

"And if she hadn't called, this would have—what?—just continued until the kid went off to college? I mean, she's already three months pregnant. I trusted—" My throat closed around my vocal cords, and all I could do was produce a strangled sound, like a seal.

"Neelie, I'm so sorry," he said. "I'm not even staying with her. I'm staying in a motel. Until we can talk. You and me. We need to talk."

"What's there to talk about?" I asked.

"I was—I don't know." He took a deep breath. "The practice was getting so busy, and I was under a lot of pressure. So stressed out, and she and I were together every night until late, and you—"

I knew that he had been getting home late. Later every week. I was leaving nice dinners for him on the kitchen counter. Love notes in his underwear while he showered in the morning, even though he had been too exhausted to have sex with me for weeks. There were phone calls during lunch, made from my cell phone while I was atop a rearing horse, for God's sake, to keep things good between us. To keep the connection.

"You were having an affair with her when I lost the baby!" I gasped, my outrage slamming my heart into my lungs.

He didn't answer. "I felt we were drifting," he finally said. "I was getting mooned."

Maybe it was marooned—I had stopped listening by now. Then I hung up.

And I realized that I had not only been deaf, I had also been blind.

Chapter Three

We are all somebody's rescues. Grace, my Boston terrier. Alley, my cat. And even Mousi. All rescues. I rescue friends from hard times, and families from crisis. I went to school to be a social worker. I was trained to rescue.

I won't bore you with all my rescues, or the details. Except that I found Grace in the middle of the road while on my way to work and Alley as a kitten, half frozen, next to the donut shop.

"Damn disposable mentality," Matt said with some disgust when I rushed Grace to his office so he could fix her broken jaw. She was maybe five months old, and we put ads everywhere and waited for someone to claim her. No one did, and I named her Grace because she was gracious enough to forgive half of the human race and love me unconditionally. I say half the human race because, after her jaw healed, all men, except for Matt, became the brunt of her fury and the recipients of her sharp little teeth, which she usually implanted somewhere below their knees if they dared to step into the house.

I found Mousi in the hands of an abusive trainer and bought him on the spot.

I suppose that I took a little satisfaction in thinking I had rescued Matt in some way. He was lonely, and he was hungry for family. He had been an only child, and had lost his parents early in life. He wanted to come home to someone, to belong somewhere. He wanted to be able to call and tell someone that he was going to be late, and have her care about it and say, "Okay, hon, I'll be waiting." He wanted to be able to say, "Oh, I'd better check first with my wife."

I gave him all that and more. I gave him a home and meals and holidays where we had to be someplace by noon, and in-laws and love. God, I loved him. I gave him my extra pillow when his neck hurt. I gave him the last piece of chocolate pie. I turned off the radio that I always kept playing, because he liked the house quiet when he got home. I left the window open in the winter because he liked to sleep cold. I *gave* him cold air!

He rescued me, too, in a sense. From being alone. From the dark sweep that overtook me because I hadn't found my way back to riding professionally yet.

Maybe Holly thought she was rescuing Matt as well. Poor overworked, underappreciated Matt, trapped in a marriage with a woman who left him alone every summer for two whole weeks at a time, so she could bring her students to silly horse shows. Handsome, deliciously unavailable Matt. It must have warmed her heart to rescue him from all that.

＊   ＊   ＊

He called me again on Friday. I was out riding a horse I had gotten in for retraining. I kept my cell phone clipped to the side pocket of my britches, in vibration mode, so it wouldn't startle the horse. I felt the buzz and asked the horse I was riding to halt, so I could check the phone. The horse wouldn't halt. She backed up, shifted herself sideways, leapt forward, then gave a series of tiny half-rears, but I got a glimpse of the phone number. It was Matt, calling from his cell, which he normally keeps plugged into his car. It meant he didn't want to use his office phone. I looked at the number and clipped the phone onto my pocket again to let the voice mail take it. I would delete it later without listening to it.

I was riding Isis, a big chestnut horse with brown coin dapples, and she hated to halt. That's why she was sent to me. She wouldn't stand still at the halt. Instead, she jumped around like Baryshnikov. I suppose somebody once tried to teach her to piaffe, an advanced dressage movement where they prance in place, and now she fretted about it all the time. So I sat on her, patting her neck and waiting. I thought about Matt and how I used to reach over and pat his hand in bed, and how he would pull it over his heart. It meant he loved me, but was too sleepy to say the words. Sometimes he pulled it down over his penis and held it there, which meant he wanted me but was too sleepy to do anything about it, and we would fall asleep like that.

Ten minutes passed and I just sat there. Twenty. I didn't ask Isis to do anything. I just let my seat slump down into the saddle. I made sure I barely touched her with my legs; I kept the reins quiet. I thought about Matt and let the tears roll down my face.

Isis never suspected how upset her rider was. She had her own problems to worry about. And I sat there, realizing that I really would have to talk to Matt again at some point. I would have to pay attention to his words.

·   ·   ·

This is why I train horses. They don't speak words, they just move. They lift their heads, twitch their ears, swish a tail, lean to one side or the other. They run away. Or they don't move forward at all and rear straight up. It all means something. I understand conversations like this. Horses speak volumes without saying a word. They never lie. They never say, "Sorry, hon, we had this emergency come in at the last minute. I'll be late," and then screw around.

I listened politely to what Isis was telling me with her body, and then I told her my side of the story. What I wanted her to do for me. All without a word being exchanged. I understood Isis when she hopped around after I asked her to halt. She was telling me that when she used to halt someone had bashed her with a whip, to make her prance. Now she was afraid to stand still. So I sat there and told her, with my body, that we were just going to stand there and do nothing until she relaxed.

I checked my watch. It was twenty-five minutes before she started chewing at the bit and let out the long snort-sigh that told me she finally understood me. She dropped her head and stood still. I dismounted immediately, which was her reward. Then I reached into my pocket and took out a sugar cube and gave her a treat. She had learned something. She had made a decision to trust me, and I was honored.

I had made a decision, too, by that time.

*   *   *

I called Alana when I got back to the house. "I need help," I said. "I have some major cleaning to do."

"What exactly are you planning to clean?" I could hear the suspicion in her voice.

"Just some stuff. Are you in?"

"Is this the sponging of rats?"

"Why would I sponge rats?"

"Expunging of Matt?"

"Exactly."

*   *   *

Alana got a babysitter for her two little girls, brought over an extra-garlic pizza, and spent the rest of that day and most of the night helping me clean every bit of Matt from the house. Every piece of clothing, every sock, every picture. She even helped me haul his favorite recliner to the curb. If I could have scraped off his DNA from everything he ever touched, I would have done that, too. I kept thinking about his remark about the disposable society we live in, and the irony of it. He had disposed of me. Neat and fast, moving right on to family number two.

"Damn disposable mentality," he had said, and, unwittingly, I became part of it. I guess everything is disposable, because now I was cutting his photos out of albums, shredding his shirts, stretching out his sweaters, tying knots in his tighty whities, and then bringing everything to the curb, where it would sit, unrescued, until the garbage truck came to whisk it away. Irony. Irony.

There was one last box, up in the attic, and it contained his stuff from vet school. Some books, an old stethoscope, a stained lab coat, a large picture of his graduating class in a plain black frame. I sat

down in the old broken Windsor chair that we had planned to refin-
ish someday, and studied his picture. There he was, standing in the
white lab coat, in the back row, because he's tall, looking very young
and serious, with a mustache. I had never seen him with his mustache, and he looked so different from the current Matt. He must
have shaved it off after he graduated. It made him hard to recognize,
but it was him. Then I looked closer.

And found out his secret.

Chapter Four

SECRETS ARE like plants. They can stay buried deep in the earth for a long time, but eventually they'll send up shoots and give themselves away. They have to. It's their nature. Just a tiny green stem at first. Which slowly, insidiously grows taller, stronger, unfolding itself, until there it is. A big fat secret, right in front of your face; a fully bloomed flower perfumed with the scent of deception.

I had Matt's picture from vet school in front of me, and I was scrutinizing every inch of it, like a microscope specimen.

I never knew that Matt and Holly had been classmates. They were standing next to each other. She had her chin tilted up, and her long, sun-streaked hair was blowing sideways. She was all white teeth, wide smile, heart-shaped face. He was looking at her, intent and serious. I know that look, and I had to turn the picture over and put it down.

"That's probably why she called him for a job in the first place," Alana said, taking the picture from me and studying it. "They had a history."

"He never told me that he knew her before," I said. I felt sick. Then I tore the picture up and dropped it into a green plastic trash bag. That's where histories go.

*   *   *

"Am I so ugly?" I asked Alana when we were finished. We were having tea in the kitchen, well after midnight. She had clients to counsel in the morning and her husband to get home to, and she had to leave soon. The radio was playing Vivaldi very softly in the background. I like Vivaldi because he's undemanding. You don't need to think him through. When you listen to Vivaldi, you can squash your feelings down and let the music fill in the spaces with its controlled, you-always-know-where-it's-going progressions.

"You're very pretty," she said. "Matt's crazy to leave you." I looked at my face in the bowl of the spoon that I was using to stir sugar into my tea. I have nice features. I have long, thick brown hair and green eyes. I am slim. I have a rider's body. My childhood trainer always complimented me like that. "You have a rider's body," she would say. The first time she said it, I was eleven, and I thought she meant there was something wrong with me. I had the beginning of breasts and hips, which I hated, and had just started my period, which I hated, and now, of all things, I had a rider's body. But she meant I was short-waisted, with long legs to wrap around the sides of the horse. "You are all legs," she would say. All legs. And then I thought, Great—because riding was going to be my life.

All legs, I think now. Did that preclude brains?

"I guess I look okay," I mumbled.

"I always thought you were striking," Alana said. "I wish I had your figure."

Alana is short and very rotund, with curly peach-colored hair and light-blue eyes and freckles. I wish I had her serenity.

And her two daughters. I was hoping to have a daughter.

We drank our tea in silence, except for an occasional burp from one or the other of us, thanks to the extra garlic on the pizza.

"Holly is something that should be hung. That's what you do with Holly," Alana finally said with some disgust. "Who the hell names a kid Holly?"

"Don't talk to me about naming kids right now," I said.

We ate a few slices of pizza in silence. "I should have gotten two pizzas," Alana finally said after we each tried to put dibs on the last slice. "This is definitely a two-pizza night."

"You can have it," I relented. "Because you're my friend."

"Well, as your friend, I have more advice," she said, sprinkling a little salt on the last slice. "Protect your finances. The house. Accounts. Double-check any CDs you might have. Make sure they are intact."

"What would Matt want with my music?" I asked her.

She rolled her eyes at me. "Bank accounts, honey. Certificates of deposit."

"Oh." I flapped my hand at her. "Matt wouldn't do anything unethical."

"Except get another woman pregnant," she pointed out.

"Money is different," I said. "There is no raging hormonal drive for money."

"That we know of," said Alana.

*   *   *

I took Alana's advice, and the very next day I checked with my bank. The clerk was very sweet and efficient and spent a very long time looking at the screen of her computer before walking away and coming back with the manager. I knew what that meant. She didn't want to be the bearer of bad news.

"All your accounts have been closed," the manager said, double-checking the screen. "The CDs are cashed out; 401s are cashed out. The only thing you have open is your checking account. The balance is two hundred and twenty-eight dollars and seventy-five cents."

"How can that be?" I asked, breathless with shock. I grabbed the counter between us to keep from slumping to the floor.

"Dr. Sterling did it all chipmunks to go," she said, impatient to hurry me along since it was Saturday and they were closing soon.

I think she said "six months ago," but what did it matter? Everything we had worked for was gone. I turned away so she wouldn't see my tears. I barely made it to my car. If there was a word beyond "stunned," I was it. I felt stunned and bludgeoned. Blunned, maybe. I hadn't suspected a thing. But then I did something I had sworn I wasn't going to do.

I got a lawyer.

*   *   *

If I were still counseling clients, I would have told the offended wife, if she wanted to salvage the relationship, to initiate a dialogue between herself and the errant spouse. To take some responsibility for the loss of communication. To consider several strategies, which would be proposed by me with great confidence, until she found the one that worked. Did she want to be self-righteous or did she want to be happy? Commence the healing process, I would have advised, and work on moving forward with it.

Great advice.

Buzz words.

When I had my practice, I found it getting harder and harder to force myself to concentrate on the problems that my clients were bringing to me. Harder to pay attention to them, to care about their words. Their sentences started to sound like those spam e-mails you get when the subject is a bunch of nonsense words designed to fool your spam filter. Snoxhill cannonball snow juice. Perimeter apple feet platinum. I didn't want to listen anymore.

People are all about words. Sentences, paragraphs, pauses, expectations. Demands. I needed to get away from all of it. Matt encouraged me to ride again. We were doing pretty well financially, he said, and he encouraged me to find my way back to what I really loved. I felt so lucky that he understood. I closed my practice and recommended Alana to all my clients. And I stumbled toward something I had once turned away from.

I have an affinity for solving problems. Troubled people. Troubled horses. They are not so different. I knew I would be able to turn the lives of problem horses around and spare them from getting passed from owner to owner or, worse, ending up in a slaughterhouse.

I _needed_ to save horses. I needed very much to save horses.

That was my secret.

Chapter Five

It GAVE me great satisfaction to tell Matt that there was nothing left in the house that belonged to him. The garbage had been collected the day before, taking everything that Alana and I had set neatly on the curb. Matt was on the phone and asking if he could at least drop by. I put my pitchfork down from mucking stalls, so I could concentrate on our conversation.

"Would tomorrow be convenient?" he asked. "I could be in and out before you know it. I'll just take my clothes."

"You have to get new clothes," I said. "To go with your new life. In fact, you need to get new everything, because there's nothing left here for you. But since you took all our money, I'm sure that won't be a problem."

He sucked his breath in sharply. "Nothing? My books? My— *Nothing?*"

"Nothing."

"Did you put it all in storage for me?" He can be dense sometimes.

"Yep, long-term storage at the garbage dump. Sort of like where you threw our marriage."

"Have you gone crazy?" His voice rose with anger. "Didn't you think I was going to need anything?"

"Oops, I forgot," I said. "Somehow I wasn't thinking of your needs. Sorry to be so inconsiderate." I was loving this now.

There was a long pause. "I told you I was sorry," he finally said. "I *am* sorry. Can you even hear me with that radio blasting? I don't know what else to say. I love you and I screwed up."

"I hear you fine," I replied. "And forgetting to take the truck in for an oil change is screwing up. Fucking someone and getting them pregnant, when you are both adults and professionals in a *medical* field, is—unforgivable. It's the—the *planning* of it—the sneaki-ness—the—"

"I get it," he interrupted me. "I get it. I am *abjectly* sorry. I don't know what else to say."

"I guess I can hang up, then," I said, brightly. "I'll have my lawyer get in touch with you."

"Wait! Neelie?" he called out. I put the phone back to my ear. "What?"

"I don't want a divorce," he said. He sounded miserable. "I love you. I never wanted a divorce."

"Did you think we were going to be a cozy foursome?" I snapped. "You, me, Good-Golly-Miss-Holly, and little *Hollikins?*"

"Oh God," he said. "Don't talk like that. Please."

"Have I offended your sensibilities?" I asked in a delicate, phony British accent. "So sorry. I meant the future Mrs. Dr. Matt Sterling and *family."* I felt nauseated now, like I had overindulged in ice cream. It wasn't fun anymore.

"I want to be with you," he said. "Maybe we can work something out. We can always make custard on the train with her."

"I don't eat custard," I said, clicked off, and turned my radio up even louder. I was into my mucking half an hour when what he said rearranged itself in my brain. Custody arrangements.

* * *

Isis was waiting for me in her stall. "Don't ever get a cell phone," I said to her, clipping the phone to my pocket. "They're a bloody nui-sance." I picked up a brush and rubbed circles against her orange-brown hair. She pushed back, obviously enjoying the attention. I brushed her face very gently, then moved the brush down her neck and chest and across her shoulders. Up across her back. I was brushing her sides when I found them. Her own secrets. A crisscross of thin, ridged lines. Old scars that ran down her flanks, extending to her rump. She flinched as I ran my fingers across them.

"You didn't deserve this," I told her, and reached down to get a softer brush. She nipped me on my shoulder as I turned away from her, just catching my sweatshirt in her teeth.

"You're right," I said. "It sucks."

I tacked her up, locked Grace in a stall, and swung myself into the saddle, steering Isis toward the trails that run along the back of our property. I didn't want Grace to follow, because she sometimes forgets and runs off on secret missions to rid the world of squirrels. Twice I've had to bail her out of the pound while she sat there like a repentant convict. I wanted my full attention on Isis.

We walked a long time before I asked Isis to halt. I was curious to see if she would connect halting out there, in the middle of the trail, given trees and low fragrant brush, and mossy footing, and birds singing in the branches above our heads, with halting in a training ring. She stopped, hesitated for a moment, then backed up and pranced sideways. She broke into a sweat from nerves.

Old secrets are hard to give up. I know only too well. I just kept bringing her gently back to a halt, then tried to sit there quietly. I asked her to halt again. Sat. Asked for the halt. Waited. Ten minutes passed. The birds stopped singing and jumped down to the lower branches to check out this odd sight in the middle of their woods. This large horse-human chimera. A deer halted in its tracks, not more than three feet away, and stared at us with large moony eyes. Isis chewed the bit in her mouth and tossed her head up and down, almost hitting me in the face.

"I know," I said to her. "But they were wrong."

Twenty minutes this time, before she finally sighed and stood there. The sweat dried up on her body, her neck relaxed, and we walked back to the barn.

*   *   *

Matt was waiting for me. My insides were screaming out how much I loved him. He has sandy hair and hazel eyes. He has the long fingers of a good surgeon, strong but gentle, extending from wide hands. He has wide shoulders that I used to press my head against and feel like he was my wall, protecting me from all the things I couldn't name. He has small love handles. His face is long and refined, betraying his Norwegian ancestry. He has a straight nose.

He had turned my radio very low, and the first thing I did was turn it back up so I could ignore him, more or less, though I had to step around him when I put Isis on the cross-ties. Then I let Grace out of the stall and got to work. There is always a ton of things to do in a barn, to occupy or preoccupy, depending on how you look at it.

"Can we go in the house and sit down and talk?" Matt asked over the music. Stravinsky now, the *Firebird*, discordant and jagged, which was pretty much the way I felt. Matt looked contrite and worried and very unhappy. Grace was making an absolute fool of herself, standing on her hind legs and scratching at his knees, frantically licking his fingers, delighted to see him again. "Please?" he added.

I spun around. "Why didn't you ever tell me that you and Holly went to school together?" I said, choking over the words.

He stepped back. "I—it was—over. She dumped me," he said. "She married someone in Colorado. It wasn't something I wanted to talk about."

"So this was your way of—what?"—I asked, fighting for control—"forgiving her? By taking her back?"

He gestured helplessly. "I don't know what I was thinking," he said. "I— There was no closure." He looked bewildered, puzzled. As though he was taken by surprise as well. It was all I could do to keep myself from comforting him, from apologizing for my anger. He had no right to look so pathetic.

"Well, consider this your closure," I finally said, turning my back on him. "Good-bye." I untacked Isis, brushed her, put her sheet over her, and put her in her stall with some hay. I gave Mousi and Conversano, my other horse, a few carrots. Then I carried the saddle into the tack room, put it on the saddle rack, and took out a small bucket, a bar of saddle soap, and a sponge. He knew I was wasting time now. I haven't cleaned my tack in five years.

"It all got so complicated," he said, taking the bucket out of my hand. "Please, let's talk." I hated that there were tears in my eyes. "Come on. Please," he said to me, his voice tender and cajoling, and he looked at me with that look that made me fall in love with him ten years ago. That sweet-eyed, want-to-touch-his-lips-with-my-fingers look. I was screaming inside how much I loved him.

I looked into his eyes. Our eyes locked.

And I slapped him.

Chapter Six

I SEEM to horrify my mother on a regular basis. She was thrilled when I was invited to train at the Olympic Team Headquarters for a spot on the Young Riders Team, because she had been my greatest fan, then she was horrified when I totally stopped riding two months later. She was proud when I got my degrees in social work, and started my career in something academic and professional, like my two brothers, and then was horrified when I closed my practice. She was delighted when I married Matt, and now she was horrified because I told her that Matt and I were divorcing. She was doubly horrified when I told her that Matt had emptied our joint checking account and cashed in all our CDs and bonds and savings accounts and maybe even our foreign-coin collection, although I hadn't checked that yet.

"How can this be?" she asked me five or six times. We were in her kitchen, and I was helping her make bread. She makes the best bread—raisin, multigrain, fruit-and-nut, cheddar-jalapeño—and usually makes a dozen loaves or so at a time, to give away, because she is in charge of the local Loaves to the World charity. They collect other foodstuff, too, because, as my mother likes to say, one can't live by bread alone. But bread is her passion and her secret vanity, since she and her archrival, Evelyn Slater, are always trying to out-bake each other. And she disdains bread machines. "The loaves come out looking like apartment houses," she says about bread machines. So, every time I visit her, I wind up kneading and rolling and shaping and braiding the compliant, warm, almost fleshy-feeling dough.

"What's going on?" she asked me, a variation of her earlier question. I couldn't bring myself to explain the whole thing, it made me feel like the dough I was pummeling down, too soft, too vulnerable.

"It's because you tune people out," she said, taking the dough from me and kneading in four varieties of nuts. "I told you that a long time ago. You're there and you're not there. Sometimes it's like talking to a wall. Maybe Matt felt it, too."

"Don't defend Matt," I said, handing her loaf pans, so the bread could rise again. I refused to think how symbolic it was, the bread taking a pummeling and rising again—I was beyond metaphors.

"I don't know what I'm defending him against." She stopped and pushed her hair back. She's attractive in a thin, hair-sprayed-mom kind of way. She and my father have been married for almost forty-two years and are happy. I have two brothers, the older happily married, the younger happily single. I had two sets of grandparents growing up, a happy foursome when they were alive. I have happy aunts and uncles. Happy, happy, happy. I think that's what fascinated Matt. That we all like being in each other's company, there were no major issues, except for my one brother liking to hunt. I grew up feeling loved and happy. I rode happy.

"I thought you two had a cheese bomb," she said.

"Cheese bomb?"

"Cheese bomb! Good God, Neelie." She shook her head. "Deep bond. That you two were so happy. And that's just what I mean about listening." I watched her brush the loaves with egg white and put them in the oven. Her lips made a thin line across her face.

*   *   *

"Take a loaf home with you," she said a few hours later, wrapping one in aluminum foil and sticking it into a bag for me. "Next time you come, I'll make you some homemade jelly donuts. You're getting too skinny. Aren't you eating?"

Actually, no. I had no appetite. I hadn't done my donut run in two weeks. Okay, maybe I went twice. Instead of eating, I was drinking coffee all day long. I chewed gum. Or I would stick a strand of hay in my mouth and curl it around with my tongue while I worked in the barn. It was because I was missing Matt like crazy, but we hadn't spoken since the day I walloped him.

＊　　＊　　＊

I got home just in time to meet with a horse client. She was in her truck, her horse trailer hitched to the back of it, and waiting for me in my driveway. I opened the gates and she drove her rig through. A brand-new truck and trailer, navy with red-painted doodads. She wore a navy-and-red sweater, navy britches, and horse bling: earrings with little rubies set in gold, and a gold horse sweater-pin. New horse-owner, I thought with some amusement. And I just *knew* that the horse's leg wraps and blanket would perfectly match his owner's outfit. Of course, all my stuff matched, too. After you've owned horses for a while, you can still match your clothes to your horse equipment, but in a different way. Everything you own is dirty and hairy with holes in it.

＊　　＊　　＊

The horse was a bay gelding. Mahogany-brown hair, black mane and tail, two white hind socks. Very flashy. And very obnoxious. His owner's strategy for unloading him was to unclip his head gingerly, drop the tailgate of the truck, and let the horse scramble out backward, while she screamed and ran for cover in the front seat. He finished his grand exit with a rear and strike, all duded up in his navy wraps, matching navy-trimmed red blanket, and red nylon halter.

"Can you fix him in a month?" his owner asked me, making sure I had him under control before she left the safety of the truck.

I grappled with his lead line, trying to keep him from rearing. "I don't know," I yelled over my shoulder. "I'll try."

"My daughter is afraid of him," she yelled back.

Smart girl.

The horse's name was Delaney, eight years old. He had somehow learned that he could get out of work by throwing his front end up in the air and then running away as soon as he touched back down. The woman had purchased him for a lot of money, only to find that he had this odd little quirk of being totally unridable.

"Rearers and kids don't mix," I had told her over the phone. "It's an accident waiting to happen." As far as I was concerned, rearers are like cars with blown transmissions, and you were morally obligated to let the owner know. She agreed to put him up for sale to a professional rider, after I retrained him, and now he was rearing himself toward my barn in gravity-defying leaps.

I led him to his stall and then looked over his health records. His back had been checked for soreness, his legs and feet were fine, eyes and teeth in good working order. Apparently, the only thing wrong with him was his crappy attitude. The woman shook my hand.

"Good luck with him," she said. "You have a terrific reputation."

I nodded and looked back at the horse. He was busy spooking at his stall door.

"I have someone interested in buying him," she said. "So—try not to hurt him."

"I don't do that," I answered. She looked relieved and jumped back into her truck. I opened the gate again to let her out.

"Your berries are contagious," she called out, waving good-bye to me.

I waved back.

The problem is, I'm not courageous at all.

. . . Chapter Seven . . .

WHO INVENTED night anyway? It's just day, slowly losing consciousness. Night closes in like death, your vision fails, things go bump, you escape into sleep, and if you can't sleep, you are trapped in nothingness.

At eleven that night, I had a peanut-butter-and-jelly sandwich and went into my bedroom, where I had a DVD playing Mozart. Not the *Elvira Madigan* one, I wouldn't have been able to bear that, just a few controlled little piano pieces that didn't need attending to. Actually, I stood in the doorway of my bedroom and just stared in. The sight of my empty bed felt like a reproach, like it was telling me that Matt was with *her* right now. That he was taking her hand and moving it across his body, and holding it there. And just the thought of it—

I finally sat down on the edge of the bed to think. He had been screwing her for almost two years. When had it started? When he closed his equine practice and began specializing in small animals? It seemed to me that there was a connection.

He had made the decision to switch to small animals without even discussing it with me. Not unusual for him. Sometimes he was distant and busy, like he was phoning in his half of the marriage. And that's not counting the times when he was distant and not so busy. But it was always okay with me. I had my own long-distance phone plan going on, as well. When I questioned him about dropping his equine clients, he shrugged it off.

"Money," he said. "I'm putting together a really good business strategy to take advantage of the fact that small-animal vets make more than equine vets."

I knew that part of it was true. Equine vets work long hours—driving in the middle of the night to get to an emergency, then driving to the next barn, miles away. Standing in bitter-cold half-lit barns in the middle of winter, trying to treat large hard-to-manage animals. Vets stand in mud puddles. They stand in hot, dusty paddocks in the blazing heat of summer. The time they spend driving from barn to barn is unproductive and they don't get paid for it. Sometimes they get to a barn and no one is there to help, and they are in the unique predicament of having to lasso their patients before treating them. The odd hours wear a lot of equine vets down. They get terrible back problems from holding up horse legs or wrestling medicine down their patients' throats. In addition, they get kicked at and stomped on, rare for practitioners of human medicine.

Still, Matt's decision took me by surprise, because I thought he loved the work. I thought he loved it more than we needed money. We were doing okay. Now I realized that it was probably a decision he made with Holly-Greedy. Or for Holly because she complained about his being out of the office so much. She wasn't much for farm work because she would have gotten mud on her Gucci loafers. And all the while, I hadn't suspected a thing. I thought he had done it for us, so I could continue to build up my horse business.

*   *   *

It was too quiet, even with Mozart. Grace jumped on the bed and settled down on Matt's pillow, and promptly fell asleep. Her snores accompanied Sonata No. 15 in C. Alley Cat was on his other pillow, purring and doing her kneading routine, which reminded me of my mother making yeast bread. I scratched Grace behind the ears and thought maybe I would get a few more dogs, and another cat or two, so they could fill up Matt's entire side of the bed. I definitely needed more warm bodies. And more horses to keep me busy. More something.

I threw myself back against my pillows and waited for sleep.

*   *   *

There is a peace that comes when I am with an animal. I don't have to strain to listen to words, I don't feel pressured. They speak volumes, without one word passing between us. And I can feel the tightness across my shoulders ease, feel the clench in my jaw, the coil of memory that winds around the inside of my head, unwrap itself. I keep the music playing for the same reason. So I don't have to think. So I don't have to listen to my own head.

Three a.m., and I realized that I wasn't going to sleep. I pulled on my sweats and sneakers and went out to the barn to check on the horses. Grace followed.

It's spiritual for me, the darkness, the soft sighing when the horses are lying down, or chewing their hay. Mousi always makes a nest for himself with his hay, then settles down in the middle of it like a big white marshmallow, so he can be cushioned while slipping strands out from underneath his great body. Isis stands in a corner, her head pressed under her hay rack to protect her from everything. Conversano, my three-year-old, still sleeps like a foal, flat on his side. He isn't saddle-broken yet, doesn't know that life is about working.

I was curious how Delaney, the new horse, slept.

Grace and I walked across the back lawn under a half-moon, following the bouncing yellow ball from my flashlight. I ducked under the door-guard and into the barn. The sound of the horses breathing instantly relaxed me. I glanced around. There was Mousi, asleep in his nest; Isis, in her corner; Conversano, flat out and snoring loudly. And Delaney, awake, vigilant, ready. He scooted back as soon as I approached him. I ignored his behavior and just casually threw him some "quiet" hay—trying not to rustle it, so I wouldn't wake up the others. I would need time to figure him out.

I stood outside the barn for a few minutes after that, looking toward the house. It was no longer a house I recognized. It was dark; there wasn't anyone sleeping inside, waiting for me. No one that I could crawl back into bed to and reach over for. It was all empty.

"Come on, Grace," I said. The night was pressing against me now. The cool, quiet air bringing a chill. The streak of half-moon throwing haunting shadows across the ground. Then I thought I heard him.

"Grace, come!" I had to walk fast now, to get back into the house, because, for one moment, I thought I heard him in the distance. I held my hands over my ears and practically ran, but I could still hear it. The faint, faraway sound of a horse whinnying for me.

It was why I never listen. It was why I don't allow myself to hear what is going on around me. Why I don't attend to voices, to conversation.

I didn't deserve to.

"Grace!" My back door was just a few feet ahead. Maybe it was the wind. The wind can sound like that sometimes. Like the last call of a horse. Distant, dying.

It was the one sound I couldn't bear to hear.

Chapter Eight

PREDICTIONS ARE the hubs that turn the wheels of life. Predictions glide you through every situation, because, if you know how the other person is going to react, what they're going to say, what they need, you can be ready. You predict what time they will be walking through the front door, you can predict their mood just by the way they are holding their lips, you can predict that they are going to be there for your birthday and New Year's and that they'll bring you tea when you have the flu. Predictions make everything comfortable and comforting.

"Meet me tomorrow at the Hudson Inn." My mother called three weeks after my marriage exploded. I could have predicted that she was going to wait a discreet two weeks after she found out before prying. "We'll have afternoon cocktails and lunch."

"Mother," I began to protest. "I have a dozen—"

"You need to get away. You're letting yourself get depressed. When's the last time you got out and socialized?"

I couldn't remember the last time I ate a whole meal. I was planning to live on one jelly donut a day. I imagined that's what people do when they have no money and their life is falling apart. Jelly donuts are a cheap source of happiness.

After we hung up, I wondered if my mother was right. Can you *let* yourself get depressed? Do you invite it in, like the proverbial dinner guest that won't leave? Or does it slip over your shoulders like a coat, and get heavier and heavier, and you just keep adjusting to it until the weight brings you to your knees? I really didn't want to go anywhere. I didn't want to change out of my sweats. I didn't even want to ride horses, although it was the one thing I did force myself to do, despite wishing I could spend all day in bed, cuddling with Grace and going through two or three boxes of tissues. But I couldn't disappoint my mother. I'm sure she knew that I wouldn't disappoint her.

And I predicted my mother would be wearing her pale-gold blouse, and beige skirt with the long, matching beige jacket. Tan-and-white pumps. Brown-and-wine paisley clutch bag. Antique gold earrings and her favorite pearls.

"You look perfectly awful," she said, as the hostess seated us. She was wearing her gold blouse, beige suit, et al. I had showered, run a comb through my hair, and found some strength left over to pull together a mildly rumpled outfit that had only one small stain.

We started with cocktails, of course. You can't have afternoon cocktails without the featured item. She ordered her usual Bay Breeze. I had a glass of wine. She fingered the little luncheon muffins, evaluating them with the eyes of an expert.

"Lemon-and-poppy," she said. "Good."

I propped the menu up in front of me. I knew what was coming.

"So, Cornelia, are you ready to talk about it?" she asked, gently, carefully.

I shook my head and kept diligently studying the menu.

"I can make an educated guess," she said, then took a sip of her glowing red concoction. "You caught him cheating."

I shrugged. I did not want to cry in the middle of the Hudson Inn, so I shredded a neat fringe around the edge of my tissue, then fiddled with the lunch menus, balancing them across each other like little tents, then rolled my linen napkin into bunny ears. I concentrated very hard on these tasks until the waitress came back.

"Caesar salad," I told her. "With lots of anchovies."

"Grilled salmon." My mother handed back her menu and smiled at me. "After lunch we can go to that donut shop you like and get some donuts for dessert. Although you know they don't hold a candle to my personal donuts."

She always said that.

It was all about predictions. I knew she would have grilled salmon for lunch. I knew Matt would have ordered something like a bowl of chili or a hamburger platter and then covered it all in salt and hot sauce. Part of being secure in life was having the predictions you made about the person you love come true. It meant you knew that person intimately. You knew what they were about. Predictions ease you through all the social rituals and turmoil and disorder that the world throws at you. You can predict outcomes and consequences. A prognosis is the prediction of how an illness will progress. Sometimes you can even predict death.

Sometimes.

The waitress came back with our lunches, and I realized that I really wasn't hungry.

"Who did he cheat with?" my mother asked. "That snappy little blonde who works with him?"

I must have dropped my jaw, because she laughed.

"I could smell her type a mile away," she said. "Little husband-snatching bitch."

My mother's words surprised me. She never talked like that. "I didn't think you knew about those things," I said.

She looked down and poked at her salmon as though she found something very interesting under the lemon slice. I stared at her. I stared at the lemon slice. Nothing was forthcoming from either one of them.

"I will tell you something, because mothers and daughters should—well . . ." She dug around some more under her salmon. The capers that were decorating the top of it rolled onto her grilled vegetables. "You're my only daughter, and I want you to have glistening teeth."

Forget teeth. She didn't say "glistening teeth." _Listen to me_, she had said. _I want you to listen to me_. I knew that she was about to give me advice. To tough it out. To salvage the relationship. To forgive and forget and love Matt anyway, because he was really a decent man. Stuff I didn't want to hear.

"Remember Mrs. Campbell?" she finally said. Mrs. Campbell had been a friend of my parents. A young widower. Black hair, DD bra.

"She wasn't that pretty," I said, not wanting to know and now knowing.

"Cornelia, when men want to cheat, they aren't thinking about anything above the waist."

I sat back in my chair.

"But you—and Dad—are—*happy.*"

She squeezed her lemon over her fish with a little too much force. The pit flew across the table.

"Happiness is a decision," she said softly. "I wanted my family intact. I told your father that unless it stopped he was going to lose everything. Everything. He returned to me and begged me to forgive him. And then I told him that I had earned the right to an affair of my own. Whenever I chose. Those were my terms."

I couldn't believe it. My mother, with her coiffed dark-honey hair and perfectly made-up clear brown eyes and small patrician breasts and flawless complexion and perfect posture and antique earrings. My mother—so untouched, so unfazed—bread-maker to the family, maybe to the world, sipping the last of her Bay Breeze with tranquillity.

"Did you ever—um—exercise your—option?" I managed.

She shook her head and smiled. "No, darling, but he knows the choice is always there." She paused for a moment. "For both of us," she added.

"But you're—*happy.* Right? Aren't you happy?" Please be happy, I thought.

"Of course," she said, and signaled for another cocktail. "He treats me like a queen. But he's on his toes all the time. He doesn't dare take me for granted. And that makes me very happy."

I never would have predicted that.

Chapter Nine

DELANEY WAS a bastard to work with. He was sneaky and sullen. He was all anger and deceit. He rode great one day, gently pressing toward the reins in my hands the way I asked him to, forward and full, with a relaxed, easy trot, and then, when I least expected it, he would rear and bolt away. He nearly got me out of the saddle several times.

"What the hell are you trying to do to yourself?" Alana asked me. She didn't know much about horses, but she had come down to the barn so her daughters could watch me ride. The girls loved standing on the bottom rail of the fence around my riding ring and peeking between the top two rails, because they were too small to see otherwise. I was hoping they would eventually want to ride and had promised Alana I would find them a nice little school pony, which they could keep with me, and I would give them free lessons. But she had always demurred. It might have had something to do with her watching me ride problem horses for the past five years. Delaney was proving to be no exception.

He had been awful for the whole ride. He bolted to one side of the ring, tossed his head up into my face, reared two or three times, each rear preceded by a huge grunt. I caught Alana covering her eyes at one point, while her girls laughed and applauded.

"Do you think I'm gonna let my kids ride after watching that?" Alana remarked later, when we were sitting in the kitchen drinking hot chocolate. The girls were watching a video.

"At least you won't have to take them to the rodeo," I said. "I'm a full-service friend. Entertainment followed by refreshments."

"It could have been entertainment followed by an ambulance ride," she said. "Do you really need all that *agita?*"

Alana is not Italian, but she's a big believer in *agita.*

"I know what I'm doing," I said. "And I'm poverty-stricken now, I have no choice. Besides, the kids would probably love the ambulance—the sirens and flashing lights—"

"For some reason, watching you get crunched up doesn't sound all that appealing," she said. "And you want me to get them a horse! I'd be terrified, letting them get up on a horse."

"Pony. And they would love it," I said. "I promise they would love it. I would find them something safe. Something crippled from arthritis, with bad asthma."

"Why would I want a pony like that?" she said, puzzled.

"You want one that's too crippled to run away with them," I explained, "but if it does, you want it to run out of air, and have to stop to catch its breath. The perfect kid's pony." It was an old horseman's joke, but Alana laughed.

When the girls finished their hot chocolate, they ran off to torture Grace, who loves it.

"So—what's happening?" Alana said. "Are you still an avocado?"

"Still," I said. And I was. Almost totally incommunicado. I was not answering Matt's messages, not calling my mother back, not even my own lawyer. No one, except for Alana.

"I guess I should be honored," she said. "That you allowed us to come over today."

"I like the girls to visit."

I did. I liked their little round heads and funny pumpkin-colored braids, and small shoulders, and big eyes. The way they cuddled up to me when they said hello and good-bye.

"Thanks," she said. "They wouldn't miss it for the world."

*   *   *

Grace lay next to me in bed that night, her toenails painted a flamboyant pink, with matching hot-pink bows taped around each ear, courtesy of Alana's girls. Debussy was playing on the stereo, very sweet, very fitting for pink.

"You look like Slut Dog," I said to Grace, pulling off the ribbons. She wagged her stumpy tail. Matt had spayed her as soon as her broken jaw healed. I suddenly felt very sorry for her and began to cry.

"You can never have puppies, you know. Never," I whispered to her. "Maybe you would have wanted a family."

This struck me as very tragic, and I rolled over and cried myself to sleep.

Chapter Ten

THE PHONE rang, and I grabbed it without checking the caller ID. It had been over a month now, and I still didn't want to talk to Matt, or my mother, or my lawyer. Or, sometimes, even Alana.

"Hi, Neelie? It's Richie. How are you guys?" Richie Chiger and his wife, Jackie, were good friends of ours. Richie was general manager and vice-president of the Wycliff-Pennington Animal Sanctuary. Jackie painted humorous little animal watercolors and sold them on their Web site.

"Hey, Richie," I said, trying to keep my voice normal. "Great to hear from you."

"I figured Matt'd be at his office this time of day, but his secretary told me he was on vacation."

Vacation? Matt was always in his office. Had he stopped going to work?

"How are you guys doing?" I asked.

"We're great!" Richie's voice contained a catch of excitement. "So—is Matt around?"

"Not today." Which wasn't exactly a lie.

"I have to talk to him right away." Richie said. "We got something going on—I tried to talk to Dr. Scarletta, but she blew me off. Apparently, she isn't interested in large animals."

Ah yes, poor Holly-Golly didn't like the inconvenience of treating anything bigger than a breadbox.

"What kind of large animal?" I asked. I had always accompanied Matt to the sanctuary, because I liked visiting the animals. The place has almost everything, from alligators all the way through the alphabet to two cranky zebras. Animals saved from stupid people or injured in the wild and unable to be returned, animals adopted from petting zoos that have no business owning animals. Matt had been their vet for years, even after he sold his equine practice, treating the animals for free, until the sanctuary got a wealthy sponsor and was able to pay him.

"I don't want to talk about it over the phone," Richie said.

"Why not?"

"Security reasons. Can you have him call me as soon as he gets in?"

"Security? You're kidding," I exclaimed. "Did something happen?"

"No, no," Richie said. "I can't talk about it, just have him call me. Please."

"It might be a while before he does," I said. "Let me give you his pager, you can check with him directly." I paused; it wasn't like Richie to be so mysterious. "Why can't you talk about it?"

I loved Richie and his wife. They were among our closest friends. Richie was short, and bearded with a wild halo of graying brown curls, and a certain childlike enthusiastic sweetness about him. He had spent most of his life traveling and rescuing exotic wildlife before working for the sanctuary. Jackie always wore her hair pulled back into a long dark-brown ponytail and wore Birkenstock sandals and cooked a lot of couscous with steamed vegetables and tofu.

"It's top secret. Honestly," Richie continued. "Matt can tell you after I talk to him in person—I just hope he comes on board with this."

"Sure," I said.

After we hung up, I sat down on the kitchen floor to cry. Beethoven was playing, and I shut it off. Beethoven is too heavy when you are already bummed out. Not only had I lost Matt, I realized I was losing connections to all the things we had done together. The sanctuary and our best friends, and dinners and barbecues, and Halloween costume parties and summer vacations—every piece of my life was being unraveled, stitch by stitch, like an old scarf, and I couldn't stop it.

•   •   •

I wondered, a few days later, if Richie had been able to get in touch with Matt. Okay, I was really wondering what this vacation deal was all about. Had Matt run off somewhere to establish residency so he could get a quickie divorce?

Richie's cell phone was busy, busy, busy, and I had to search for the number of the sanctuary, since they always kept that phone number unlisted. They don't want to be bothered with people asking if they could walk through and stare at the animals. Richie takes the word "sanctuary" very seriously. I found the number, jotted down in Matt's handwriting, on a piece of paper hanging on the refrigerator, behind an old dental-appointment card. Matt's handwriting. I ran my fingers over the scrawled numbers. It was the only thing I had left of him.

After three or four tries, Richie answered the main phone. "Richie, it's Neelie." I felt stupid calling him to find out where Matt was.

"Hey!" he said. "I'm so happy that Matt is going to help."

So Matt had been to the sanctuary. He just wasn't going to work.

"I'm happy you're happy," I said.

"Of course," Richie said, "he has to get his shots and check his passport, make sure it's current. Oh, tell him I talked with Tom Pennington himself. We will have plenty of security. He gave his word." He took a deep breath. "Incredible, eh?"

"Thomas Pennington himself?" Thomas Princeton Pennington was a multimillionaire who lived part-time in New York City and part-time all around the rest of the world, and funded animal rescues with his pocket change. He was a major supporter of the sanctuary. His name was always in the news.

"Yep—he even came up here, to check the big barn and get some work started on it. We have to bring in heating and reinforce the walls."

"Reinforce the walls?" I exclaimed. "What on earth are you getting in?"

"Didn't Matt tell you?" Richie sounded puzzled.

"Matt hasn't discussed it with me yet," I said. "He's—been so busy."

"Oh?" He paused. "Are you guys okay? Matt seemed—distracted."

"We have some things going on here," I said. "What's the passport for?"

"I don't want to talk over the phone. Ask Matt," Richie replied. "By the way, did he tell you we rescued two draft horses? Sisters. You're gonna love them—so bring peanut-butter cookies. Jackie says they like peanut-butter cookies."

"Sure."

"It's been too long since we've seen you," he said affectionately, "and we miss you, so drop by soon."

I hung up and decided I would go to the sanctuary and visit Richie and Jackie. Some things just can't be unraveled.

And then I worried. What if I ran into Matt up there? I couldn't bear the thought of running into Matt, and falling apart in front of him. Or him and Holly, because, in my mind's eye now, they were joined at the hip.

I decided I would have to change banks, change supermarkets, change gas stations, change everything. I was going to have to be more careful about where I put in appearances.

I would withdraw from the world and become a recluse and speak to no one and go nowhere, except out to my barn every day to ride, and then I'd return immediately to the house. I would allow myself nothing else. No contact with the outside world. Nothing.

I was, by turns, heartsick and angry and morose and angry and filled with despair. And angry.

And the stupid thing was, I couldn't see that I was doing most of it to myself.

Chapter Eleven

How long can you sleepwalk through your life? A few weeks? A few years? Ten or twenty years, if you're not paying attention?

I had lost track of time. Were it not for the calendar hanging in the barn where I notate every ride, I wouldn't know what day of the week it was. I just didn't care.

I didn't open my mail. I avoided the phone. I deleted the answering-machine messages without listening to them.

My lawyer called half a dozen times, until, finally, I picked up the phone.

"Hello, Neelie," he started. "I have to talk to you, bubbee."

I took a deep breath, turned down my radio, and forced myself to listen. Bubbees could be breasts or Jewish grandmothers, and I knew I had to concentrate on the rest of the conversation, because context was going to make a big difference.

"Matt got a lawyer," he said. "I have the papers on my desk. Matt said that he'll pay all the court costs. My fee, too."

I felt like I had been kicked in the stomach by a horse.

"Neelie?"

"Yes."

"You guys just have to come to an agreement over the house. Probably you'll have to sell it to straighten out all the finances. Matt's attorney says that Matt's still paying off his practice, so that money will be tied up for years."

"I can't sell the house," I said. "I need the barn. How am I going to be able to afford another place with a barn?"

"You live in an equitable-distribution state."

"But he took all the money. The accounts, the DVDs—"

"That's music," he said. "You mean the CDs. And selling the house is the only fair way to work things out."

"As fair as him having a baby with his girlfriend?" I was shouting now. "Why am I the one who has to play fair?"

"I don't think Matt will pay if you start getting difficult," he said. "A fight could get you buggy spandex."

"Spandex?"

He sighed loudly. "Maybe you need a hearing aid? I said a fight could get ugly and expensive."

He was right, but giving up the barn meant I had to give up my riding business, because I didn't make enough to pay for everything on my own. And it would kill me to give up the barn. It would be the coup de grâce.

I lay awake all that night and moped around the house all the next day. I would have to open my practice again. Rent an office. Fight over how many therapy sessions some insurance clerk felt my clients needed. I would have to listen to problems and suggest life-management strategies. And, of course, long hours of work meant there would be no time for a horse, so what was the purpose of keeping a house with a barn? Good old Matt had managed to screw two women at the same time.

•   •   •

I put on my boots and headed for the barn to ride Isis. Mousi watched me from over his paddock fence, his dark eyes following me and Isis as we trotted and halted and halted some more. Mousi didn't appear jealous—just curious. He was probably wondering why I would bother saddling up a horse if I spent the whole time just sitting on it, doing nothing. The good thing, though, was that Isis was actually halting. And the time we spent at it had been trimming down over the past few weeks, to ten minutes, then seven, then five, until this morning, when she finally just glided to an immediate soft halt and stood there quietly. Gloriously calm. And for that moment, I forgot everything that had been eating away at me. Isis was standing perfectly still in the middle of the ring, trusting me, waiting for me to cue her, perfectly quiet and submissive. The sun fell on my shoulders like a warm hand, and splashed a bright patch across her neck. Time stopped. I held my breath, thinking I had become part of something greater, some odd place that connected the energy of people and animals, and somehow Isis and I had both found each other there. I hated to ask her to trot again, but I had to. I asked her to trot and then halt again, and each time she came to a full and quiet stop. It was a moment of exquisite joy.

Of course, that meant my next challenge would be to teach her to piaffe, which was going to be tricky, but that was a problem for another day.

I had stopped riding Delaney. My plan was to let him observe me from his paddock. Let him watch me riding Isis. I think horses can sometimes learn from other horses—modeling, it's called in psychology—and I was hoping that he would learn from Isis that I was someone who was okay. Plus it gave me the advantage of being able to observe him without a rider.

He browsed through his hay like a normal horse. Every once in a while he would lift his head and grunt before bolting across his paddock, like demons were on his tail. It struck me as curious that this behavior seemed to have little to do with anyone's riding him, and I made a mental note of this. I put Isis away, pleased with her progress, and I decided to do a quick donut run before I rode Delaney later that afternoon. I headed for my car. My brother's car was parked behind it in the driveway.

Reese, my kid brother, was in the kitchen, his head in my refrigerator. He's really not a kid—he's thirty-three and has his own apartment near my parents. We share the same genes for height and brown hair and green eyes. He's good-looking. For a brother.

"How did you get in here?" I asked. I had taken to locking the door while I was in the barn now, in an effort to Matt-proof the house, just in case he and Holly-Sneaky wanted the furniture.

"I took the screen out of your kitchen window and climbed in, over the sink," he said. Sure enough, there was a sneaker print in the middle of the sink. Also a few across the floor. Luckily for him, Grace was with me in the barn, or he would have been dabbing at micro-bite wounds by now.

"I did knock," he said, "but I thought you probably couldn't hear me over Metallica. Why do you keep music playing so loud when you're not home?"

"Because I will be coming home at some point, and it has to be there," I said, watching him shuffle my one egg to another shelf. "If you're looking for food, I have none."

"I saw." He straightened up and shut the refrigerator door. "Actually, I was putting food in. Mom sent it over with me. She's worried."

"I'm fine," I said.

He sat himself down at the table. "Make coffee," he said. "She also sent over some corn bread."

I put up coffee. "How's teaching?" I asked. Reese teaches math in a junior college.

He shrugged. "Same old same-old."

Grace came into the kitchen and raced over to him and, thinking it was Matt, almost wagged her tail loose from her back end. When she realized it was Reese, she lowered her head and growled.

"NO BITE," I yelled at Grace. She looked disappointed.

"So—how's it going?" Reese asked, picking Grace up and plopping her onto his lap to rub her ears. She liked ear rubs more than she liked biting, and was admirably restraining herself. "Have you heard from Matt?"

I didn't answer him.

"Hey," he said. "Don't tune me out."

"I wasn't," I said defensively. "If you have to know, everything sucks."

"It may not be too late for you guys. Maybe you should talk things over with him. You know, find out what he wants and needs."

"Like a layette?"

"Maybe it's not all his fault."

"Oh?" I asked, my voice heavy with sarcasm. "Like, *I* used his penis to get her pregnant?"

"Maybe he was looking for someone to talk to, someone who could listen to him," Reese said. "For a change."

"I was always there for him!" I said, slamming his mug of coffee down onto the table. I turned my back on him on the pretense of getting a sponge to clean up the spill, but really to dab at the sudden tears in my eyes. "There's no milk," I said hoarsely.

"Black is fine." Reese took the mug. "Maybe if he didn't feel like he was married to a stone wall, things wouldn't have happened."

I spun around. "Reese!"

"Oh, come on, Neelie." His voice was soft, tentative. "It's time someone brought this up with you. So there was this big horrible accident," he said. "You were sixteen, and you couldn't have done anything, for God's sake. So get over yourself already."

I could hardly breathe. "Shut up," I said, and put my hands over my ears. Reese got up and walked over to me and pulled my hands away and then put his arms around me.

"Everyone tiptoes around you," he said, patting me on the back like he was burping a baby. "Come on. How long can you play the elephant card?"

I pulled away, tears running down my face now. "What are you talking about, elephant card?"

"You know," he said. "You *know*. You carry it with you. All the time. It's like there's always an elephant in the room with you. It's time you let it go."

Chapter Twelve

WELL, I knew there was at least one elephant I had to face. Matt. I didn't want to, but I absolutely had to talk to him and see if there was some way I could keep the house.

I debated between calling his cell phone and calling his office, then thought better of doing the latter. I didn't want the sympathy or curiosity of Crystal, the dyslexic secretary that had come with the practice.

I put it off for almost a week. My lawyer left a few messages to ask how things were coming along. Working things out between us before the divorce would save money, he said. I didn't care about saving Matt money, but I did care about saving my barn. My lawyer also said something about licorice puppy cups, but I didn't have the patience to listen a second time to figure it out. A quick hit of the delete key solved the problem.

I waited a few more days, but I just couldn't make the call.

"Call him," Alana advised. "It'll get Holly all worried that you're in touch. Right now, she has the upper hand. Give her a little *agita*."

I paced away the whole afternoon until, in the early evening, I couldn't stand the thought of going through the torture all over again the next day, and finally called his cell phone.

"Neelie?" He sounded happy. I could have sworn he sounded happy. "I'm so glad to hear from you."

"We have to talk," I said. "About the house and stuff."

He readily agreed and asked if I'd had dinner yet. I said no. Then he asked me to dinner.

We were going to meet at the diner. It was the only place that had no special memories for us. And I decided to dress a bit for the occasion.

Form-fitting jeans, my tightest, since I knew Holly-Belly would be showing by now. And a nice little sweater with a scooped neckline that showed just a little cleavage, not enough to make the other patrons drop their forks, just enough to show Matt what he had given up. Matt used to love my hair, so I feathered it with a pair of cuticle scissors, because it had gotten a bit wild around the edges, then bent over and straightened up fast, which in theory was supposed to make it fall around my shoulders in carefree, voluminous waves. I dabbed on some makeup. Dark moss-green to bring out the color of my eyes. A light-rose blush across my cheekbones to heighten their angles. I stood back and looked in the mirror. The effect was what I wanted. Revenge dressing.

He noticed.

"God, you look incredible," he whispered to me as the waitress led us to a booth in the back. We sat down on opposite sides of the table and I flashed him a sexy smile. "I missed you," he added, then looked at me again with *that* look. "God," he said again. "How I missed you."

He ordered the hamburger platter, and I ordered the diner version of Caesar salad.

"The house," I said, in my most businesslike manner. "We need to work out your portion of the house versus my portion of your practice. Plus you have to pay back the DVDs you cashed in."

"CDs," he said. "DVDs are music."

"CDs used to be music," I said. "Whatever is money, I want half of it back."

He stared down at his side of fries. "I don't want to sell the house."

I didn't understand. "You don't want to sell it to me? Or you don't want to sell the house, period?"

"Neither one," he said. "I want you to keep the house."

I leaned back in my chair and stared at him. He had lost weight, his love handles were gone, and he looked like he did when we got married. Sexy hollows in his face, longish sandy hair. If I wasn't so broke and angry about being broke, I could have pushed aside the condiments and jumped his bones right on the table.

"What do you mean, keep the house?" I said, fighting to keep my voice even. "My lawyer said that I would have to give up the house. Which means I have to give up the training business. So I decided I could saddle-break Conversano and sell him for money to live on until we work out all our assets."

"I thought you loved that horse." He poured ketchup on his burger. Predictable, I thought. I knew he was going to use a lot of ketchup, followed by a big splash of hot sauce. Then heavily salt his fries. He shook the hot sauce on his burger. Here comes the salt, I thought, but he ate his fries without it. I must have been staring at them with some surprise.

"No salt," he said, grimacing. "My blood pressure is sky-high. Jeff said to cut out the salt." Jeff is our family doctor and friend. I made a mental note to change doctors, too.

"I think Conversano is very talented," I said. "He's got a trot to die for. With some schooling, he should bring in big money, which, I might remind you, I desperately need. He's got good breeding and he's still a stallion."

"Don't sell him," Matt said.

"I need the money," I said. "You closed the joint account and left me with two hundred and twenty-eight dollars and seventy-five cents in my personal account, which, after the past month and tonight's meal, will be down to twenty-one dollars and—"

He held his hand up to silence me. "I'll give you some money," he said, reaching into his pocket and putting his wallet on the table. "And I want you to keep the house. We can still keep both our names on the mortgage." He pulled out some money and pressed it into my hand. I stuffed it into my handbag without looking at how much, because looking would have made me feel so . . . *mercenary*. Then he took a bite of his burger, and I waited patiently for him to finish chewing and explain. "We have plenty of time to worry about what we're going to do with the house."

I was puzzled. "I don't even know if I can carry the whole thing myself. I might have to open my practice again anyway."

"I'll keep up the payments and the bills."

I smiled a little. "Should I have brought a tape recorder to get this down? Because it sounds awfully generous." He was being the usual Matt, hard to fathom, hard to figure out. "Or is this because you don't want me to claim part of your practice? Which my lawyer says might even cancel my part of the house."

He shook his head. "My practice is tied up in knots right now," he said. "I bought some fancy equipment last year, modernized the whole operating suite. I have more equipment coming in." Then he put down his burger and stared me right in the eye. "I wasn't trying to hurt you, Neelie. Honest. I thought—things got so crazy—" He fished around for the words. "I'll make it up to you. I swear. Don't give up the bus."

"What bus?"

He furrowed his brow. "Bus?"

"You said 'bus,' " I said.

"I said, Don't give up on us." he said. "I messed up. I was a total jerk." Then, before I could protest, he took my hand into his. I pulled it away.

"No," I said. "It's like cheating on your future wife."

"Holly and I—" He stopped and gave a weary sigh. "Never mind for now. Listen, did you throw out my passport?"

"Passport?" I mentally sifted through all the stuff that Alana and I had carried to the curb. "Where was it?"

"In the attic. In the blue suitcase. The front zipper compartment."

I hadn't. Because we jointly owned the suitcases, and because I didn't think there'd be anything Matt-ish in them.

"Can I come by and get it?"

I fiddled around with the salad. It was really just romaine lettuce and some goopy dressing with a few croutons, trying hard to resemble the real thing. Maybe Matt's repentance was like the diner salad, also trying hard to resemble the real thing. Maybe there was some fiendish plan behind Matt's offer to help with the house, and it wasn't as obvious as bad food—maybe he was trying hard to resemble caring and contrite, and then would drop another bomb, like how much Holly-Baby-Hatcher wanted to live in the house. After all, she had seen the bedroom we had once optimistically fixed up for a nursery. The gray ponies I had stenciled all around the walls, with pink and blue halters and sparkles. How could I know what his motives were?

"What do you need your passport for?" I asked. "Quickie divorce somewhere, followed by a long honeymoon?" I didn't want him to know I had spoken to Richie, because Matt's a very private person. If he thought I was talking to Richie about him, I knew he would shut down and I would totally lose any chance to talk things over with him. Or maybe I had already lost all my chances. Diner food is sometimes hard to figure out.

"Neelie, don't." He finished his burger, then took a long drink of his diet soda. "Richie Chiger asked me to help him with something," he said. "Out of the country. It'll pay me a lot of money if I go, so I'm going."

"And you can't tell me?"

"No."

"Why not?"

He leaned over the table, accidentally catching his shirt pocket in his ketchup. I dipped my napkin into my water glass and offered it to him. "Why not?" I asked again.

"Because," he said, looking down at his pocket and swiping hard at it, like a little boy who had just gotten his party clothes dirty, "the trip could be very dangerous."

      *   *   *

He followed me back to the house in his car. As soon as he walked into the house, Grace went crazy, jumping in the air, yelping like a puppy, racing circles through the rooms. I followed him up to the attic, where he found his passport, and was still behind him when he stopped at our bedroom door.

"Nothing left?" he asked, peeking inside. "I'm going to need the rest of my jeans. And my heavy stable-boots."

"No," I answered. "It's all gone."

"Oh," he said sadly. "Oh."

He said nothing else. And I felt terrible.

I followed him downstairs. He stood at the front door a long time, looking at me, then down at his shoes, then back at me. I knew he wanted to kiss me. I knew it. The truth was, I wanted to kiss him, too—wanted him to hold me and put everything back the way it was—but it was too late. There was, as Reese put it, an elephant in the room. This time it was Holly and the baby. Matt put his hand on the doorknob.

"Let's talk some more," he said. "When I get back."

"Back from where?"

"I can't discuss it yet," he said. "I was kind of sworn to secrecy."

"That shouldn't be a problem." I opened the front door and smiled brightly. "You're so good with secrets."

Chapter Thirteen

I HAD to know.

I had to know where Matt was going and why it was dangerous.

And the only person who could fill me in was Richie. So I broke my self-imposed vow of silence toward the entire rest of the free world and called him.

"Neelie! Great to hear from you! Matt did a terrific job on the bear. Claw's almost healed."

"Great," I said. "How are the new draft horses?"

"Matt wormed them, did their teeth, routine stuff." He paused. "Didn't he tell you?"

"He's been so busy lately," I said, "we practically never get around to talking. You know how it is."

"I guess so," he said, but it sounded more like a question. Then the conversation ground to a halt.

"Maybe I'll drop by this week," I ventured.

"Would you mind bringing a few more syringes? Matt forgot to leave extras," Richie replied. "Turns out, one of the lions needed antibiotics—"

"Sure," I said.

Things were getting complicated. Syringes were not usually at the top of my pantry-supply list. I wanted Richie to think that Matt and I were still together, and now I had to come up with syringes. Lies always do that—pile up on one another like a game of pickup sticks, and you can't touch one without upsetting the whole heap. Of course I wasn't going to bring anything but a box of peanut-butter cookies for the horses. I would just pretend that I had forgotten the syringes.

•   •   •

The Wycliff-Pennington Animal Sanctuary sits on 750 acres off a secluded road, ten miles from us. It was founded twenty years ago by Elisabeth Wycliff, a recluse and an animal-lover, who rescued two badly treated lions from a roadside zoo. Over the years she added to her collection, never turning away an animal, paying for everything out of her own pocket. It was an enormous expense, but she persevered. With some publicity, she secured a sponsor, Thomas Princeton Pennington, who supported the sanctuary without a lot of fanfare. He had inherited a family fortune and increased it with legendary business acumen. He was always on television and in the papers, and I would read about him from time to time as he dated starlets or attended Greenpeace rallies or argued before Senate hearings about the environment.

Even with Thomas Pennington's full support, the sanctuary that bore his name wasn't a glamorous place. Just a farm, really, with a few large barns and lots of strong fencing, but the animals were fed and treated well. For the past nine years, I had frequently accompanied Matt when he was called to work there.

Now I drove up the long gravel driveway, past the big house where Mrs. Wycliff lived, then past the more modest house where Richie and Jackie lived, past the isolation barn for newly acquired animals, to Richie's office. I got out of my truck. Richie was loading a battered black farm truck with hay and plastic bins of raw chicken legs and bags of frozen bluefish. He waved hello as soon as he spotted me. I waved back.

"Peanut-butter cookies," I said, holding up the boxes as I walked toward him. "Coffee and jelly donuts for us." I smiled, hoping he had forgotten about the damn syringes.

"Good to see you," he said, taking his coffee and donut. "Come with me, it's feeding time at the zoo." He opened the passenger door, and I climbed in. We bumped down a gravel path, and I watched the farm roll past. It was peaceful; only an occasional loud grunt or call broke the silence. The only humans to be seen were a handful of volunteers, who were now busy cleaning out the barns or filling water tubs.

Richie parked the truck in front of a large pen, and I followed him out of the cab, carefully trying to avoid the deep, slick mud. He threw several squares of hay over the fence, and a herd of imperious-looking camels walked over and began eating. We got back into the truck, and he drove up to a grassy enclosure where two old lions were batting a basketball back and forth. They were the happy recipients of the raw chicken legs. A grizzly bear sat contentedly in the middle of a pond next door and watched Richie fling two or three fish at him before he was motivated enough to wade over and check out his lunch. We drove on to still another fenced field, where we got out of the truck again so Richie could toss more hay over the fence.

"I'll call the girls," he said, then whistled through his fingers. Two sorrel draft horses trotted up to us. They were carefully groomed, but their ribs and spines stood out in bas-relief, and their hip bones looked like coat hangers.

"Wow," I said. "Thin."

"Believe it or not, they've put on about two hundred pounds apiece," Richie said. "You had to see them when they came in."

Richie watched them snuffle the cookies from my hand for a few minutes. I was just starting to relax about his request when he brightened. "Oh, hey," he said, "did you bring the syringes?"

"Oh no!" I gasped, doing an Oscar-worthy performance of embarrassed incompetence. "I *totally* forgot!" But I felt very guilty about the infected lion.

He nodded, not looking very surprised. "That's okay. I'll ask Jackie to stop by Matt's office. I can boil the ones I have until she picks up new ones."

"I'm really sorry," I said, relieved he was able to come up with a solution, but not able to look him in the eye. I fed a few more cookies to the horses, wondering how to bring up the subject of Matt's traveling off to somewhere dangerous without sounding like I was prying. As Matt's wife, I really shouldn't have had to ask where he was going.

Richie watched me quietly. The horses finished the box of cookies. I gave them a final pat.

"So what's going on, Neelie?" Richie asked. "Matt looks like hell, and, frankly, so do you. He hasn't said anything, but I can tell something's very wrong."

"Maybe I need some time at a sanctuary," I joked. "You got any room here?" The two horses were pushing each other out of the way to beg for more cookies.

"You didn't come to feed the horses," Richie said.

I looked down at the mud oozing over my shoes. "No."

"So—what's the deal?"

I stared out at the fields. Seven hundred and fifty acres of generosity. Of kindness. They even had a hippo somewhere back there, and bison, and a big monkey house with an outdoor pen where rescued lab chimps lived in comfort.

"Come on," Richie said. "Spill."

"I'll tell you a secret if you tell me a secret," I finally said.

"Deal," said Richie.

I took a deep breath. "Matt and I are divorcing."

"Shit," said Richie. "Jackie and I kind of suspected as much. But why? I thought you two guys really had a good thing."

"Dr. Holly-Slutkins is having Matt's baby."

His head snapped back with surprise. "Double shit!" he exclaimed. "I didn't know *that.*"

"Not one of his proudest moments," I said. "Now it's your turn. Why does Matt need a passport?"

Richie looked around quickly, as though the draft-horse girls were planning to spy on us. He didn't answer for a moment, then he spoke, his voice both hushed and straining with excitement. "You can't tell anyone." I shook my head a definite no.

"We have to keep it confidential because—you know—first of all, it's very, very dangerous, and, secondly, there could be diplomatic problems if it leaks out to the press."

"Diplomatic? Like international?"

"Like an international incident if it doesn't go off."

"I promise."

He continued. "Okay, then." He stopped, started again. "Okay. We're going to Zimbabwe. We're . . . we *have* to . . . steal an elephant."

I stared at him, speechless, then giggled a little with embarrassment. "You know, I have this hearing thing," I said, laughing at the absurdity of it. "So—I thought you said 'steal an elephant.'"

He laughed, too. Then he said, "I did."

I had to think about that for a minute. He had said "steal an elephant." I looked him in the eye and said, "Really?"

"Really."

And I thought about Matt and how much I loved him and wanted to be with him, and that maybe I should fight for him, danger or not, and then I said, "I'm in."

Chapter Fourteen

"ZIMBABWE?" ALANA repeated, her voice rising with incredulity. "Are you sure you didn't hear Richie say you're in a bad way? Because you are."

Of course the first thing I had done when I got home was call Alana and tell her all about it.

"I'm positive," I said. "They're rescuing an elephant from Zimbabwe. And I volunteered to help."

"You have to admit, it's not your everyday activity," she said, "like could you please get my dry cleaning, and, oh, it just might be a little out of your way, but could you also pick up an elephant from Zimbabwe?"

"Well, what do I do now?" I asked her frantically. "There's a meeting Friday night for everyone. Richie's counting on me to come."

Alana had no sympathy. "You've been hoist with your own petard," she said. "And, yes, you heard me right."

"What happens if Matt's there?" I asked. "And what if he brings Holly-Folly?"

"Of course Matt's going to be there," she said. "So withdraw your offer to go. You have no business rescuing elephants anyway. Besides, I think you're just doing it to stay in Matt's life. And if you want to do that, then just spare yourself more *agita* and find a way to work things out with him in your own country." She paused. "Are you listening?"

"No."

"I didn't think so. So—go get yourself an elephant."

•   •   •

Of course Alana's suggestion was sensible. I should just tell Matt I still loved him, and I would work on forgiveness, and in the meantime, he could come back to me. I didn't have to go to Zimbabwe to do that.

Except I could never bring myself to tell him that I forgave him and wanted him back. It was the equivalent of saying it was okay to cheat on me.

And that would never be okay. Never.

•   •   •

"I've been hoist with my own petard," I said to Isis while asking her to halt in the riding ring. "And I did it to myself, and I don't even know what a petard is."

She flicked an ear back and forth and stood motionless at the halt. I patted her neck and praised her lavishly, and then asked her to move forward into an energetic trot.

"I have a meeting Friday night to learn how to rescue an elephant," I said as we trotted around the ring. "I don't know anything about elephants." Then I asked her to slow her trot into half-steps, half the length of her normal trot stride. "What happens if Matt doesn't show up?" Isis slowed her trot, slow, slow, until she gave me one prancelike step, which is exactly what I wanted. I praised her again, and asked her to trot a few more times before another half-step. It was just the beginnings of a piaffe, this half-step, half-prance that she offered me, and I dismounted right away and fed her handfuls of sugar cubes, marveling at how she was beginning to understand.

"Richie says they're leaving for Africa in a week," I told her as I groomed her in her stall. "I have enough problems understanding my own language. What am I going to do in a foreign country?"

Isis had no answer for me, and I finally had to swear her to secrecy like I did with Alana.

*   *   *

The meeting was at seven o'clock in Mrs. Wycliff's living room. I came late, deciding that I could slip out the door if I spotted Matt with Holly-Breeder. He wasn't there when I arrived, but I still took a chair near the door.

The living room was spacious but plain. Two sofas were covered with afghan throws and several cats of various colors, there was a practical-looking Berber rug on the floor, and a carved mahogany table by the bay window with violets in little ceramic elephant planters.

In all the years I had accompanied Matt to the sanctuary, this was only the fourth or fifth time I had seen Mrs. Wycliff, and she hadn't changed one bit. She still looked like she was in her mid-seventies, still wore no makeup, still kept her gray hair pulled back in a hastily made bun, and, as far as I could determine, was still dressed in the same jeans and white Irish knit sweater that she was wearing the day I first met her. She poured us all tea and passed around lumpy homemade cupcakes, which told me she was more interested in spending money on her animals than in lavishly entertaining. Richie and Jackie were already sitting in the two upholstered chairs by the window. They gave me sympathetic smiles when they saw me walk in. I did not want sympathetic, because the second part of that word is "pathetic," but I smiled back anyway before glancing discreetly around. There were about six other people seated, and I didn't know any of them.

I sat in a chair at the edge of the room and waited for Matt. It was getting late, and I was trying not to jump every time I thought I heard something near the door. Several times it turned out to be Mrs. Wycliff's two apparently weak-bladdered black Labs that had to be let out, then in, then out, only to come back in. Conversation buzzed all around me—everyone seemed to know each other—and I overheard words like "poaching" and "hostile environment" and "dangerous." I just sipped my tea and let the voices jumble on. Richie's cell phone rang and he jumped, checking his watch, before taking the call in another room.

"That was Tom," he announced, coming back. "He should be here in an hour. He got stuck in some traffic coming up from the city."

Thomas Princeton Pennington. The man with the money.

Richie's phone rang again. He answered it, and I saw him glance quickly in my direction. I knew this time it was Matt.

Richie made his second announcement. "Well, Dr. Sterling— the vet who will be helping us—just called. He can't make it tonight. He's doing an emergency surgery."

Oh, those late-night emergency surgeries, I thought, but kept my face parked in neutral, wondering if it would look bad for me to get up and leave now. Too obvious, I realized, and stayed put and studied my cupcake.

It was vanilla-frosted, and I chastised myself for not taking a chocolate one. Atop the frosting was a blue sugar-wafer elephant, and I spent some time sucking its head off, followed by each individual foot. One hour and two more cupcakes later, both chocolate, Thomas Princeton Pennington arrived.

He wasn't what I expected at all. I expected a fifty-two-year-old polished tycoon wearing a custom-made suit and crisp shirt and custom-designed tie, like the images I had seen in the media, but Thomas Pennington was dressed in jeans and an old sweater and heavy construction boots. He looked to be just a little taller than me, with longish, neatly trimmed white hair, and an open, intelligent face saved from being preternaturally handsome by a jagged scar down one cheek. His presence was mesmerizing, the way he took instant command of the room, radiating energy, charging the air around him like an electron accelerator. I couldn't take my eyes off him. _Don't stare,_ I scolded myself, but I couldn't help it. He was that compelling. _He's used to being gawked at,_ I defended myself, but did try to be more discreet, forcing myself into occasional glances at the half-eaten cupcake on my napkin, as if it provided worthy competition for my attention.

Richie jumped up to shake his hand. Mrs. Wycliff bustled over to give him a quick peck on his cheek and hand him a mug of tea, which he took, and a cupcake, which he turned down and I instantly coveted. Richie introduced him to us simply as Tom. He greeted us with a quick smile, then strode across the room and, in one motion, grabbed a folding chair, gracefully swinging it around so it faced backward, and sat down. He braced his arms across the back of it and leaned into the room, a contained volcano, anxious to get started, anxious not to waste a minute, ready to erupt with commands and action. Our eyes caught for a moment, and I felt my heart stutter and the color rise in my cheeks. Then he shifted his gaze toward the rest of the group.

"We leave for Zimbabwe in exactly one week," he said in an accent that was a fusion of American and European. "Richie will hand out a list of shots that you need. We will be splitting into teams. One team will come with me northwest to Makuti, and one will work here to ready things for when we get back." He glanced around. "Where's the vet?"

"In surgery," said Richie. "But his wife can give him all the information." He pointed me out. Thomas Pennington looked at me again. I didn't want to meet his eyes this time. I didn't want to see the shutting-down look that men get when they find out you are married, even if I was doing this whole thing to get Matt back and shouldn't have cared.

"He needs to come and work with our vet in Africa, and learn everything he can. Elephants can be tricky to treat," he said. I looked up at him and nodded. He gave me a quick smile and then addressed the rest of the room. "Okay, first I have to start off with a few warnings about the dangers involved."

When Richie mentioned "dangerous" to me, I assumed that the danger would come from getting squashed by an excited elephant, and that I would just stay vigilant and jump out of its way, should things come to that. Like a horse, I figured. If you stand at a horse's shoulder, you are pretty much out of range of flying hooves and in a good position to pivot away from spooks or rears. I would just make sure I stood to the side of the elephant. It seemed intuitively simple.

Or I would just run very fast. I was on a sugar high now and was actually picturing myself outrunning a rampaging elephant.

But Thomas Pennington went on to list dangers I hadn't even heard of. Trypanosomiasis, rickettsial infection, dengue fever, filariasis, not to mention a very hostile political climate, with renegade soldiers running loose, and armed poachers roaming the bush. Then he enumerated the vaccines we needed so that we wouldn't contract additional diseases. Typhoid, hepatitis, polio booster. Getting squashed under an elephant was never mentioned.

I tried to give Richie my best "you've got to be kidding" look by raising my eyebrows up and down a few times, but he was busy nodding in agreement with Thomas Pennington's suicide list.

Then Thomas reached over, swooped up his briefcase, and opened it. "Everything's been printed out, so make sure you take a packet of information back with you," he said, pulling out a ream of paper. "Destroy it when you are through with it. I guess we can go right into the interviews."

I looked at Richie again and now tried to signal my panic by opening my eyes very, very wide. He came over to me. "Don't worry," he whispered. "Let me do the talking."

I wondered how Thomas Princeton Pennington, obviously no fool, was going to interview me if Richie planned to do the talking, but it looked like it could be a win-win situation. If I didn't pass, I could get out of my promise to Richie without losing face or my health. If I passed, I would be with Matt.

One by one, Thomas Pennington summoned each person in the room to sit next to him and answer some questions. He spoke to them all in a quiet voice. Some left smiling, some not. And then it was my turn.

Richie took me by the arm and introduced me. "Tom," he said, "Neelie Sterling here is trained to handle all sorts of animals."

"Mostly horses," I mumbled shyly.

Thomas Pennington studied me carefully. Dark gray-green eyes met mine, and I felt a stir, an exchange of some sort, a recognition of something happening between us. *He probably has this effect on every woman he meets,* I thought.

"Ever work with elephants?" he asked, sounding amused at my awkwardness. "Because the trainer I was planning to use can't get away."

"Neelie's the best animal-trainer around here," Richie said.

"Well, mostly horses," I mumbled again, suddenly anxious that he would find me lacking and trying to spare myself the embarrassment of rejection. Horses are not elephants.

"She's a quick study and has all the right instincts," Richie added. "Her husband is the vet, and she's used to assisting him. You won't get better. I can vouch for her skills."

"Mostly hor—" I started, but Richie pinched me. Thomas Pennington nodded. "Okay," he said. "It sounds like you'll be the one working with the elephant when we get her back here. I trust Richie's judgment. See you next Friday. Give Richie your name tonight, as it legally appears on your passport, so I can arrange for plane tickets. I need to do that right away. Every day we waste is a day we could lose her. I'll put you on my payroll starting from the time you leave New York."

I was in. In for what, remained to be seen.

Thomas Pennington took a few more questions from some of the group and then apologized that his driver was waiting, and left. The room deflated like an old balloon when the door shut behind him. I took another cupcake. The meeting was over.

I turned to Richie, as people filed out the door. "I don't know anything about elephants," I said.

"You're a quick study," he replied. "So start studying. I want you to go. I love elephants more than anything, and I want this elephant. Tom's always promised me an elephant to care for."

"Thanks," I said, "but why is it so important to you that I go?"

He gave me a quick hug. "You and Matt are really good friends," he said, "and Jackie and I love you both. So I figure you'll be helping us save an elephant, I'll be helping you save your marriage."

Chapter Fifteen

CHAOS WAS not only a theory, it was the current definition of my life. I still had Delaney to ride, and Isis to retrain, lessons to give my eight students, the daily running of my barn, clothes to pack, elephants to study, Matt to cry over late at night, and a week to get it all done.

The next two people I swore to secrecy were my mother and Reese. They were both appalled. No, Reese was appalled, my mother was just horrified. Again. But I needed my mother for moral support and maternal advice, and my brother to take care of the horses while I was gone.

"Running away from your problems is not the way to solve them," my mother lectured me. We were in her kitchen again, and she had decided to make several batches of sticky buns for me to take on the plane. You know how well sticky buns travel.

"I'm actually running away *with* my problems," I said. "Matt will be going, too."

"And his girlfriend?" my mother pursued. "Is she—"

"Don't call her his girlfriend," I interrupted her.

"What, then?" my mother asked, pouring lots of syrup and pecans into the pan, the way I like it. "Fiancée? Intended?"

" 'Whore' works for me," I replied.

"So you are going on this crazy trip just to be the other woman?" My mother stopped her work to look up.

"I'm Matt's wife," I said. "I can't be the other woman. I'm the original woman."

"You know what I mean," she said, popping the pans in the oven. "Penguins are not as sweet as you think."

"You are so wrong," I disagreed. Revenge can be very sweet.

* * *

After Reese got over his initial dismay at the dangers involved, he actually approved of my trip to Africa, even volunteering to house-sit for me, which relieved me of the burden of begging him to. He brought a bag of Liver YumYums to ingratiate himself to Grace, and fed them to her handful by handful until she forgave him on the spot. We were sitting in my kitchen and drinking coffee one afternoon.

"She can't live on snacks, you know," I commented as he opened a second bag. "Make sure she gets dog food, too."

"The lady will get what she desires," he said. "So I don't wind up with holes in my ankles. When exactly do you leave?"

"In four days," I replied.

"Africa or bust!" he cheered while slipping more Liver YumYums between Grace's delicate lips. "Bag a big one for me."

He's the brother that hunts.

"We're not going to shoot it," I reminded him. "We're bringing it back alive."

"Even better," he said. "We can shoot it in the comfort of our own backyard."

I made a face at him, and we finished our coffee and the banana muffins my mother had sent over with him.

"Let me show you how I run the barn," I said, opening the back door.

"I like Matt," he said to me encouragingly as we walked to the barn together. "I think it's great that you're willing to fight for him. Don't let him slip through your fingers."

"He didn't slip through my fingers," I said. "He sneaked through. And I'm going more because I'm really interested in rescuing an elephant from terrible circumstances."

"Right," he said, looking sideways at me. "Look, Neelie, when I said there was an elephant in the room I didn't mean it literally, that you should go get one."

"It's too late, Reese," I said. "I already made the arrangements."

* * *

I showed him what the horses ate and how to clean stalls, and how to bring all the horses out to their paddocks without killing either them or himself. He used to ride as a kid, so he wasn't too intimidated.

"I'll just get up early and feed them, and turn them out, and then clean stalls when I get home from teaching," he said. "Piece of cake."

I led out the first piece. Delaney. He raced out of his stall, nearly knocking me and Reese over. I yelled and backed him up into his stall again, and asked for a rerun. This time he came out with manners.

"Okay," said Reese. "I get the routine. Lead 'em out, scream, slap 'em on the chest with the lead line, scream, jump out of the way, scream some more, and put 'em in their paddocks. If you can do it, I can do it. Still a piece of cake."

I love sibling rivalry.

* * *

I called my students and told them that I would be away for a week or two and that their riding lessons were going to be put on the back burner for just a bit. I swore them to secrecy.

I called the woman who owned Isis and told her how wonderfully her horse was doing, and how I didn't want to rush things, and that, by the way, I was leaving for Africa for a while, but when I came back, she would be the first person to actually see her horse halt, which seemed to mollify her. It's not every day you can have a special, private showcasing of your horse standing still.

Then I called Delaney's owner.

"But you promised to have my horse fixed in a month," she said.

"Your horse is a nut job," I said. "I said I would *try* and fix him.

And if I can't do it, nobody can, but you're welcome to take him somewhere else."

She didn't miss a beat. "I'll leave him with you."

"Fine," I said, and swore her to secrecy, too.

              •   •   •

I had to give Richie all my information right away, so that Thomas Pennington could get our tickets. I read the packet of information that Thomas Pennington had given me. I had checked and rechecked my passport, and had gotten cholera and typhoid shots and a polio booster, all of which gave me a fever and a bad headache and made my muscles ache for three days. The trip was becoming more scarily real, I thought, as I swallowed another handful of Tylenol. And if the shots were this bad, how awful was I going to feel after I got trampled by an elephant?

              •   •   •

I was packing my jeans and sweaters and pairing off my socks when the phone rang. I grabbed it.

"I know what you're trying to do." It was Holly-Hotcrotch. Apparently, Matt was doing some swearing to secrecy himself. I caught my breath and sat down on my bed.

"Your plan won't work," she announced.

"Plan?"

"You think if you run off to Africa with Matt he'll fall in love with you again." She paused for effect, which, I had to admit, was pretty effective. "It's over. He's not in love with you anymore."

"He's still my husband," I said. Hardly a snappy remark, but my head was spinning.

"They say if something is truly meant to be yours it comes back when you set it free," she said, now coolly morphing into Holly-Hallmark. "So I guess we can leave that up to Matt."

"For your information," I said acidly, "he told me he *does* want to come back."

"Only until the divorce," she replied. "He's just trying to spay your feather brain."

I could barely listen. What was she saying? What was she saying? I think she said Matt was sparing me further pain, but it really didn't matter. All I could think of was that we used to be friends, and she had gone behind my back and pushed the war button.

"We'll just see how things go," I managed to choke out, but my feather brain did catch her last words.

"Oh," she said, very clearly, "did Matt tell you the baby is kicking now?"

* * *

Alana was furious. "What a bitch," she said. "I think she wants to keep you here because she's obviously insecure about Matt's feelings for her."

"Should I go?"

"Oh, Neelie, it's so dangerous there. Don't you watch CNN?"

"Should I *go?*"

"What are you trying to prove?" she asked.

"I'm not sure," I replied. "Maybe make him love me again? Or maybe just be with him without distractions, so I'll know what to do about us?"

"I would call an elephant a major distraction," Alana said.

"Yes," I agreed, "but it's not a *romantic* distraction. I picture the two of us sitting around a campfire, and baring our souls and drinking champagne and singing 'The Lion Sleeps Tonight' and finally snuggling together under a leopard-print bedspread in the hotel room."

"Is that before or after you bag the elephant?"

"After. When we're celebrating."

She thought it over for a long time. "Bring sunscreen," she said. "I would say about six hundred SPF."

* * *

By the end of the week, I had read so much about elephants I had a nightmare that an elephant was sitting on my chest and I was suffocating, and I woke up panicking and gasping for air. Alana said it was just a manifestation of my anxiety and I should try her lucid-dreaming technique. Manipulate the situation, she said. Tell yourself it's all a dream and make it go the way you desire. In my next dream I was drinking buddies with Jumbo and Babar. Saggy Baggy couldn't make it.

·   ·   ·

The morning of departure, Matt knocked at my front door. Richie, who was driving the three of us to the airport, waited in the car. As soon as I saw Matt through the storm door, my fury rose. He looked so unconcerned, an expectant smile on his face. He didn't look apologetic and repentant that Holly had upset me.

I opened the door in high dudgeon. "How tacky can you get to have your . . . girlfriend call me," I yelled angrily. *"Again!"* He said nothing, and just picked up my suitcase, which was near the door. I snatched it away from him, juggling it with the big bag of jelly donuts and sticky buns I had packed for the trip.

"I can carry my own suitcase!" I screamed. "You tell her not to call me! Ever! Tell her I do not wish to listen to her bullshit! How dare she actually think she can insult me on my own phone!"

"Holly isn't like that," he said. "I rather doubt she said anything to hurt you. She's not what you think. You probably don't know that she—"

"Prays for world peace every night?" I finished for him. "Oh, dang, did I miss her canonization?"

"Neelie." His shoulders sagged. "You probably just misunderstood what she meant. I know she would nev—"

I jerked up to my full height. "Are you calling me a liar?"

"I just think . . ." He searched for the right words. "Maybe she said something out of concern for your safety, and—and, well, we all know how you are."

"We all know what? That I'm so stupid you can screw around

and get away with it, and take all our savings, and then you and your—your—lover can have a good laugh at my expense? Well, I—"

"Now, now, kids." Richie was behind Matt. He took my suitcase from me and guided Matt firmly by the arm, down the porch steps to the car. "This is not the time," he said. "You guys can straighten everything out when we all get back home."

∘   ∘   ∘

Matt and Richie sat in the front seat. I sat in the back, angrily eating my donuts. When we had to talk, Matt spoke to Richie, who spoke to me. I answered Richie, who passed it along to Matt. It was a bit circuitous but certainly kept the conversation flowing.

"Wow, next stop, I guess we'll be in Zimbabwe," I said to Richie as we neared the airport.

Richie glanced quickly at me in the back seat. "Didn't Matt tell you our itinerary?"

"She didn't give me a chance," said Matt.

"He was busy defending his pregnant lover," I said.

"She was busy attacking—"

"We've got two long flights ahead," Richie interrupted us. "Normally Tom uses his private jet, but since he can't have this mission be affiliated with his companies, we're flying—"

"A private jet?" I said. "Wow."

"No. Lufthansa. Also," Richie continued. "We're not going straight to Harare Airport in Zimbabwe, because we have to eat frankfurters first, then pick up escargots."

"Escargots?" I repeated.

"Listen to me," Richie said impatiently. "I said we first have to meet Tom in Frankfurt, to pick up the cargo plane. You'd better start listening carefully, because things could get hairy if you don't pay attention."

And I could see Matt smirking next to him.

Chapter Sixteen

WE LANDED in Frankfurt after a seven-hour flight, tired, sticky—courtesy of my mother's buns and jelly donuts—and with Matt and me still barely civil to each other.

Thomas Pennington met us at the Lufthansa terminal and led us swiftly through customs, then drove us to the other side of the airport, to a huge blue-and-white cargo plane. He introduced us to Grigoriy, his Russian assistant, and then left to oversee the loading of the plane and to discuss itinerary with our pilots, two chain-smoking, wheat-haired, unshaven Russians who badly needed a few grooming tips. Grigoriy was in his late fifties, with pale-blue eyes and unruly graying reddish hair, and was sucking at a tiny stub of a cigarette tucked in the corner of his mouth.

"Call me Grisha," he said to us in heavily accented English. We all shook his hand with great ceremony.

"Wow." Richie stood back and whistled at the size of the plane. "Where did Tom get this from?"

"Is Russian Ilyusha, the plane," said Grisha. "Mr. Thomas knows everyone. He has friend in my country—lets him use plane when he witches." He smiled up at the plane, like it was his favorite sweet-heart. "Old Russian plane, but she does good work." I watched as his cigarette burned down perilously close to his lips. "Stronger than American plane," he said proudly. "She can carry much enamels."

"Much what?" I asked.

"*Da.*" Grisha squinted against the wisps of cigarette smoke. "Mr. Thomas—shall we say—is enamel server."

We all looked at him.

"Enamel?" Matt repeated, trying to puzzle it out.

"He said 'enamel,' but he I think he means another word," Richie said, and turned to me. "Neelie, you're good at these things."

"Oh," I said. "He means animal . . . something."

It took me another moment, but I realized that he meant "animal saver." Or "savior." But I wasn't talking to Matt, and Richie had already left us to talk to Tom, so I kept the translation to myself.

The cigarette stub finally burned against Grisha's lips, and he pulled a small black-and-red box with Cyrillic writing from his shirt pocket.

"Stolichnye Lights," he said, offering them to Matt and me. "Better than American cigarettes. Strong like Russian bear." He took a fresh cigarette from the pack and lit it from the glowing remains of his old one, before spitting the stub onto the tarmac and grinding it under his foot.

We watched them load the plane for a few minutes. Two or three tons of hay, along with several big round metal barrels and dozens of pallets of medical supplies and boxes labeled "Maize" and "Soy Products."

"Maize?" I asked. "Isn't that corn?"

"You did not see maize," Grisha said brusquely. "You did not see nothing."

"Oh," I said, wondering why I hadn't seen anything.

"What are the barrels for?" Matt asked.

"Water. There is shortening of water. All Zimbabwe has drought," Grisha explained between puffs of his new cigarette. "We give enamels the water."

Our suitcases were brought on, along with food for the ten or so hours that we would be flying. Nothing exotic, just sandwiches and cases of bottled water. And sleeping bags.

"Sleeping bags?" I asked Grisha.

"We sleep in bush," Grisha answered. He took a long drag, then exhaled and gave me a mischievous smile. "Five-star bush."

My fantasy hotel with the rooms nicely tricked out in safari theme went up in a puff of smoke from Grisha's cigarette.

"But isn't Makuti only a few hours' drive from Harare?" I asked.

I had looked at maps. Harare was where the airport was, Makuti was where the elephant was supposed to be, near the western border.

"*Da.*" Grisha nodded. "Just a few cows."

It was difficult, but I understood him. Sixty minutes make one cow.

"A few cows?" Matt asked. We ignored him.

Then I got worried. "If we're sleeping in the bush, what about bathrooms?"

"Madame Sterling worries too heavy." He puffed a cloud of smoke over my head, and it wafted down across my face.

"Madame Sterling might have to pee on occasion," I said.

He gave a brief acknowledgment by nodding his head. "Madame Sterling can use *toilette*. There is *petite toilette* behind pilots."

"I meant on the road to Makuti."

"Ah." Another puff. "Many trees."

Peeing behind the pilots may have sounded a bit unceremonious, but peeing behind some tree sounded distinctly public. I must have looked doubtful, because Grisha laughed up a big cloud of smoke.

"Don't make so heavy worry, Madame Sterling," he said, casually taking yet another deep drag. "We don't watch you. Americans worry too heavy over privates."

A staircase was rolled up to the side of the plane, and we climbed aboard. Except for the cargo, the interior of the plane was fairly empty, and resembled nothing more than a long metal tube. There were some jump seats folded in the very front, where we would be sitting. Now I felt that we were really going to Africa. To Africa and back. Returning, I kept thinking, with an elephant sharing the space behind us, in that narrow metal tube of a plane. A wild elephant. I kept staring at it, until Grisha touched my shoulder and pointed to my seat. I sat down.

"We go," one of the pilots announced from the open cockpit, puffing furiously on his own cigarette, and putting his two hands together and flapping them like a bird flying, just in case there was any question of how the plane was going to get to Africa.

"Button up sit belts," said the other, leaning forward to see out the cockpit window through the haze of smoke.

I couldn't help but think that some of the dangers Thomas Pennington neglected to mention might stem from sitting in a cargo plane loaded with hay and chain-smokers.

The great roar of the plane's engines brought me out of my musings, and I watched from the window as the ground rapidly fell away and an aerial view of Frankfurt angled below us, a maze of gray buildings and roadways.

I was glad that Richie sat with Thomas Pennington—because I still couldn't bring myself to address him by his first name—and, thank God, Grisha sat with Matt. I sat next to a case of granola power bars and opened one up, though I drowsed off before I could eat it.

I awoke after a few hours and watched sleepily as the men exchanged places—Richie sat with Matt, Grisha took the granola bars—and I rose and stretched and headed for the _toilette_. Grisha forgot to mention that it didn't have a door, which gave the occupant an unobstructed view of the cockpit, while at the same time giving the pilots an unobstructed view of the occupant. While I peed, I feigned great interest in all the dials and gauges and digital displays and took heart that the plane never so much as dipped a wing, reassuring me that the pilots were not very interested in observing what was going on behind them. I washed my hands and slunk to my seat.

Matt and Richie were sleeping now. Grisha was still smoking. Thomas Pennington was sitting in the seat next to mine. I was thrilled to be sitting so close to him. The last famous person I had been near was Big Bird at a shopping mall when I was seven years old. I shyly glanced at his face; the interesting scar that ran down his cheek gave him a certain mysterious virility. He caught me looking at him.

"Hungry?" he asked.

"A little."

He got up from his seat and came back with a few sandwiches, for me to take my pick from. I felt flattered and honored. Thomas

Pennington, serving me food! He was watching me with an expression I couldn't figure out—bemused, perhaps. I chose an interesting-looking blue-veined cheese on a baguette. He put another sandwich on the seat for himself, and left to bring me a cup of coffee.

"Mr. Pennington, how many elephants have you rescued?" I asked him, once he settled down.

"Tom," he said, opening the wrapper on his sandwich. His moves were graceful, deliberate, spare.

"I feel funny calling you just plain Tom," I said. It was like calling the Washington monument Georgie.

"Tom," he said again. "I promise you, after a few days in the bush, you'll be calling me a lot worse."

"You've done this a long time?" I asked, taking a bite of my sandwich.

He closed his eyes to calculate. "Twenty years. Maybe more," he said. "Rescued maybe two or three hundred elephants."

"Two or three *hundred?*"

"At least," he said. "My first one—ah." He lifted his chin and closed his eyes, the way a man would when imagining his first time having sex. "My first one had been shot seven or eight times by one of those game-hunters for hire, and left to die. We came across him by accident, while I was on holiday. I found a way to get the poor creature to a sanctuary in Kenya, where he was treated and saved. Nice big bull elephant. Twelve feet at the shoulder. By then I was hooked."

"Hooked," I repeated knowingly.

"Yes." He glanced down at his sandwich. "I guess it's like—"

"You don't have to explain 'hooked' to me," I said. "I do horses."

"So you do," he said, and smiled at me, a smile of camaraderie. Then he lifted his gaze and stared straight ahead for a moment, lost in elephants. I understood that, too. I waited a few polite minutes, then asked, "You said this one is critical?"

"From the severe drought," he said. "There's no vegetation. The thirst and hunger are making the elephants come closer to the villages, and then the villagers attack them. Sometimes the elephants get gravely injured, and sometimes they die. She is the last of ten elephants we just rescued. We brought the others to sanctuaries in Kenya and Mozambique, but they're full up now." He took a sip of coffee. "She's badly wounded. We had a hell of a time tracking her. We think she's heading up toward the Zambezi River."

"Wow," I said. "How does one even start something like this?" I meant it more as a rhetorical question, because I felt overcome with the need to sleep. I put my head back against the seat and closed my eyes, the rest of my sandwich languishing in my lap.

"And every time it's different," Tom continued. "An adventure."

I opened one eye for another quick glance at his scar. "A *dangerous* adventure," I said, and closed my eyes again.

"It is," he agreed. "But it's an odyssey, really. Consider this an odyssey, of sorts."

I turned to look at him—he had no idea how his words struck me—then I turned my head away, squeezing my eyes shut against the feel of hot tears.

All of a sudden, I didn't care about the danger. In an instant, my going to Zimbabwe didn't have so very much to do with my being with Matt as it was for me. I was doing it for me. Maybe it had always been for me.

I needed redemption. And I realized I wanted this to be my redemption.

Reese was right. There was an elephant in the room. His name was Odyssey.

Chapter Seventeen

I WAS meant to ride. I always knew it. Why horses take over someone's life, as opposed to dogs or cats or gerbils, is probably one of the universe's great mysteries. My two brothers and I came from the same gene pool, same environment. We all rode ponies, and swam and took tennis and piano lessons. It was just part of the childhood experience. But I was the one that got stuck on horses. Lived for horses. Knew they were going to be in my life forever.

And I was a nice little rider. I quickly grew bored with jumping horses, and my mother signed me up with a dressage trainer. I liked it right away—the obsessive striving to perfect each compulsory movement that was the hallmark of dressage training, the figure eights, pirouettes, straight lines that were straight, circles that were round. It was like equestrian figure-skating, but without the fancy costumes, and instead of being comely and lightweight, our partners were four-footed, lumpy-shaped equines, dressed in saddles and bridles.

I had gotten enough good scores at the horse shows to receive an invitation to train at the United States Equestrian Team Headquarters in Gladstone, New Jersey. I was almost seventeen. If I had a successful training session, I might even make the short list for the Young Riders Team. It was an incredible opportunity.

We were to work with Captain Pierre Chandelle-Meiers, the coach for the Swiss Olympic Team. He had made himself available to help the Americans. He would give us pointers. Whip us all into shape for the big international competition.

BNTs, we call them. Big Name Trainers. They were famous in our small, insulated world of riders and competitors. Their word was law. They were almost as revered as the ODGs—the Old Dead Gods—Alois Podhajsky, Willi Schultheis, Harry Boldt, those who had literally written the books on how to train dressage horses.

I was very honored to be able to ride with Captain Chandelle-Meiers.

∘   ∘   ∘

Homer was my horse. A gift from my parents when I turned twelve and my trainer told them that I had outgrown my gentle, not very athletic first horse. His real name was Odyssey, a well-trained ten-year-old brown Hanoverian, dark, like espresso coffee, with a black mane and tail and a long white blaze down his face. Odyssey. So, of course, his barn name became Homer.

We clicked right away. He lived to please me, and I lived to make him happy. We began winning at practically every show I took him to. I loved him. All I talked about was Homer. He was my first love, my confidant, my social life. And after I had gotten invited to Gladstone, I thought life just couldn't get any better.

Captain Chandelle-Meiers was in his early sixties, with brilliant blue eyes and white, white hair that made me think of the snow-covered Alps of his home country.

He seemed tall to me, although now I realize that he was probably only five foot eight or so, but he carried himself like an oak tree. Absolutely upright. He had rider's legs, long and muscled, and a little potbelly that hung discreetly over his britches.

He dressed like a military man. Tan britches, boots shined to mirror perfection, a starched white ascot over his white tailored shirt, a navy jacket with brass buttons, and a tan cap that sat on his head like a crown. He gave us all a curt nod when we were introduced.

∘   ∘   ∘

Homer always rode well for me. I barely needed to touch him with my leg, and I held his mouth very lightly with the reins. It was the way my coach had trained me, and it was the way her coach had trained her. She had ridden with Nuno Oliveira. Another ODG. Nuno used to give exhibition rides with a piece of thread that ran from his hands to the horse's bit, just to show how light in the mouth the horse was. And that was how I rode Homer in front of Captain Chandelle-Meiers. Not with a thread, of course, but my hands held the reins so that the bit barely disturbed Homer's mouth. All my signals came from my legs and back muscles. The Captain watched me work, his arms folded, his eyes burning into my back as I rode past him in the riding ring.

"More engagement," he snapped. "He does not come through."

I knew what he meant. The horse was too tenuous, not stepping his hindquarters under his body enough to support his full weight. Not releasing his mouth totally to me. I tried harder, pressing my legs against him and inching the reins in just a little.

Homer stiffened his neck against the unfamiliar pressure. I felt bad taking a stronger feel of the rein, but I did it.

"*Nein, nein, nein.* Not good enough," the Captain said. "Come again."

I was embarrassed. I wanted to be the best. I wanted a spot on the team. I tried harder. More leg. Stronger hand.

After watching me with growing disapproval, the Captain beckoned and I rode over to him. He gestured for me to dismount, then reached into his jacket pocket and pulled out a pair of spurs. They were round, with rowels. They reminded me of the wheels that you use to slice pizza. Pizza-pie cutters.

He mounted Homer and trotted him around, taking a solid feel of the reins. Homer threw his head up and flattened his ears. I watched from the rail, pressing my hands together from nerves, until my knuckles blanched. The Captain rode Homer for about ten minutes while I mentally begged Homer to behave, to give in. To just give in. The Captain wasn't asking so much, just for a little cooperation. But Homer had stiffened the muscles under his neck until they bulged like they were cast in iron. He thrust his head out, he shortened his stride into choppy little bounces.

"This horse resists too much," Captain Chandelle-Meiers finally said, touching Homer's side once more with his pie-cutter spurs. "Get me the Gogue."

The Gogue. It sounded so light. Elegant. Like a French dance from a more courtly era. The Gogue in C Major. Ladies in long gowns, men in frocked coats with ruffles at the throat, horses in a contraption that forces their heads down and their necks into an arch of submission.

Homer fought the device right away. I could see his eyes widening, his muscles cording up. He didn't like the feeling of pressure against the poll of his head, the pull against his mouth. He stepped backward, trying to relieve it.

Captain Chandelle-Meiers was not pleased. He leaned back a little in the saddle to drive Homer forward into his hands, and touched the pizza cutters against Homer's ribs. Homer grunted and hopped forward. I leaned against the fence rail and pressed my fingers against my mouth, breathing for Homer, willing him to be obedient.

Homer struggled to raise his head, then tried to shake off the unfamiliar device. He snorted. Then he took a misstep sideways, and plunged to the ground.

In an instant it was over. Homer lay there, his neck broken in two. Broken. His nostrils flared and his eye rolled wildly around, as if looking for an answer. He whinnied a soft, faraway whinny, like a soul retreating. Dying. A dying, distant, far-off whinny.

I had been holding my breath the whole time, and I gasped hard and put my hands over my ears, but I heard him anyway. His whinny grew softer, breathy, as if straining against this new journey to death, until it finally stopped.

It was over.

In one instant.

       •   •   •

I sat in my room for days. I couldn't speak. I didn't cry. In one instant I no longer owned a horse. I no longer had a horse I loved. I was no longer a candidate for anything. My mother would talk to me, and I would just look at her, not hearing her words. My ears were filled with Homer's whinny.

I never competed again. I didn't want another horse, I didn't deserve one. Captain Chandelle-Meiers had been telling me that my horse needed to listen to him and submit to his wishes. Homer had been telling me that he was frightened, confused, bewildered by the new requests made of him. I was listening, I was listening, but my mistake was that I had been listening to the wrong one.

Chapter Eighteen

THERE ARE elephants, and there are elephants, and as we flew across the continents to our destination, I dreamed of both kinds. One lumbering and gray, one graceful and dark brown. One needing to be rescued. One beyond it.

We were all asleep when we touched down at Harare Airport.

"Mr. Thomas," Grisha called out, and the rest of us snapped awake. "We make the landing."

I looked out the window across an ultra-modern airport, bustling with planes and trucks and cars. Ahead of us, the terminal gleamed in the brilliant sun, an enormous windowed building with huge green awnings that were half closed, like heavy-lidded eyes. The yellow, green, red, and black striped flag of Zimbabwe flapped vigorously in the wind. On one side of the terminal was a very high, rounded tower that looked like a cross between a pineapple and a pine cone.

"That's the aerodrome," Tom said when I pointed it out. Then he rose from his seat and walked to the front of the plane. "Listen," he said, "we'll be going through customs in a few minutes, and then I plan for us to leave the airport right away. Stay close to me. Let me do all the talking. There should be a jeep waiting for us. Be discreet."

We followed Tom from the plane and into the terminal, clean and brimming with light. Tom took charge of everything without appearing overbearing. The customs agents were casual and friendly, but I couldn't help noticing that over every door hung a portrait of President Mugabe, sternly overseeing all the proceedings. Tom surreptitiously passed out packets and packets of colorful bills to just about everyone who worked for the airport, so that the cargo on the plane could unload without being examined.

"Do you need anything?" Tom turned to me once we got through customs. "There's a loo here where you can freshen up. It's in pretty decent order. Take some Zims with you, in case you want to buy toiletries or anything."

He reached into his pocket and pulled out another impressive fistful of Zims, the Zimbabwean dollar.

"You're too generous," I protested, taking one or two from what seemed hundreds. "This is enough."

"The black-market exchange is insanely inflated," he said under his breath. "Over a hundred thousand Zims for one U.S. dollar—at least for today—so take whatever you need."

I enjoyed using the bathroom sans audience, then hurriedly washed my hands and face and combed my hair before rejoining the group. Tom pulled me aside.

"I've cautioned you about the political situation," he said, his voice still kept low, "so you are more than welcome to remain in Harare until we get back with the elephant. There's a Sheraton I can call."

"I want to go with everyone," I said.

He gave me a long, searching look. "Okay."

He quickly led us outside, across a large parking lot where a safari jeep waited with a driver. The jeep was big enough to seat ten people, and had metal crossbars that arched over our heads and supported its roof. Grisha loaded our luggage, extended a hand to help me up, then gestured for Matt to climb in next.

"And Mr. Doctor can take seat with Madame Sterling," he said, giving a little bow of his head.

Matt sat down next to me, and I immediately moved to the seat behind him and flushed when I saw that Tom had caught me doing it. He climbed in next and sat in the seat facing me. Richie and Grisha settled into seats in front of us. After everyone was aboard, Tom reached down and pulled out a large khaki blanket and tossed it at my feet. It was a warm day, and I gave him a puzzled look.

"Be glad if you don't need it," he said.

The jeep sped off. We were to meet the rest of the crew about one hundred miles outside the city.

In my silly ignorance, I didn't know what I expected from Harare—maybe something along the lines of Tarzan huts hung with leopard skins—but we drove down wide boulevards lined with tall, modern buildings, and colorful billboards advertising products like Koo Smooth Apricot Jam and Chibuku Shake Shake, a beer that apparently came in purple plastic bottles and needed mixing before drinking. We drove through tunnels made by lush red bougainvillea and jacaranda trees heavy with purple-blue blooms. But there was little traffic.

"No petrol," said Tom, when I questioned him. "I bring my own."

I didn't ask how he managed that, but hoped it wasn't on the same plane that had just transported all the hay and Grisha's ever-present cigarettes.

After the sophisticated main avenues, we drove through a city in calamity. Men huddled under tarps, slumped over small campfires they had built on the street curbs; mountains of garbage overflowed the sidewalks, almost blocking some streets. And men scoured through the garbage looking for scraps of food. Thin, starving, desperate men. Ragged, bony children ran behind us, with their hands out, and dogs lay dying, too weak to move or even bark.

"Very bad," Tom said. "It is very bad. No money for food. No money for petrol, not even for the government trucks to pick up trash."

"*Da,*" Grisha agreed, turning around in his seat to talk to us. "The golden-mint has lost control. Now they have elated prices." I nodded at him, which only encouraged him to expound further on the Zimbabwean political crisis, the severe inflation, the weather, and the plight of both the people and the wildlife.

"How did you get interested in elephants?" I asked him when he paused to light a cigarette.

He pursed his lips and took a long drag on his cigarette. "I work in Vietnam during American war many years in the back. American golden-mint napalms all the elephants." He looked down, his face darkened. "Very bad. I commence work to save them."

"Oh God," I said, covering my mouth with my hand. "Don't tell me any more."

"No," Grisha agreed.

We drove on. There was no place to turn my eyes. One street after another was a study in deprivation.

"Why isn't anyone helping them?" I asked.

"Golden-mint very bad here," Grisha said, standing up and leaning toward us, to make a point. "Mr. Thomas distrubumates maize and fruits to the peoples." He shook his head. "Loaf of bread cost peoples sixty-one thousand Zim dollar. Mr. Thomas gives all free."

That needed no translation, and I looked at Tom, now realizing why Grisha had informed us that we hadn't seen the pallets of maize. Tom was smuggling it into the country. "Bread is only about fifty-five American cents, but it is more than most can afford," Tom commented.

"Mr. Thomas has big peoples' charity to boots," Grisha added. "But everything is heavy secret."

Tom looked uncomfortable. "It's dangerous here," he said softly. "Mugabe is extremely sensitive to outside criticism, even if it puts his own people at risk. I have formal charities, of course, but the money becomes diverted once it gets here. I do what I can—I bring in food and . . . remove an elephant or two."

"There's no sanctuary you can bring them to right here in Zimbabwe?" I asked.

He shrugged. "There is Chipangali Rescue in Bulawayo, but they're strapped. And then there're all the complications . . ."

Words, words, and the money thing again.

We headed for the outskirts of the city, and then beyond. We drove past dozens of plantations that had been seized and now lay abandoned and fallow, and miles and miles of desolate, dried flatlands. Another hour passed; we ran out of gravel roads.

"The camp is farther west," Tom said. "I have to keep moving it, but the driver knows the way."

The jeep bounced along with alarming swoops and dips from the badly rutted dirt road. I saw Matt fly out of his seat twice, hitting his head on the crossbar above him. One more good jounce and he changed seats, which disappointed me. I was hoping he'd get a few more good thwacks before we arrived at our destination. After several miles, I noticed a large truck following us on the otherwise empty road. I leaned forward and poked Richie and pointed with my eyes.

"Truck," Richie said to Tom.

"It's okay. They're our supply truck," Tom answered. "They're just catching up. They had to unload the plane and disperse the supplies. The rest of it is for the elephants."

"*Da*," Grisha said. "The enamels get twisty and rummage the village chairs."

I had no idea what he was saying, but made a sympathetic noise, which seemed to please him.

We had lost the dirt roads by now and were driving over an endless stretch of dried yellow pampas punctuated by stunted plants, and round clumps of grass that resembled large, golden, long-haired guinea pigs; we drove past thorn-acacia trees, with lacy umbrella-shaped tops that looked too delicate to support the baboons that swung through them, following our progress. Impala startled and leapt away from the sound of the jeep, and herds of gazelle stopped grazing to watch us with cautious posture.

Africa.

I closed my eyes and took a deep breath. The air was scented with grasses and brush and wildflowers and dust. And there were new sounds. I needed to listen to these sounds. The huge flapping of birds overhead, whistling and calling, the screeching of animals unseen, roars and barks and grunts I didn't recognize. I wanted to memorize the noise of Africa, to absorb it and lock it away. I looked over at Richie, who was wide-eyed. I glanced at Matt. He was entranced as well, but said nothing. He had never turned around to face me during the drive. Not once.

Tom suddenly stiffened and pulled out a pair of binoculars. The merest wisp of dust was spiraling up in the distance. He leaned over and pulled the khaki blanket from under my feet.

"Get down," he ordered me.

"Down?" I was confused by his request.

He unfolded the blanket. "On the floor," he commanded. "Cover yourself completely and don't move."

In a minute I knew why. Two old trucks bucked and belched along the horizon, then slowly turned toward us. I followed Tom's orders immediately. Our jeep came to a halt, and so did our supply truck. I could hear Tom's men jump from the back of the supply truck, the clack of their rifles as they immediately positioned themselves around both vehicles.

"Renegade soldiers," Tom said under his breath. "Either from Mugabe or fighting him. Once you leave Harare, it can get pretty lawless. There are rifles under your seats. I want everyone to grab one."

I had time to reach beneath my seat and pull one of the rifles close to my body. I had no idea how to use it, but it made me feel better.

The trucks pulled close, and I heard the doors open, then slam shut, followed by men shouting in another language. Tom stood up in the jeep and shouted back at them in their own tongue.

Their exchange lasted for several minutes, while I lay under the blanket, holding my breath. Finally, there was the sound of laughter, and the trucks pulled away. After a few minutes, Tom reassured me that I could take my seat again.

"They call themselves war veterans," Tom said to us. "But they are poachers. Or looters. Or both. Some of them kill for fun." He paused, then looked at me meaningfully. "Some do worse." I shivered involuntarily.

"What were they laughing at?" Richie asked.

"They asked me what I was doing here, and I told them I was

going to steal their elephants," Tom replied. "And they laughed and said they are pests, not so good for eating, and we should take them all or they will kill them."

We drove another two hours without incident, but I sat co-cooned in the khaki blanket, and reflected on how far away I was from home, and how different Africa looked, the contrast of the golden savannas with the green mountains of New York State, how different the animals were, elephants and horses, and, sadly, how very much the same they both were sometimes treated.

Chapter Nineteen

MATT AND I had managed to avoid speaking to each other for the entire trip so far, but it was getting harder and harder to act as though things were normal.

Nightfall brought a rose-colored sky and a sudden electric storm. By the time we pulled into camp, we were thoroughly impressed with Africa's capricious rainfalls.

"I thought you said there was a drought," I said to Grisha. I was now using the khaki blanket as a raincoat.

"Heavy chowder," Grisha agreed.

"It won't last," Tom commented. "And it won't be enough to do any good."

The jeep pulled into camp just as a long, sizzling bolt of lightning revealed one large tent and about two dozen smaller white-plastic domed tents behind it, glistening in the rain like a city of huge, half-sunken golf balls. The outline of a grounded helicopter flashed silver against the wet grass. Three large trucks, now including our supply truck, were parked nearby, and dozens of men bustled around, impervious to the rain, carrying supplies and shouting exchanges in ChiShona. Tom, Grisha, and Richie jumped from the jeep and immediately busied themselves. That left Matt and me, and we still weren't talking.

"I'd better try and find the elephant vet," Matt said, more to himself than me. I turned my face away and stayed in the jeep, propping my legs up on the opposite seat. I was dry, protected by the jeep's roof, and was sleepily watching the lightning flash in sheets across the sky.

"You're sure you want to sit there?" Richie called out to me from inside a nearby tent.

"I absolutely cannot move," I called back. "I'm exhausted. I'll wait till it's over."

"Metal feet," he said, raising his voice over the crash of thunder.

"No, they're leather." I lifted my legs to show off my shoes. Then I caught on, and scrambled down. "Right." I agreed.

Metal jeep. And you don't want to be sitting in one in a lightning storm.

We were ushered into the larger tent, which was illuminated by the wavering lights of two battery-operated fluorescent lamps. Tom introduced Dr. Billy DuPreez, elephant veterinary specialist, and Donovan Hobbs, the helicopter pilot.

Donovan Hobbs reached out to shake my hand. "He's a Bateleur," Tom explained.

I wasn't going to touch that one. I nodded and smiled like I understood, and patiently waited. Matt, who was standing behind me, asked, "What's a Bateleur?" Bingo.

"They're a group of pilots from South Africa who have donated their time and planes to fly animal-rescue missions," Tom explained. "They named themselves after the bateleur—it's a type of eagle."

"Bateleur," I said, savoring the name. It sounded wild and noble. Donovan Hobbs smiled and bowed his head at me. He had curly red hair and was very tall and had an impenetrable South African accent, as did Dr. Billy DuPreez, who was dark-haired and short.

"This your first ellie?" Dr. DuPreez asked me.

"Ellie?" I thought I had misheard him.

"Elephant," he said. "We call them ellies."

"My very first," I said.

"Rack of lamb sidewise." He put his hand on my shoulder and smiled. "It'll grow onions."

I smiled and nodded. In fact, that's basically what I did for the entire hour, listening to him and Donovan Hobbs; I didn't understand one word being spoken by either of them, a personal best.

"We'll dine now," Tom finally announced, as though he were graciously hosting a dinner party in his home. He called to one of his workers, and soon platters of something called *mopane* in a peanut sauce were passed around. I spooned some onto my plate, and was eating it when Richie whispered in my ear.

"Like that?" he asked. "It's an African delicacy."

"Mmm," I said, lifting a second forkful into my mouth. "But it has an odd texture."

"Fried worms would," he said. I coughed and pushed them to the edge of my plate.

This first course was soon followed by plates of fragrantly spicy meat and roasted yams, and, having passed on the *mopane,* I hungrily dug into the new food on my plate.

"Delicious," I commented to Grisha, eagerly taking a second plateful from him.

"Da," he agreed, exhaling a long plume of smoke that totally surrounded my head and face. "Better than American cheeseburger."

"What kind of meat is it?"

"Barbecued warthog," he replied.

I went through every mental permutation I could think of, trying to figure out what he had really said, before coming to the conclusion that it was, indeed, barbecued warthog. I handed him back the plate, the food untouched. "Sure fills you up fast," I said.

Tom bade us all good night and left the tent, but not before greatly urging us several times to get some sleep, as though we would all be opposed to such a preposterous idea.

The storm had passed by now, and I stood outside the tent to look around. Grisha was at my side in a flash, careful to point out that Madame Sterling could employ the nearby very large trunk of a baobab tree to duck behind, for her *toilette,* which, he hastened to add, included the amenities of having very nice leaves to use for toilet paper, but to make sure that I was accompanied by either him or one of Tom's men if I should decide to pay a visit in the middle of the night.

"Why do I always have to pee in front of an audience?" I asked testily.

"Madame could take chance of intimate liaison with lion," Grisha replied, puffing on his ubiquitous cigarette. "They like—"

"Don't tell me," I said. "I taste better than American cheese-burger."

He opened his palms in a gesture of helplessness at the truth.

I eyed the tree and I eyed Grisha. "I'll call you," I said.

Richie walked over to me, carrying a sleeping bag. "This is for you." He transferred one into my arms. "Those small tents are for us to sleep in. I'm sharing one with Grisha and the pilot."

"For your sake, I hope Grisha doesn't smoke in his sleep," I said. Richie laughed.

I looked around. "Which tent is mine?"

"Over here." He gestured for me to come. "I'll show you."

"Great." I picked up my suitcase and followed him to one of the smaller tents.

"There's only one problem." He turned to me and gave me a rue-ful shrug. "You are sharing it with Matt."

Chapter Twenty

BE CAREFUL what you wish for, my mother always said. The gods had heard me. I was to spend the night with Matt in cozily intimate sleeping quarters in an exotic setting. Except I had changed my mind. I didn't want to share the continent with him, let alone a cramped tent.

Matt was in his sweats and fiddling with his sleeping bag by the time I ducked into the tent. There was a small flashlight perched upward, distorting his arms and body into liquid, eerie shadows as he moved. I wordlessly placed my sleeping bag as far as I could from him, a full three feet away, and pulled over my suitcase. The air was humid and warm, and the tent was filled with his scent—the scent I had sniffed at his pillows for, only a few weeks earlier. I studiously avoided meeting his eyes as I scrambled through my suitcase to find something lighter to wear overnight.

"Aren't you going to talk to me?" Matt asked.

A dilemma is always presented when someone you are not talking to asks if you are talking to him. To say no, you have to talk. And that inevitably leads to more conversation. I ignored him.

"Neelie?" He stood there, waiting for me to answer. I couldn't look at him. His hair was tousled, and his face vulnerable and tired, his voice inviting.

"Neelie?" He said my name again, softly.

"No," I finally said.

"How long can you punish me?" he asked, flipping open his sleeping bag and unrolling it across the plastic floor-mat.

It was my turn to answer, and I wasn't going to take the bait. I pulled out a pair of cutoff jeans and a tee shirt, then realized it meant changing in front of Matt. He was in his sleeping bag by now and lying on his back and smiling up at me, his head resting on his upwardly folded arms. If I didn't change my clothes, I would have been living in my present clothes for the past two days, which actually didn't faze me all that much. I had set a minor record wearing the same clothes the first few weeks after learning of Matt's betrayal. However, I did want to change my underwear. I had done at least that. But I was not going to do it in front of Matt. I eyed my sleeping bag and tried working out the logistics of a wardrobe shift inside of it. Matt caught on.

"Come on, Neelie," he said softly. "We're still married."

"Marriage terminated," I said.

"It doesn't have to end." He held his sleeping bag open. "You can come in here with me."

"Privileges terminated," I said. I pulled a pair of rolled-up panties from my suitcase. They unrolled before I could stop them and flapped in front of his face.

"You won't need your underwear," Matt added, a hopeful note in his voice.

"Not gonna happen," I snapped.

He sat up. "Isn't that why you came?" he asked. "To work things out with us."

"Wrong," I said, getting into my sleeping bag with an armful of clothing.

"Why else?" he asked. "Why would you make a trip like this? You don't know anything about elephants."

"Neither do you." I was wriggling out of my clothes while lying on my back, and my words were coming out in gasps.

"But *I'm* going to be treating her. Dr. DuPreez is going to teach me so I can take care of her after we get her home."

"And I'm going to be training her so you can treat her without getting stuck between her toes," I said. I had my jeans off. Undies were next. I tossed them out of the bag and slipped into clean ones, followed by my cutoffs.

"I know you love me," Matt continued. "And I love you. Come

inside my sleeping bag." He gestured for me to come to him. It was all I could do to turn away.

"We can work it all out," he added.

I turned over to face him again. "You meant to say we can *all* work it out, don't you?" I snapped. "You're forgetting Holly-Makes-Three."

"Stop it," he said loudly. "She's in a very difficult situation. You just don't underst—"

"Like my situation is all roses," I raised my voice, too. "How dare you make *her* the victim."

"I told you I was sorry." His voice was filled with pain. "I don't know what else to do. I'm a pail full of flounder here."

"Pail full of flounder?" I repeated acidly.

"Isn't that just like you," he said, "to retreat back into your safe little shell when I reach out to you. You never heard me when I needed you. You never did. I said I was painfully floundering."

"I heard what I heard," I muttered, turning my back on him. He turned out the flashlight.

"I *need* you," he whispered.

"You come with too much baggage," I said.

He sighed loudly. "She can be as much a part of our lives as you will allow," he said.

"You don't understand," I answered. "I don't want that bitch in my life at all."

"I didn't mean Holly," he said. "I meant the baby."

I paused for a moment to let that sink in. My heart felt like it was imploding, shrinking into itself, and turning into a hard black stone, then plummeting through my body in a free fall of agony as it tore its way through my guts.

"It's a girl?" I asked.

"Yes," he said across the dark. "I've seen the sonogram."

Something inside my mind got sucked into a black hole. I jumped out of my sleeping bag and ran from the tent. There was nothing but pain inside the tent, but there was nothing outside to ease it. The night was blinding black; above were the sharp crystal points of faraway stars. The humid air became a suffocating presence, pressing against my face. I had jumped from one black hole into another, and I needed to get away. I needed to stop thinking that this should have been *my* daughter.

I groped my way forward, trying to remember where the jeep was, thinking I would curl up in the back seat, under the khaki blanket, and try to regain my composure. It was a girl, a girl, and I heard a soft cry escape from me without my consent. Where was the damn jeep? I stumbled against something and felt an arm around my waist, catching me.

"You can't wander around without a rifle," Tom said softly, into my ear. "You are not at the top of the food chain here."

"I'm not at the top of the food chain anywhere," I said, choking on my tears.

"So I heard."

"You heard?" My face flushed with embarrassment, although I knew he couldn't see me.

"The night carries sound very well." He was still holding me. I could feel the warmth of his breath close to my face. "I was walking about, checking on everyone before I turned in."

I turned my head away. "I'm sorry," I said. "It's just that—it's—a girl."

He turned me around and took my face in his hands, his warm fingers pressed against my cheeks. "Listen to me," he said in a low voice. "This is a patriarchal society. Don't disrespect Matt here. My men won't help him if they see him as"—he groped for a word—"weak."

"I'm sorry." I stood motionless, unable to think. "I'm going to sleep in the jeep," I finally said.

"It won't be safe."

"I don't care," I said. I didn't. It didn't matter to me anymore if I became fast food. I turned to where I thought the jeep was parked. "My life is over." I started walking.

"Don't talk like that." He grabbed my arm, restraining me for a moment. My skin burned from the touch of his hands. He smelled of mint and wild grass. "Don't be foolish."

"I can't stay with him," I whispered. "He took a lover—and the baby—the baby is a girl."

"Come with me," he said, and took my hand, leading me behind the tents so that we avoided a group of men sitting around a campfire, and then to his own tent, on the other side of the camp, walking through the darkness with sure-footed ease. It wasn't until we were inside his tent that I realized he had a large rifle slung over one shoulder. He leaned it against the wall. I waited there, in the dark. Some of the men who were sitting around the campfire were singing and clapping now, to the accompaniment of sweet, haunting chimes.

"What is that?" I whispered. "It's so beautiful."

"It's a folk song, 'Muka Jona,'" he replied.

"The chimes," I said, "the chimes."

"A *mbira*," Tom said, "a thumb piano."

Their voices rose and fell in a rhythmic chant-song; the clapping broke against the still of the night; the chimes floated behind, like feathers caught in the wind. I felt calmer, comforted. There is dark and there is dark.

He rested his hands on my shoulder. "Use my sleeping bag," he whispered. There was heat in his hands, in his voice. There was something else there—a steadiness, the sympathy I didn't know I wanted, there was strength, and the excitement of him standing just close enough. I reached out to touch him, to dare touch him. I wanted him to kiss me. I wanted to feel desirable again. I wanted to tear my heart into pieces and throw away the parts that held Matt, and take the rest and press it together so that it would beat properly again, and send life and feelings through me once more. I wanted Tom, for crazy, unthinkable reasons. I wanted to hurt Matt until he was crumpled with pain. I wanted to feel arms and shoulders and hands touching me, reaching through the shadows and pulling me back, into desire.

I could feel his face coming closer to mine, his breath against my face, and I reached out and put my hands on his chest. I leaned toward him and raised my face to him. Suddenly he put his arms around me and kissed me. I wanted him to, yet it caught me off guard. The hardness of him, the heat in his lips, in the urgent way he pressed them against mine. Time stopped, the moment held us, suspended like a drop of water hovering from the tip of a spigot. It was all heat, burning through my clothes, my skin, burning into me. A piece of star had fallen from the sky and caught us, spinning us along in its gravity. It was a minute, it was forever, until we broke apart and stood wordlessly, the only sound our breath. I pressed my hand to my mouth and stepped back.

"Get some sleep, Neelie," he finally said.

"Yes," I said. "Yes." I dropped to my knees and crawled inside the sleeping bag. "But where are you going to sleep?" I asked. I could feel him standing over me, the smell of mint sharp and compelling.

"I'll be right here."

I reached up and touched his hand. "Please, you can sleep with me," I blurted out, wanting him more than anything, and ashamed of it, and ashamed that I had to ask.

He knelt beside me and stroked my hair. "This isn't the right time," he said gently. "You know that."

Chapter Twenty-one

THERE IS a distinct difference between implosion and explosion: one collapses into a heap onto itself, the other collapses outward onto everything else. They both break your world apart. The damage is just done differently.

I curled up in Tom's sleeping bag and silently wept, a little bit from embarrassment over offering myself to him and getting rejected, and mostly because I was heartsick over Matt's remarks about the baby. Tom placed my head on his lap and continued to talk to me, patting my head like I was a favorite dog and telling me that I was a beautiful woman and a fine person and I would be all right.

"There are losses that etch themselves forever, deep into your soul, and losses that can be replaced," he said, very softly. "Peace of mind comes when you learn to tell the two apart."

"I guess so," I said. Here was Thomas Princeton Pennington, sitting on the ground on a piece of plastic and cradling my head.

"I'm sorry," I murmured to him.

"For what?" he asked.

"For this," I said. "For—you know—for coming here—with all my problems and—stuff." My words refused to come out smoothly. "I was hoping that this trip . . . would fix things between me and Matt." How foolish I must sound, I thought, hoping to save my marriage by running off to Africa, and then propositioning the man who had brought me there.

I could hear Tom breathing in the dark. He ran his fingers over my face. "Yes, well, I noticed in the jeep," he said quietly, "the tension between you and Matt. I knew right away there was something wrong." His fingers traced my nose, my lips. "I should not have kissed you," he said. "You're a beautiful woman, but I—I was out of line."

I tried to sit up, but the sleeping bag didn't give. "I wanted you to," I said. "It's my fault, too. I feel so stupid. You must think—"

"Shhh," he said, gently putting a finger to my lips.

There was quiet between us. "I'll still work hard," I said. "I'll do whatever I have to do for, you know, the elephant."

"I know you will, Neelie," he replied. "Everything will be okay." I lay down again and let him rub circles in my hair until I drowsed off, and slept like a baby for the rest of the night.

* * *

Tom apparently had gotten up much earlier before dawn, because I awoke alone. I crawled from the sleeping bag, rolled it into a corner, and stepped outside. No one noticed me; everyone was preoccupied, packing up the city of tents.

Dawn was just breaking over the savanna. The navy sky dissolved into fingers of rose, threads of gold wove themselves upward, upward until everything was cast in gold. The grasses shimmered gold, the tops of the trees glowed with rose and gold. I stood outside my tent and stared, astonished at its clarity and beauty, moved by the pure light.

I took off for the nearest baobab tree, then came back to camp and found a large bottle of water and a tin basin in Tom's tent, placed there by Grisha, so I could wash. I scrubbed the scent of mint from my face and neck, fixed my hair into one braid, and rubbed insect repellant on my arms and legs before stepping outside.

Grisha brought me a breakfast of *mealie sadza,* a thick corn porridge, and fruit and coffee. "Madame Sterling sleeps well?" he asked. I didn't know how to answer. "Mr. Thomas gives peoples amusing account how he sleeps the night in jeep," he remarked, casually handing me the tray of food.

"Thank you," I said, now understanding that Tom had taken care of protecting me.

Everyone in camp was busily folding tents and checking equipment and loading the trucks to get ready to track the elephant. It was a whirlwind of movement, with Tom at its center, directing traffic, checking maps, consulting with his crew, burning enough energy to fuel a nuclear reactor.

He had at least thirty workers, recruited from the villages. Local tribesmen, with strong, proud, upright bearing and dark-brown skin and sinewy arms and muscled legs. They worked hard, talking among themselves, an organized, efficient army of rescuers. I wandered through the camp, trying to stay out of everyone's way, until I ran into Tom. He was stowing an elaborate-looking radio in the back of our jeep. He looked up at me, his face closed. I understood.

"Good morning, Neelie," he said in a casual voice. "Did you sleep well?"

"Yes, thank you," I replied. He nodded and went back to work on the radio. He left for a moment to direct some of his men, then returned.

"What do your men do when they aren't working for you?" I asked him.

"I have a don't-ask, don't-tell policy." He made a face. "They need to earn a living, and I need them. Plus I bring them food. But when I'm not here . . ." He shrugged. "They need to survive . . ."

I went back to Matt's tent for my suitcase. The tent had been folded; the suitcase was standing next to it. So was Matt, drinking a cup of coffee. His face brightened when he saw me.

"I tried to go after you last night," he said. "But it was so dark. Where did you disappear to?"

"I slept in one of the jeeps," I lied. His eyes were tired, defeated, and I wondered if he would turn out to be one of the replaceable losses Tom was talking about. I picked up my suitcase. "I'm floundering, too," I said.

"Give me time," he said, giving me a tenuous smile. "I know we can work things out."

I refused to smile back. He took my suitcase from me, just brushing my hand with his fingers in the process. "Please forgive me," he said. "I'm so stupid. I didn't realize what I said last night—how it would affect you."

"How things affect me seems to be last on your list," I replied, then glanced around, remembering what Tom had cautioned me about. "This isn't the place to discuss it."

He looked relieved. "We'll talk about everything when we get back," he said.

"Sure."

Donovan Hobbs, the helicopter pilot, came over to inform Matt that Tom was ready, the crew was ready, and they were leaving in a minute or so. Matt would be flying along with him and Dr. DuPreez, to learn how to tranquilize the elephant with a dart gun. They would be flying ahead of us and would radio her position back to the trucks just before darting her, so that the men could locate her immediately and load her onto the truck.

I would be in the jeep with Tom, Richie, and Grisha, the trucks behind us. Tom would stay in touch with the helicopter by radio. We had been given packages of biltong to chew on if we got hungry, a sort of salted jerky, consisting of whose meat I didn't want to know, and a pail of fruit. Donovan Hobbs started up the helicopter, and dozens of lavender and crimson birds screamed into the air. Billy DuPreez and Matt climbed aboard, and a moment later, the helicopter took flight. Grisha hopped into the jeep and motioned for me to sit next to him.

"Sit with me," I begged Richie under my breath. "I'm going crazy trying to understand Grisha."

He laughed. "And I thought you two were hitting it off so well."

.   .   .

Our jeep followed the helicopter, tracing our way across the savanna toward Makuti, leading two big open trucks, one transporting a huge wooden crate with twenty men standing next to it in the open bed, the other holding another ten or so men sitting in the back and chatting. Our driver had to gun the engine to keep up with the helicopter. Richie was studying the horizon with binoculars, while

Grisha chatted his ear off. Tom and I made polite conversation, as though we hadn't spent the night together. We were jolted and bounced around for another two hours, until, slowly, Makuti bush country revealed itself, the green and yellow grasses, tan-green bushes, and long patches of rocky, dried-out, concrete-hard dirt giving way to thickets of odd-shaped trees. Tom named them for me, *majanje,* red and gold *msasa,* acacias, *mpane*s, strangler figs that hosted huge brown puffs, nests built by weaverbirds. There were termite mounds the height of a man. Giraffes observed us in stately groups as we drove past, buffalo ran next to us, hyenas loped away in small packs laughing eerily; a straggly lion continued to sun itself without showing any interest in us.

The jeep bounced over the thick grasses like an unbroken horse. I held hard onto the bar over my head to keep from flying out of my seat and braced my legs against the floor. Hours passed and we continued tracking.

Then I saw them. A troop of baboons. They were sitting under a tree, busily grooming one another, swatting at the flies that hovered over them, chewing on pieces of bark. A female moved from the group to pass near us, her baby clinging to her back, its arms and legs wrapped around her, buried in her thick brown coat. She hesitated for a moment, and stared at us, worried, most likely, that we were a threat, then she moved on. The baby looked back at me with its dark human-like eyes. An infant. I could feel something rising inside of me and took a deep breath. "Stop, stop, stop," I admonished myself and looked away.

●   ●   ●

Dusk came and we had to make camp. The helicopter found a flat spot to land, and the tents were erected nearby. Dinner appeared quickly, and we ate a chewy meat and some vegetables and washed it all down with strong coffee.

I avoided Matt—I didn't want a replay of the previous night— and I sat in the jeep, wondering where to sleep. Tom came up to me.

"Take my tent," he said. "I'll stay out here tonight."

*   •   •   •*

I slept fitfully—maybe drinking two mugs of black coffee hadn't been the best idea—and was up early enough to witness another dawn as incredible as the first. I watched the day break over us and wondered how a land so rich with beauty could be so poor in spirit. So broken.

The trucks were packed in record time, the helicopter lifted off, and we were back in the jeep as it flew northward.

"Every day that passes, we could lose her," Tom muttered.

I dozed under a hot sun, and the dust settled over me, coating my face and my hair. I kept my eyes shut. The scent of the grasses filled the air—woody, spicy scents—and I drifted along with them.

"She's ahead," the radio crackled loudly and I snapped awake. "We're trying to get a fix on her." There was a static-filled pause, and Tom leaned forward, his ear pressed to his radio as the volume nearly disappeared.

"These are fresh batteries," he complained, fiddling with the knob.

"Trying to get a fix." I recognized Billy DuPreez's Afrikaans accent come back on the air. The helicopter circled around and over the jeep. "She's gone off into the bush," Billy declared into the radio. "I can't get a clear aim with the dart gun." I looked up to see him hanging out the helicopter door, the dart gun poised on his shoulder.

They circled again and made another pass close to the trees, but to no avail. The elephant had escaped into the bush. Donovan Hobbs landed the helicopter on a plain of grass and shut the engine down. Matt and Billy DuPreez jumped out, carrying dart guns.

"We have to dart her on foot," Billy called over. "Let's go." He and Matt ran ahead toward the trees.

"You stay in the jeep," Tom barked to me as he climbed out.

"I want to see," I said.

There was no time to argue. I followed behind Richie and Grisha as Tom, Matt, and Billy ran ahead, racing across the thick grass. The crewmen in the trucks were on the ground now, dropping ramps and chains, working all of a piece, in well-practiced precision.

My heart beat wildly with anticipation. This was it. In only a few minutes, we were going to rescue an elephant.

Chapter Twenty-two

⟜_____I FELT her even before I heard her, a soft throbbing under-current, a thrumming, that my body, rather than my ears, was pick-ing up. A quiver ran through the leaves overhead; there was a pulse that penetrated the base of my skull and seemed to synchronize its rhythm to my heartbeat.

I followed the men for another ten feet or so, across the stiff, knee-deep yellow grass and hardpack sand, passing an area that had been flattened and bloodied, where she had earlier taken rest. Then we moved toward the closure of trees, tracking along a path of bro-ken and hanging branches. The men quickly convened around Tom. She was in there, they agreed, just ahead, and they formulated a strategy to get her. Several of Tom's crew were dispatched to drive her from behind and into our trap. They slipped among the trees like shadows.

Richie and I were motioned to the side, to give her plenty of room, while Billy and Matt raised their dart guns, waiting for her to come out. I saw that Tom had a gun, too, the big, ugly one he had had in his tent the night before.

"What kind of gun is that?" I whispered to Richie. It had a wide, ominous-looking barrel, and I was afraid of his answer.

"It's an elephant gun," he whispered. "A .458 Winchester Magnum."

"An elephant gun?" I repeated. *"Gun?"*

"To save our asses," Tom, who overheard me, brusquely whis-pered back. "I've never had to use it, but it's powerful enough to kill her if she starts stampeding and one of us gets into trouble." I put my hand over my mouth to stifle a gasp. I wasn't sure what I would do if I had to watch Tom shoot her. "If you want to save her life, stay out of her way," he added, and I was sorry I hadn't stayed in the jeep.

Behind us, the trucks had been positioned, and now the workers were ready, poised. They had worked together like a machine, thirty men, each one doing his part, lowering the ramp, pulling the electric rollers in place, securing the wooden crate with large chains. Some of the men acted as sentries, pacing the perimeter of the work area, eyes constantly searching the horizon, guns perched on their shoulders like crows. I could barely breathe from anticipation.

I heard the men in the bush. They let out a low, keening, rhythmic sound, and rattled the trees for effect. The elephant responded with a guttural rumbling, just before she crashed through the bush, back to us.

Suddenly there she was. Bigger than I could have imagined. A noble monolith of mottled gray. Standing motionless except for her huge ears, flapping the buzzing flies away from her face, her tail lifted with apprehension. She took a step, but it was agony for her. There were open oozing wounds on her legs, on her trunk, wounds that carved out great pieces of flesh from her flanks. She shut her eyes with pain. I could smell the rotting infections and turned my face away. My legs trembled with rage at what had been done to her. The tranq guns went off, phfft, phfft, finding their mark in her right thigh, and the rescue was set into motion.

It would take about seven minutes for the tranquilizers to take full effect, and everything had to be coordinated. The large wooden crate was opened and pushed closer to the conveyer belt; chains, ropes, all were stretched and held ready.

She staggered forward a few steps, while the men behind her urged her toward the trucks. Toward us. Richie grabbed my arm and jerked me aside. Tom held the gun up, waiting. She took another step and, with a deep groan, crashed to the ground.

Thirty men were ready for this moment. Tom threw his gun into the jeep and ran toward the crate. Black, sweating faces intensely concentrating on their work, black arms ropy with straining muscles, the crewmen calling out to each other in ChiShona, and though I didn't know one word, I knew exactly what they were saying. They wrapped thick, soft white cotton ropes around her legs, which I recognized as the kind of ropes I used for training horses, and they pulled her, inch by inch, into the crate. I drew closer to watch. The heat and humidity made me feel like warm dough, struggling to rise against the thick air. I had to sit down in the jeep while thirty men, sweating and heaving, moved an elephant.

A chain caught, locking onto a corner of the crate, and Billy DuPreez straddled it, trying to free it with his hands. Tom jerked it and the chain lurched upward, hitting Billy between the legs.

"Hey!" he yelped, jumping out of the way. "Watch it! I've only got one ball left after my run-in with that hippo last year!"

"Watch it yourself," Tom yelled up at him. "There's a lady present."

"Half a lady," I announced. "I've only got one ovary."

Tom looked at me with surprise and then roared with laughter, before giving the chain a final tug. In an instant, the electric rollers eased the crate onto the hydraulic lift and slid it upward onto the back of the truck, where the men strained to right it.

I checked my watch. It had taken forty-five minutes.

Billy DuPreez and Matt jumped onto the truck, behind the crate. Billy filled another syringe with the antidote.

"She can't be sedated for long," Richie explained to me. Billy and Matt slipped inside the crate to administer the shot, then quickly ducked out. The crate was closed and locked, and Billy waved his hand at the driver. The truck started and strained, its wheels chewing at the dried yellow grass and packed dirt and spitting it out again, the truck engine whining its loud complaint. Finally, the truck rolled forward.

Tom grabbed my arm, and I followed him back to the jeep. His crew jumped into the second truck and, at a wave of his hand, gunned forward. The elephant trumpeted loudly. And the convoy started back for Harare.

Grisha glanced at his watch. "A few cows and we are back in Harare," he announced, pulling his cigarettes from his pocket. Our jeep jerked to life.

"None too soon," Tom said. "She's worse off than I thought."

We had just started rolling across the dried grass when I thought I heard something. Something faint. Barely audible. A distant call. Plaintive.

The elephant trumpeted again and pushed against the wooden slats of the crate. They squeaked under the pressure.

I thought something echoed back from the woods. Perhaps it was an answer from another elephant in her herd. Perhaps it was the dry, hot wind. Perhaps it was my imagination. The trucks rolled onward, crushing the dry brown and yellow grasses into whispers, and I turned my body, straining to listen.

"I think I hear something," I said to Tom.

He shook his head. "Ellies make a lot of odd noises," he said.

"Just enamel," Grisha agreed. "Sometimes they make noise for several cows, all the way to Harare."

"Can't we just check the trees one more time?" I asked.

"We can't lose the daylight," Tom replied. "We don't want to camp overnight with her. We'll have poachers up our ass, ready to finish her off for her ivory. Kill us, too."

She trumpeted again, but it sounded like a cry to me. A call to something she had left behind. And I thought I heard it again. A murmur of grasses, or leaves, really nothing. Hardly a sound, a just-perceptible shiver in the air. A ghost of a call. Like a dying horse. Slipping away from us, as we drove on.

Then I knew. She had left another elephant. Maybe even more wounded. Maybe lying there obscured by the tangle of trees, maybe dying. I tugged at Tom's arm.

"Was there another elephant?"

He shook his head no. "There was no sign of anything else. We checked thoroughly. But if she calls enough, she could bring other elephants. Strong ones. We don't want to get stampeded."

I sat back and strained to listen. Above the grind of trucks making their way through the grasses, and the screams of birds, annoyed at our intrusion, and the high cackling of a few nearby hyenas, I could hear it. I could still hear it. Distant, dying. Was it coming from the trees? Or echoing back from my own past? I closed my eyes tight and strained against the noise. And then I was certain. I was crazy with certainty.

I tugged at Tom's arm. "There's a calf," I yelled. "We can't leave it. We have to go back."

"There was no sign of anything," he said calmly. "We looked."

"No!" I screamed. "No! No! We have to get it. We have to. We have to."

"We have to get this ellie to Harare and stabilize her," Billy called down to Tom from the back of the truck, where he was standing, balancing himself against the crate. "She's in bad shape. We can't waste any more time here."

"You don't understand!" I pulled the door to the jeep open and jumped out, falling into the sharp blades of dried weeds and scraping the skin off my arm. I didn't care. I leapt to my feet and began running back.

"Jesus," I heard Billy exclaim, "somebody shoot her with the tranq gun."

Our jeep lurched to a stop, and the truck in front of us started braking. I was becoming a spectacle for thirty solemn black men, staring at me with disapproving eyes. Matt jumped down from the back of the elephant truck and ran after me, catching me by my shoulder and spinning me around.

"Neelie, stop it," he yelled. "You're acting crazy."

Tom jumped from the jeep now and caught up to Matt. "Stay with the other vet," he ordered. "I'll get her back in the jeep if I have to carry her."

But I had wrested Matt's arm from my body and was running toward the trees again, toward the sound. "I'll find it myself," I screamed back at them. "I don't care. I hear it!" I ran as fast as I could.

"Neelie!" Tom caught up with me and grabbed my shoulder. "She doesn't look like she's lactating. There's nothing back there except maybe a lion." I pulled away. He wrapped his arms around my arms, pinning them to my sides and dragged me backward. "A lion or a hyena that's just waiting for you to come back."

"You can't let it die," I choked, trying to free myself from his arms. "Please. She has a baby. Please." I didn't care that I was making a fool of myself in front of him. "You can't let it die."

"I won't," he growled into my ear. "I won't. I promise. I believe you. And if there's something there, I'll find it. Now get back in the jeep."

*   *   *

Twice I had felt my life implode, turn inward, pulling my world in around me. Pulling in the words I was hearing, the trust I had that things would work out, and, finally, pulling me in as well. Now everything was exploding, coming apart in great pieces of death and pain. I screamed at Tom, at the trucks, at the vicious beauty of Africa, at the heartlessness that lay beneath, and let Tom take me back into the jeep. I lay down on the seat, under the khaki blanket, and while Tom awkwardly patted my shoulder, I cried all the way back to Harare.

*   *   *

In the end, Tom diverted the second truck and sent it back with Billy DuPreez and they found her. A very young calf, dehydrated, lying inside a nearby grove of trees, about a half a mile in the bush, too weak to move, maybe dying, calling back to her mother. Mother and daughter. Or maybe its mother had been killed and we had taken her aunt. Elephants, in their matriarchal wisdom, will adopt each other's babies. The men carried her onto the truck. It took only a few men. Billy started an IV, and they brought her to Harare just an hour and a half after we arrived with her mother. They loaded them together. To be saved. To live. Together.

And I thought, Implosion, explosion, it's not so much about the direction as it is about where it takes you.

Chapter Twenty-three

BABY ON board, I repeated to myself, baby on board. Like those signs you used to see in car windows. Only we had a baby elephant in a trailer.

We were going home. The cargo plane left Harare, and flew directly to New York, where it and Tom were met by USDA officials. The paperwork was smoothed over, and the elephants were loaded onto a large trailer, as Tom had prearranged. We have elephants, I thought with some awe, as I watched them march slowly up the ramp into the trailer. We have elephants!

Matt was solely responsible for them now. He had restarted IVs in both mother and baby, to stabilize them as the trailer lumbered along the familiar highways that curved through the mountains of upstate New York.

We left Grisha with the cargo plane, for his voyage home to Pulkovo Airport. And now we sat exhaustedly in the cab, Richie, Tom, Matt, and I, too tired to say much of anything, our heads resting against the back of our seats, only able to grunt half-words, hoping that the others would understand and respond, and spare us the effort of forming whole sentences.

Despite my nervousness, the plane ride had been uneventful. Matt kept the elephant mildly sedated, enough to examine her. And he bottle-fed the baby, coaxing her to take weak, fitful sips of the special formula that Billy always carried with him. I slept sporadically, trying to keep a watchful eye on Grisha's cigarettes, and Tom busied himself going over importation papers that he would need for the USDA.

And now we were driving to the sanctuary in a small tractor trailer, carrying one large and one very small elephant.

Every so often the trailer behind us swayed from the adult elephant's shifting her weight. A camera and microphone were trained on her, and we could hear her grunting and barking in an effort to reassure her baby. The calf had dropped down into the straw, too weak to move, and we watched the monitor as her mother ran her trunk reassuringly over her head and body. Several times the mother trumpeted, and I smiled inwardly, thinking how startling it must be to the other drivers on the road to hear the trumpeting of an elephant.

The volunteers had the barn ready for us. The cement floor had been scrubbed clean, overlaid with thick rubber mats, while one half of it was banked deeply in hay. The wooden walls had been whitewashed and then protected with thick metal rods; the heat lamps were already turned on. There were crates of carrots and apples. An office had already been set up with medical supplies.

Matt taped the IV lines to the mother's body before Richie dropped the ramp on the trailer. The elephant, blinking against the barn lights, stepped out cautiously. Richie and Matt guided her forward while Tom and I helped the baby follow, supporting her body with the ropes. She was barely past my knees, tender and small and vulnerable and very thin from her ordeal. She trembled alarmingly as she held tightly on to her mother's tail and struggled to follow her into the barn. She dropped into the straw as soon as we let go of the ropes. Richie covered her with a thick, warm blanket.

We turned our attention to her mother again. That's when I noticed the chains. A heavy chain wrapped around each front ankle. They must been put on while she was sedated. Richie quickly attached them to chains that were cemented to metal brackets in the floor. The sight of them upset me. There is something repulsive in seeing a wild animal in chains. A moment later, she felt the restraints and tried to lift her leg, but they held her fast. She struggled against them, trumpeting loudly.

"Why is she in chains?" I demanded of Richie. Matt was busy adjusting the IV. My voice rose. "Why is she in chains?"

She tried to lift her leg, found it secured, tried to shake off the chain, and began screaming with rage and frustration.

"Oh God," I said, putting my hands over my ears. "I can't bear it." She thrashed her trunk back and forth with fury, aiming first at Richie, then Matt, trumpeting all the while, the whites rimming her brown eyes. Her baby, startled, tried unsuccessfully to struggle to her feet.

"Take them off!" I yelled. "Look what it's doing to them."

Matt just ignored me. He went on examining her wounds with his bright flashlight, while dodging her trunk, then rinsed out the deep pockets of necrotic flesh with sterile water and filled them with handfuls of white cream. Richie restrained the baby, talking to her in a gentle voice.

"Oh God," I said again.

Tom grabbed my arm and steered me outside the barn. "Calm down," he said firmly, after we stepped into the fresh air, "before you get the elephant even more upset. How else is Matt to treat her, without getting hurt?"

"She doesn't belong in chains," I whispered. She didn't. No more than Homer belonged in a Gogue.

"Bracelets," he said. "They're called bracelets. They'll come off as soon as they're finished working on her. It'll be okay." He put a hand on my shoulder, like a clamp.

I could hear the elephant screaming in panic, and the sound sickened me. I wanted to run to her, but Tom's grasp held me in place and I began to weep with frustration.

"I can't listen to this," I cried out.

"Stop it," Tom commanded sharply. "They have to do this. It's the only way we can help her." There was an edge of impatience in his voice. His hand remained tight on my shoulder.

I knew it was necessary for her to be restrained, for us both to be restrained, because I knew I would have foolishly run to her—to do what, I didn't know.

I was embarrassed at Tom's annoyance with me.

"I'm sorry," I said.

He put his arms around me in a great hug and rocked me, then stepped back and dropped his arms to his sides. "I'm sorry too," he said, "but you have to let things happen the way they need to happen."

He was so close to me, I could feel his presence in the dark night. I could hear him breathing, and I remembered the feel of his body when he had kissed me. What was wrong with me, that I was thinking of this?

We stood outside the barn for a little while more, but it seemed like hours. We said nothing, only listened to the elephant raging at her confinement. I looked up at the stars and thought that they had looked so different in Africa, but they were really the same stars, and we were still the same people. All the flying back and forth had changed nothing. Or had it? I looked over at Tom. Then it went quiet.

"You can come in now." Richie poked his head out from the barn, and we followed him in. I took a deep breath and forced myself to look at her.

The bracelets were still around her ankles, but unclipped from the floor chains, and she was able to move about. Her wounds were covered in salve, big white patches melting into her gray skin. She lowered her trunk and poked at the hay in front of her, then slowly sniffed the bars. Her baby was down again, asleep in a pile of hay. Matt eased himself from the enclosure and locked the gate.

"I gave her a shot of long-acting antibiotics," he said to no one in particular. "And I put some Silvadene on her wounds. The stuff's great for infection. I'll be back tomorrow to clean things up again."

"I'll stay with her tonight," said Richie.

"Good idea," Matt agreed. "Check her temperature at least once overnight, and call me if it goes up. Also, try to get some more of that formula into the baby."

"Will the baby make it?" I asked Matt, forcing myself to look at him.

He shrugged. "I don't know. She's very sick. The first two weeks are going to be critical, and Billy said that baby elephants are very fragile."

We turned to watch our new charges. The mother had lowered her head and closed her eyes, her trunk now resting on the floor.

Tom turned to us, like a commanding officer. "Well, good job, everyone," he said. "Thank you for your work."

"Thanks for bringing her here." Richie shook Tom's hand. "I can't tell you how thrilled I am. She's my first elephant."

"You're an enamel server," I joked to Tom.

"Ah. Grisha." He gave me a knowing smile. "He's a good man. Been involved in animal conservancy for years."

"What will he do now?"

"He'll go back to Africa. Maybe sneak back into Zimbabwe, keep an eye on things. Mugabe proclaimed all the elephants there are Presidential Elephants, and he promised to protect them, but they are still being hunted like crazy. Some of it to spite him. When Grisha finds an animal that needs me, he'll let me know soon enough."

"I think we should let them sleep now," Matt suggested. He gave me a long look and walked outside, hoping, I think, that I would follow him.

"Good idea," Richie agreed. He lowered the lights, and we followed Matt into the night. He and Richie stepped aside to discuss medications and treatment, in low tones.

I turned to take one last peek. Even in the darkened barn, I could see the outline of her huge body, the shape of her bony head, the big fan ears, and it thrilled me.

"She's magnificent," I said softly to Tom.

"You can have the privilege of naming her," he replied quietly.

"I'd rather name the baby," I said.

He raised his eyebrows, then touched my arm. "She won't be the last baby in your life, you know."

"Maybe not." I caught my breath. "But she's my first."

We stood outside the barn in a circle of triumph and immense fatigue, reluctant to let the night go.

Matt stretched and yawned and looked over to me. "Want to grab a cup of coffee?" he asked. "And then I can take you home."

"No thanks," I replied.

"Oh," he said. "Okay. Okay." He turned from me and walked to his car.

"I'm going home to shower," Richie said to me. "And then I'll set up a cot and take the first shift. We can do one week on and one week off."

"Let me know when you want me to take over," I said.

"Yep." He gave me and Tom bear hugs and headed down to his house, leaving us standing together in front of the barn.

"What are you going to name her?" I asked Tom. "The mother, I mean."

"Maybe Margo," Tom said, "after my mother. I never got to name one after her."

"Margo," I repeated. "Yes."

"Do you need a lift home?" he asked. "I'm taking a cab back into the city tonight. I could drop you off."

"Thank you," I said.

Half an hour later, we pulled up at my house. We had been too tired to make much conversation during the ride. Tom took my luggage from the driver and carried it to the front door for me.

"Maybe I could call you in a day or two," he said, his voice carefully noncommittal. "See if you've recuperated."

"I don't know how much I'm going to recuperate, sleeping with an elephant every other week," I said, "but I would like that."

"I'm concerned about you." He raised his arm to touch me, then seemed to think better of it.

"Thank you," I said. He stood next to me as I fished through my fanny-pack for my keys. I didn't want to ring my bell and bring big-mouth Reese to the door. "I'll be okay," I added, thinking I would give him a way out, if he wanted one.

"I think so, too," Tom said. "But I'm not sure you believe it yet."

"Will you be checking on—Margo?" I asked.

"I'll come up here once in a while," he said, "when my schedule permits. I think you and Matt and Richie can handle things."

"Oh." I felt disappointed. And annoyed with myself for feeling

that way. "You must be very busy, of course," I said. "It's probably going to be difficult for you to find the time."

"I'll find the time," he said. He stepped toward me and lifted my
face with his fingers and brushed my hair back, tucking it behind my
ear. I looked up into his eyes, because eyes can tell you everything,
but I couldn't read his. He has careful eyes, I thought. Then he
leaned toward me and gently pulled my face to his, and kissed me.
If his eyes were careful, his lips betrayed him. They pressed against
mine with heat and urgency and the answers I was searching for. He
found me desirable. Desirable. I wanted to know that. He kissed
me, and I wanted more. I kissed him back, and he held me to him,
covering my face with kisses. Suddenly he backed away a step and
cupped my chin and grinned. "I'll find the time," he said. "I always
find the time if something's important to me."

Chapter Twenty-four

PLATE TECTONICS. It's when the plates that make up the surface of the earth slide against each other, the resulting friction causes mountains to rise, earthquakes to rumble, and volcanoes to erupt. And I now had plate tectonics going on inside my head.

I thought I would come home and take a long, hot shower, fall across my bed, and lapse into an immediate stupor. The fact was, after mumbling a few quick greetings to Reese and Gracie, who was miffed at my absence and would not let me pet her, I lay awake for most of the night, feeling plates shift across my brain. Mountains sprang up and disappeared, earthquakes of emotion left me staggered, boundaries were colliding and collapsing. I wanted to hate Matt, and I couldn't. I didn't want feelings for Thomas Princeton Pennington, and I had them. Rivers of tears overflowed their banks. There was a huge sensation of continental drift going on. I was a geographical mess.

Grace, who finally thought better of snubbing me, was now all forgiveness as she jumped onto my bed. She gave my face a big welcome-home lick and made herself comfortable across my chest. Alley Cat tucked herself under my armpit, and we all fell asleep together.

. . .

The next morning, Reese was standing by the sink, gulping down a cup of coffee, ready to dash off to school.

"Good morning," he said. "So—did you bring him back alive?"

I poured myself a cup of coffee and let Grace out the back door.

"Her. It was a female. And we brought two of them back alive. She had a baby with her."

"I meant Matt," he said. "I expected you to be hauling him in here all hog-tied, and you smiling in triumph."

"I have nothing to smile about," I said. "Everything's still a mess. I'm a mess."

Reese put his hands on his hips. "Okay, this should cheer you up. How do you shoot a blue elephant?"

"Not now," I replied.

"With a blue-elephant gun," he said. "So—how do you shoot a red elephant?"

"It's not funny, Reese." I opened the refrigerator and looked for breakfast.

"Squeeze it by the neck until it turns blue," he answered himself, "then shoot it with the blue-elephant gun!" He guffawed and slapped his knee. "I have another one. What is red and white on the outside, and gray and white on the inside?"

I whirled around. "Didn't you hear me?" I snapped. "I'm not in the mood."

"What's gotten into you?" he asked. "Didn't you have fun in Zimbabwe?"

"No," I said. "People are dying there, animals are dying, and the land is dying. It wasn't fun at all."

"Oh," he said contritely.

I looked back into the refrigerator.

"Why are these in here?" I demanded, annoyed at the largesse of four half-empty pizza boxes stacked neatly on the top two shelves. I had left him eggs and juice and bread and bacon and fruit. And a roasted chicken.

"After I ate everything in there, I bought some extra snacks," he explained. "I was starving."

"Ironic," I said. "There's starvation and there's starvation."

"I'm sorry," he said, peeking into the refrigerator behind me. "You can finish the rest of the pizza."

"No thanks," I mumbled. "I don't feel like eating pepperoni pizza for my first breakfast home."

"Well, there are a few beers left, behind the boxes," he said as he grabbed his jacket and headed out the door. "Help yourself."

•   •   •

I did my donut run. The shop owner handed me my coffee and donut, and I stood for a moment, mesmerized by the bins and bins of fresh-baked pastel donuts. The smell of coffee, the sight of people lined up, casually ordering lattes and eggs on bagels as they did every day, it all felt strange to me. I glanced down at my own coffee and then at the line behind me. Every one of them would have a different request and expect to have it filled, without much thought about how easy it was. A dozen donuts, please. A chocolate donut. A Bavarian cream. No one would know about Zimbabwe and the men picking through garbage looking for something they could eat, for some stray cast-off piece of food they might bring home to their families. Men who would never know about the donuts here, stacked in huge fluorescent piles, fresh and inviting and so easy to obtain. Stacks of donuts, just waiting to be bought. Donuts that are always waiting here, that would be stacked and waiting here tomorrow, too.

"Anything else?" the shop owner asked me impatiently.

"No," I said. "No thanks." And I mused how even the simple act of buying donuts now seemed miraculous to me.

•   •   •

I put Delaney on the cross-ties and spent a good amount of time grooming him. He was a puzzle. Inconsistent in temperament and work, he was my most challenging horse so far.

Today he had good manners and stood quiet and respectful, letting me brush him and clean out his hooves. He even looked like he enjoyed it. He let me saddle him and mount him. Maybe I had made some progress in the weeks before I left for Africa. Perhaps he had talked things over with the other horses and decided to reform.

I walked him into my riding ring, and after a few minutes of warm-up, we picked up a trot. His body felt tight—I could feel it in his back, in his jaw, in the way he braced his neck against me—but he was manageable. The last time he had misbehaved with me, I had tapped a whip against his flank and urged him into a strong trot that settled him. Maybe that was all he needed, a firm hand and a secure rider who would insist he behave properly.

Fifteen minutes later, he threw me. It was sudden. A violent twist to the left that left me no time to react, no time to regain my balance. I hit the dirt, unhurt, and sat on the ground, watching him gallop madly around the ring, like a crazed merry-go-round horse. I got up, dusted off my jeans, and caught him. He stood trembling while I examined him. When a horse reacts like that, it is usually the result of unexpected pain—maybe a pinch from the saddle or an insect sting. I ran my hands over his body, his legs, across his neck, trying to feel for something out of the ordinary. There wasn't a lump or heat anywhere, and my saddle fit him well. I was stumped. I mounted him and cantered him around the ring. He rode fine, and I dismounted and led him back to the barn.

"What is _wrong_ with you?" I asked him as I brushed the saddle marks from his back. At the sound of my voice, he turned his head to me and opened his eyes wide. I braced, prepared for him to act up again, but he let out a long sigh and dropped his head. I studied him for a moment, puzzled. He didn't strike me as spiteful, and then an inkling of something crossed my mind. It was an answer I didn't want.

I can fix just about anything, except crazy.

*   *   *

Alana called me that afternoon to welcome me home. "So you came back in one piece," she said.

"How did you expect me to come back?" I asked.

"Frankly, deep in the bowels of a lion."

"Which would make me a pile of shit," I said. "Which I feel like anyway."

"I didn't mean it that way," she said. "How are things with Matt?"

"We had a big fight."

"Of course you did," she said. "Emotions are running high. You're resentful, and rightly so. And he's defensive, and—"

"I know all that crap," I said. "Tell me how to fix it."

"You ought to know," she said. "You need to talk it through. Define your goals. Decide if you want to be righteous or married."

"Can't I be both?"

"No," she said. "You have to pick one."

"Can I pick Tom?" I said. "He's very nice."

"You can't have Door Number Three," she said. "That's a different game."

"Anyway, Door Number Three rejected me," I said. "I invited him into his own sleeping bag, and he turned me down to sit up all night on a pile of boots."

"He knew it was Rebound Sex," said Alana. "And he didn't want that. He probably wants you on his terms."

"It would have been Consolation Sex," I said. "I'm not ready for Rebound Sex, because I'm not on the rebound yet."

"You'll thank him later," said Alana. "Besides, you don't know if he's in a relationship or not. You don't know anything about him."

"I don't seem to know anything about anybody," I said. "Everyone's just full of big surprises."

"Well, here's another one," said Alana. "I want you to find my kids a pony."

＊   ＊   ＊

Reese surprised me, too, early that evening, with an anchovy pizza, so I wouldn't have to cook, and a tape cassette he found somewhere, of old elephant theme music. I'm not crazy about either anchovies or Henry Mancini, but I'm less crazy about cooking. We finished the pizza with a bottle of wine, he told me the answer to his morning riddle was Campbell's Cream of Elephant Soup, we listened to "The Baby Elephant Walk," and I went to bed early. Grace and Alley were sharing my pillow, so I curled up with Matt's pillow, trying to put everything together. I had to rethink Delaney; my mind danced around the idea that the horse just had a screw loose somewhere. I had to rethink Matt and try to decide if my marriage was worth pursuing. I had to rethink Alana, who had watched me ride all sorts of bad horses over the years and now was brave enough to let her kids start riding. And I had to rethink Tom. Was I finding meanings in his gestures that didn't exist? I needed him to touch me. I needed to know that it was still possible. Was there anything wrong with that? What did I actually hope to prove?

The tectonic plates were shifting all over the place.

Chapter Twenty-five

SHE WAS ten feet at the shoulder, a wall of thick, wrinkled gray skin with sparse, bristle hair. A week had passed by now, and it was early evening and my first night to sleep with her. I stood outside her enclosure and stared in, studying her. I had never been all alone, so close to an elephant. She stood on large, round platter feet and had four toenails, like teacups, on each front foot. She had tusks that curved outward, like crescent moons, and large palm-leaf ears the shape of Africa, and small, intelligent caramel-brown eyes that stared through the bars, stared right through me, stared far off, past the confines of the barn, seeking something else, perhaps the comforting trees and bush and tall yellow grasses of Zimbabwe.

"You will be okay," I said. "I'll take care of you." She lifted her great head, but she wasn't really listening to me. She just stared through the bars, fanning her ears slightly, as though straining to hear the calls of her herd.

I pressed my face against the bars and continued to speak softly to her. "Good girl," I whispered. "Good Margo." She was indifferent to my words. Depressed. Grieving. And I felt ashamed to be human in the face of her suffering. "No one will ever hurt you again," I promised her.

Her wounds were grave. Deep gouges that still oozed bloody fluids, washing away the traces of ointment that Matt had spread on them. He would apply more tomorrow, to help fight the infection, inch by inch, until the violated skin closed and healed. I stood there quietly, until she finally closed her eyes and dozed. I glanced at the IV, to make sure it was still in place, and wondered how I would ever reach her enough to gain her trust.

I had read everything I could on elephant training, and most of it employed brutality: electric prods and sharp hooks and chains. I would have none of it. In the meantime, Reese's jokes ran through my mind, and I couldn't stop them. How do you train an elephant? Carefully. How do you know there's an elephant in the room? By the peanuts on its breath. There were hundreds that Reese had been telling me, nonstop, since I got home from Zimbabwe. Now, standing next to a real elephant and looking at her wounds, I wondered where the joke was.

I lowered the lights even more, so that the barn was dim and the shadows melded together, and then I sat down on my cot. Richie and I had given the baby a liter bottle of formula earlier in the evening, and she had finished most of it before she fell asleep in the hay. She was one very small, very sick baby elephant. Billy DuPreez had calculated her to be less than two months old. A mere infant. A two-hundred-pound infant. And she was underweight.

Margo suddenly let out a long, breathy groan and sank to the floor. I jumped up and unlocked the gate and pulled it open, ready to summon Richie, but she only draped her trunk over the sleeping form of her child before she lay flat-out, next to her in the hay. Exhaustion, I realized, and I shut the door to leave them alone.

A few minutes later, I was back on my cot, in the warm, elephant-scented air, and listened to the animals breathing next to me. I was trained to rescue, I thought. I rescue horses, and I used to rescue people. Now I even helped rescue an elephant. I lay on my cot, in the silent barn, without my radio. Without my music to fill my head. How would I manage the next twelve hours, I wondered, without my music? The room was filled with the breathing of elephants. The room was filled with their soft grunts as they slept. I pulled the blanket over my clothes and closed my eyes and listened to their sounds and hoped it would be enough to get me through the night.

*   *   *

It wasn't.

I lay awake. I sat up. I lay down again. I finally got up and walked softly across the floor and rolled the barn doors open to reveal a warm night and a full moon. I slipped outside to stand under a pale-silver sky and wonder how this was all possible, this sleeping with elephants. I wondered what the stars looked like right now in Zimbabwe. I wondered where Tom was right now, and ran my fingers across my lips to capture what he had felt like. I wondered what the African day would reveal tomorrow. How many animals were waiting for help. Wondering what Tom was feeling.

Wondering how both Africa and Tom had gotten so much under my skin.

Chapter Twenty-six

ᐁ─Aт SOME point I must have fallen asleep, because Richie
woke me up when he came in to feed. I jumped from the cot, embarrassed that I hadn't already been up and checking on Margo.

"How did it go all night?" he asked as he carried in several bas-
kets of fruit from the back of his truck.

"The baby finished two bottles," I said. "And then they both
slept pretty well."

He looked them over. "Good," he said, and threw in fresh hay.

Margo watched us vigilantly, always managing to place her large
gray body between us and her baby. The baby who still needed a
name. I could see the calf looked a bit stronger today, better than
yesterday, maybe a bit more responsive. A week of care had made a
real difference. She was standing more, and now she was peeping
out from behind her mother's knees, curious about me.

"Hello, Margo," I called out softly. "Hello, baby. Hello."

The baby flapped her ears and squeaked like a door hinge that
needed oiling. That, I knew, was a greeting flap. Margo growled and
flapped her own ears, before rumbling to her baby to stay put. That
was a warning flap. I understood ears. Ears are terrific indicators of
animal emotion. Horses and dogs and cats pin them when they are
angry. Elephants flap. I stood, not moving a muscle, until the ear
flapping subsided, and Margo browsed her hay again, daintily picking through it with her trunk and lifting it toward her mouth with a
delicate finesse. She would have done fine, I thought, dining with
my mother at the Hudson Inn. I wondered how I could join their
small world. It would all depend on how fast Margo got socialized.

"You know, we'll be able to treat Margo without those leg

bracelets," Richie said, as though reading my mind, "as soon as you get her socialized."

"Me?" I asked.

"Yep," he said, "Wasn't it your job to train her? That's what you signed on for."

"Oh, right," I said. "I just have to figure out how."

Richie handed me some fruit. "First of all," he said, "you can start trying to hand-feed her. Through the bars. Don't get all brave and go in there by yourself."

"Like I'm just dying to get intimately acquainted with the bottom of those feet," I said, holding a banana out to her, through the bars. She looked at me and then her baby, then back at me, suspicion and worry written across her face. She was afraid to leave her baby's side, even though she seemed to want the fruit.

I waved the banana again. She grunted and flapped her ears.

"You have to command her respect," said Richie. "Make yourself her target by calling her name, and then immediately reinforce it by holding out a piece of fruit."

"Right," I said, but couldn't help thinking that becoming the target of a wild elephant might not be the best career move of my life. I took a deep breath. "Margo," I said commandingly, holding the banana up so she could see it.

She let out an angry trumpet and several impressive ear flaps before rushing the side of the enclosure and giving my hand a hard slap with her trunk that knocked the fruit across the floor and left my fingers stinging.

It's not that I thought any of it was going to be easy—I wasn't picturing the two of us running toward each other through a field of daisies, my arms outstretched, her trunk waving at me—but I was hoping for some sign of recognition. She trumpeted again and finally did give a sign, of sorts. She turned her rump to me and dropped a large mound of poop. I decided that was my signal to leave.

"Coming back tonight?" Richie asked as I walked out with him. "She didn't get to you?"

"Of course." I replied. "I've had plenty of shit in my life, these past few months. You think one more pile is going to discourage me?"

"Great," he said. "That's what she needs. Daily contact, so she can trust you enough to let you work with the baby. You have to blow very gently in the baby's trunk so that she'll always recognize your scent. I already did it."

"You're kidding. Like playing a trumpet?"

He nodded "Almost." Then paused for a moment. "Listen, why don't you come by a little earlier than usual, like around four?"

"Isn't that when Matt usually gets here?" I asked, squinting with suspicion.

He shrugged and gave me a lame grin. "I'm still trying to help you two," he said. "I don't hold out much hope, but I'm still trying."

•   •   •

How can you tell if an elephant's been in the refrigerator? By the footprints on the butter. What do elephants take when they get hysterical? Trunkquilizers. Reese thought that one was especially funny. I found an elephant cap with big plastic ears and bouncy accordion-folded trunk that Reese had bought in a dollar store and left on the kitchen table along with a five-pound bag of peanuts tied with a pink bow. I found a banana propped in my coffee mug. Elephant socks on my dresser. A stuffed gray-and-yellow-checked elephant on my pillow. I knew Reese was doing his goony best to cheer me up, but I really wished to be alone, so that I would have the luxury of brooding over the fact that I was alone. I finally told him so.

I had worked the horses for the day and showered, and now Reese and I were having an early dinner that wasn't pizza. It was a bag of McDonald's. In an hour or so, I would have to return to the barn for another night with Margo. I was trying not to gulp down my cheeseburger; Reese was savoring his, wearing the elephant hat.

"I think that one should always dress formally for dinner," Reese commented, opening the wrappings on his second burger.

"Don't you have a life?" I replied.

"Mom thinks I should hang out here for a while," he replied. "She thinks you could use a campy Rottweiler."

"Is that a recognized breed?"

"Company for a while," he repeated. "Honestly, Neelie. How did you ever get along in Zimbabwe with your hearing problems?"

"Except for one or two skirmishes with Matt and Richie, I had no problems at all," I said. "None." And then I put my cheeseburger down and thought about how odd that was.

Chapter Twenty-seven

"WHAT DO you think of 'Dorothea'?" I asked my mother. "I might name the baby Dorothea."

We were having lunch again, at the Hudson Inn. She was sipping a Bay Breeze, I had a vodka martini.

"The baby?" She put her drink down and looked at me. "Did something happen in Africa that you're not telling me?"

I gave her a big smile. "For the baby elephant," I said. "I have to name her."

"Dorothea is a lovely name," she said. "Your grandmother's name. I thought you were going to save it as a middle name for your first daughter."

"This baby is," I said. "Kind of."

"And do you think your grandmother would be honored to have a . . . a . . . *wild animal* named after her?" she asked primly. "I think it would have broken her heart."

"It's a very nice elephant, and she's going to grow up big and strong," I said, slugging back the martini. "Big elephant, big honor."

"I'd be embarrassed to death to have an elephant share my mother's name." She stabbed up a tiny forkful of salmon.

"Or Amanda," I said.

"Now, there's a good idea," she agreed. "Your dad's mother. I wouldn't have any objections to that."

I pushed away my Caesar salad—I had little appetite for it—and waited impatiently for my mother to pick through her salmon. She looked up at me.

"Are you in a hurry?" she asked.

"What makes you ask?"

"I hear your feet tapping on the floor," she said. "Are you too much in a hurry for dessert as well?"

The jelly-donut tradition. "I have to work three horses this afternoon and teach two students," I said. "I spent the whole morning with the elephants, and my workday is only one-third over."

"Aren't you spreading yourself too thin?" she asked, taking another morsel.

"Listen, are you going to finish your lunch?" I asked in exasperation. "I can't spend much more time."

"We can always skip going to the donut shop," she said.

"No, we can't," I said.

We wound up skipping sitting with coffee, though I did buy a bag of donuts. I grabbed them from the shop clerk and practically pushed my mother out the door.

"So what's happening with you and Matt?" she asked, following me as I race-walked to my truck.

"I have no idea," I said, peeking inside the bag to make sure I had been given six raspberry jellies. "I don't even think about him."

"You can't hide behind this elephant forever," my mother chided, kissing me good-bye. "You have a space flight."

"A space flight?" I asked. "Are we going to the moon now?"

"Face life," she said. "Face life!"

"I *am* facing life," I said to her. "In my own peculiar way."

•   •   •

I spent that afternoon being alternately disgusted and jubilant, depending on who I was riding. Delaney was still a problem child—riding well, then spooking across the ring. I couldn't get a handle on him. I tried being firm, strong, demanding, as well as sympathetic, and I was still hanging on for dear life as he skittered away from something that existed only in his mind. Isis, on the other hand, was giving me more and more piaffe steps, in perfect rhythm. Soon it would be time for her owner to take lessons on her. That was great, because I would get paid not only to train the horse but also for training the owner to ride the horse. And getting paid was a very good thing.

"That's your dinner?" Reese asked me with alarm, when I put all six jelly donuts on a big plate, with a mug of warm milk, in preparation for eating them in bed. I had finished a week of sleeping with the elephants and was greatly looking forward to actually sleeping with my mattress.

"That's *your* dinner?" I asked, pointing to the pizza with mushrooms and pepperoni that he had just brought home.

"At least mine has vegetables and protein," he said. "So it's healthful."

"And mine has fruit and grains," I said. "Equally healthful."

We stared at each other for a moment, then took our respective dinners to our respective bedrooms for a night of TV and junk food. I was very tired. Tomorrow I would rise at dawn, race to the sanctuary to try to get Margo interested in fruit, race back to clean my barn, then work Isis and Delaney. I had no time for my own horses; Mousi was giving me lonely looks over his fence, whereas Conversano seemed to be firmly convinced that his life of loafing was just about perfect.

I was up to donut number three, and watching people eat worms on television to prove how brave they were, when the phone rang downstairs. I ignored it. I had taken the phone out of my bedroom right after the first phone call from Holly-Hateful. I heard footsteps on the stairs.

"It's for you," Reese said through my door. "Tom something?"

I leapt to my feet and opened the door. "I'll take it in here," I said, grabbing the phone from him with shaking hands and shutting the door again for privacy.

"How are things?" Tom asked after I said a breathy hello. I was surprised by how glad I was to hear his voice.

"Margo's doing okay," I announced, settling back against my pillow. "She's eating her elephant chow and alfalfa hay and—"

"I meant you," he said.

"I'm okay," I said.

"Are you sure?" he asked.

"No."

"Well, then, I'd better come by and check on you," he said with a little laugh. "Maybe we can meet at the sanctuary tomorrow and go for a proper dinner?"

"I'd like that," I said. "I kind of miss the barbecued warthog."

"I don't know if I can promise you that, but there's got to be a nice restaurant somewhere in your region."

"Maybe one," I said.

"I'll ask around," he said, then paused. "You say Margo's doing okay?"

"I'm feeding her bananas," I said, then thought, dang, I had just given him a wrong impression. I hoped he didn't think I was *personally* feeding her bananas, because I meant I was *technically* feeding her bananas by letting her slap them out of my hand. There was a big difference.

"Wonderful! She needs that personal contact," he said. "You're on the right track."

"Actually, I'm—" I started, but he interrupted me.

"Damn, sorry to cut you short," he said in a rush, "but I'm being paged. I've got to get to a dinner and I'm running late, but I'm looking forward to tomorrow."

He clicked off.

I heard a noise outside my bedroom door. Probably Grace. I opened the door to let her in. It was Reese, bending down like he was tying his shoelaces, except that he was wearing socks.

"You were listening in," I accused him.

"How could I hear anything over your TV?" he asked. "But who is he?"

"He's the elephant man," I said. "I'm going to have dinner with him tomorrow."

"Elephant man?" he repeated, then looked very sympathetic. "Oh. Wow. Sorry. I didn't realize."

"Not that kind of elephant man, you idiot," I snapped. "The elephant man I went to Africa with."

"Oh. Right." Reese said. "Listen, would you mind asking him a question for me?"

"Sure," I replied. "What do you want to ask?"

He took a deep breath. "How do you know if there's an elephant under the bed?"

My shoe just missed him.

Chapter Twenty-eight

THE NEXT day proved to be very ecclesiastical, because I spent most of it praying. I prayed all the way to the sanctuary, that Margo wouldn't make me look incompetent in front of Tom. I pictured myself blithely handing her bananas and Margo trumpeting and throwing them right back in my face.

"Please let the elephant take my bananas," I prayed, sending to heaven perhaps one of its more unusual requests. That prayer was quickly followed by "And please let Tom still be talking to me when the day is over, because I'm going to look like a real fool."

. = .

Tom arrived at the sanctuary office promptly at one o'clock, looking fresh and handsome, in a distinguished, silver-haired gentleman-farmer kind of way. He was dressed in acid-washed jeans, Movado watch, expensive loafers, and an immaculate, freshly pressed blue dirndl shirt. My heart jumped at the sight of him.

"How are you doing?" he asked, giving me a salutatory peck on the cheek when he saw me and Richie.

"Pretty good," I said. "I'm over my jet lag."

"Glad to hear it," he said. "You look none the worse for wear."

Matt, on the other hand, arrived late, drooping with fatigue, needing a shave and a haircut, and wearing a shirt and pair of pants that looked like they had seen a lot of veterinary work.

"How's it going?" Tom asked him, as I stood behind him, making faces at Matt's obvious lapses in hygiene. Matt noticed.

"Horrible," said Matt, giving me a withering look. "I haven't slept since we got back, and I've had to take over my whole practice."

"That's because his partner is busy being pregnant," I offered helpfully.

"To err is human," Matt said between his teeth. "Are you familiar with that quote?"

"How about this one?" I retorted. "To love and honor, forsaking all others."

"Let's check on Margo," Tom said, diplomatically stepping between us and leading us to the barn. Richie quickly secured Margo's bracelets to the floor chains, and Matt administered a mild tranquilizer before carefully washing her wounds and applying huge handfuls of Silvadene ointment. He finished by giving her another shot of antibiotics. The wounds that had covered her hips and legs were starting to close up; her ears and trunk showed new, healing pink skin. Even the baby looked stronger.

"Come on in," Richie invited me and Tom into the enclosure when Matt was finished. Tom approached Margo slowly, talking softly until he reached her side and was able to run his hands over her legs.

"I see real improvement," he said. "I'm very pleased. Then he turned to me. "How are you coming with her training?"

I took a deep breath. "I've been holding up bananas so she will regard me as the source of her treats," I said. "I want her to learn that I'm her target and focus on me." Richie gave me a thumbs-up from behind Tom's back.

"Excellent," Tom said. "And how's it working?"

"Working?" I repeated, wondering how I could tell him it really wasn't.

"Margo took a banana right from Neelie's hand," Richie added.

"Slapped it, really," I said.

"Wonderful," said Tom. "At least she's interacting with you."

"Right," I said. It appeared that everything had gone well, and I was relieved. My prayer had been answered, Tom was pleased, and I still had my fingers. I turned to leave the cage.

"Can I watch?" Tom asked.

I spun around in surprise. "Watch what?"

"Her take a banana from your hand?"

I looked at Richie with mounting panic, hoping he would save me from humiliation. He held out the basket of fruit, without any expression on his face. I didn't know what to do. Margo hadn't been civil to me since we both got to New York. I took a banana.

"Move a little closer," Richie suggested.

"Oh, right," I said. *"Thank you."*

I moved another two feet toward her and held out the fruit.

"Margo, take the banana," I said, praying silently that she wouldn't separate my hand from my arm in the process. *And hurry, before the sedatives wear off,* I mentally added. I could see she was getting the flap back in her ears.

Then I remembered what Richie had told me. "Look *here*," I commanded, standing tall and holding the banana in front of me like a waitress serving a customer. *Hello, my name is Neelie, and I'll be your target for today.*

She faced me. Her trunk touched my arm and ran down my hand. My heart was pounding. Her trunk stopped at the banana. She yanked it away from me, and stuffed it into her mouth. I marveled at my good luck.

"See?" said Richie to Tom, while I composed myself. "This is just the beginning. Next week, Neelie will be feeding her inside the cage without the leg chains."

Tom beamed and patted my shoulder. "Great," he said. "Great. You're doing wonderfully."

I thanked heaven for small banana-shaped favors, Richie undid the bracelets from the floor chains, and we closed the gates.

It was time to go, but Matt seemed to be spending an unusually long time in the small office attached to the barn, checking his supplies. Several times he peeked out. I realized that he was waiting for Tom and Richie to leave so we could be alone, but Richie was chattering on about the lions. Tom kept nodding pleasantly, Richie kept talking, Matt kept stalling. We were in gridlock.

Matt finally got paged, made his apologies, and drove off. Richie ran out of small talk and had to feed the other animals. That left Tom and me.

"I thought they would never leave," Tom said. "Ready for a late lunch?"

My small victory with Margo had worked up a huge appetite. "I'm ready," I said.

*   *   *

Warthog was not on the menu, though I hadn't really developed a taste for it, and I was too thrilled to eat much of my dinner anyway. Though I had shared a tent with Tom in Zimbabwe, it felt different to share a table. He looked more important, more distinguished, more handsome. He was animated and witty, and though we drank wine, and ate good pasta, and talked about saving elephants, his eyes lingered a second too long each time he looked at me. We talked of everything. Books and music and good food and traveling. And elephants.

"It's terrible that elephants even have to be rescued," I said.

He nodded in agreement. "It's terrible that we have to teach humans to be humane."

I took a piece of bread. He studied me, gray-green eyes steady, solemn, filled with—what?—amusement? "I admire you for following this whole project through, you know," he said. "Not too many women would agree to something so dangerous."

"Have you ever been hurt?" I asked. "I meant, by one of your rescues?"

He rubbed the scar on his cheek. "One of my early elephants," he said ruefully. "Before I learned to dodge tusks."

"Wow," I said. "And here I've been wasting my time worrying about falling under their feet."

He laughed and clicked his glass against mine. "I'm impressed with you," he said. "You've done more than I had a right to expect." I studied him as he took a sip of his wine. His face was lean, his nose was straight, linear. There was a certain assurance about him, as though all the plans he ever made fell right into place, as though he would brook no other outcome. Commanding. "Your devotion to Margo amazes me, especially considering what you've been going through. Divorce is not fun."

"Have you ever been through a divorce?" I asked.

"Twice." He made a sour face. "And I think it's easier to save an elephant than a relationship."

I guess he had experienced failures, though there was a sense of control about him. And serenity. I liked the serenity.

We finished our lunch and lingered until Tom checked his watch. "It's getting late," he said. "If you want, I can follow you so that you get home safely, and then I'm off to the city. I didn't use my driver tonight, so I don't want to be driving back when I'm tired."

"Right," I said. Our eyes met and something passed between us. Neither one of us looked away.

"I don't mean to pry," he began, "but are you officially single?"

"I'm extremely single," I said. "I'm just not papered yet."

He laughed, then looked down at his plate with an embarrassed grin. "I feel awkward," he said. "Because I'm sort of your boss, but I would like to ask you something."

"What?" I asked.

"Maybe we could see each other once in a while?" he said. "Without elephants?"

"I would like that very much," I said. Then blurted, "Would you like to come back to my house for coffee?"

If he was surprised, he didn't show it. "Thank you," he said. "I would like that very much."

Then I remembered Reese. "I just have to run to the ladies' room—I'll be right back."

I phoned my house from a stall in the ladies' room.

"Go home," I said to Reese, after he picked up the phone.

"What?"

"Go home," I repeated. "I am bringing the elephant man back with me and I want some privacy. Take your pizza boxes and go home."

"Can't I go home in the morning?" he asked. "I was just getting comfortable."

"This is important to me." I was getting irritated. "And I really don't need a babysitter."

"I'm under Mother's orders," he said.

"For what?" I asked.

"Because she's worried about you not eating, and dundering around Africa, misunderstanding everything that goes on around you."

"I don't have time for this," I whispered fiercely into the phone. "I am coming home in about twenty minutes, so please don't be there."

"Am I to understand that you have given up on Matt?"

"Whose team are you on?" I hissed.

"There are teams?" he asked. "If I join yours, do I get a free jersey that says Team Elephant?"

"Twenty minutes," I said, and disconnected.

Tom was waiting for me when I returned. I got into my truck, he got into his hunter-green Bentley, and as we left for my house, I was praying that Reese would be gone, and that maybe something would work out between Tom and me, and then I wondered if I was being too presumptuous to send up this last fervent prayer for the day.

Chapter Twenty-nine

SOMEONE UP there was listening, because Reese was gone by the time I got home. I led Tom into the house, where Grace sniffed his shoes for an embarrassingly long time before finally nipping him in the shoelaces. I pulled her off. "NO BITE!" I growled into her ear.

"What does she have against Bruno Maglis?" Tom asked, retying his shoelaces.

"She has issues," I explained, then excused myself to lock her in the bathroom.

When I got back, Tom was staring at a mug on the drain rack that Matt had always used for his morning coffee. It was a big blue mug with a shaggy dog on the front, and it read "World Class Vet." Reese had started drinking out of it. I turned it to face the other way.

"My brother was here," I said. "I guess he was using it."

Tom raised his hand to my face and ran his thumb across my cheek. It left a trail of sweetness.

"Would you prefer I go home?" he asked gently.

"No," I said, reaching up and clasping his hand in mine. I didn't want him to go. I wanted to let go of Matt. I didn't want it to be his and my house anymore. I wanted to cleanse him from everything. I wanted to begin a new life.

I stood awkwardly in front of Tom, painfully aware that everything in the house had once belonged to Matt and me, and I was standing in it with another man.

"I guess I'll make coffee," I said.

"Not now," he said. He was being very polite, but I could see him looking around. I loved my kitchen, but I realized how modest and small it must have seemed to him, although earlier that morning I had thought it was perfectly comfortable. We stood there for a moment, awkward and aching for more from each other, and afraid to move, until I got an inspiration.

"Would you like to see my horses?" I asked.

"I thought you would never ask," Tom said, maybe a bit relieved, and followed me out through the back door.

Mousi was asleep in his hay nest, a big white mound; Isis was sleeping with her head under her hay rack; Conversano was vacuuming up the remains of his dinner; Delaney watched us with great suspicion from over his stall door. I introduced them all, until we got to Delaney. Tom reached out to pet him, and Delaney reared sideways before scooting away.

"I got him in for retraining," I said. "He's got—issues."

"Good God," Tom said, "does everything in your life have issues?"

"I had a jelly donut this morning that didn't," I said.

We returned to the kitchen, and I stood there wondering what to do next. Reese had left the elephant music playing loudly on the stereo for me.

"Would you mind if we turned the music down a little?" Tom asked, looking toward the stereo. "And what on earth is that playing, anyway?"

"It's my brother's music, he lent it to me." I said. "I always keep music playing."

"Always?" he asked. "Why?"

I just shrugged, embarrassed. I didn't know how to answer him.

"Another one of those issues?" he asked, and stepped toward me. The anticipation left me breathless. I wanted to feel his arms, wanted him to pull me to him, wanted to feel the heat and strength of his kisses again.

"Is it okay?" He tilted his head sideways, waiting for my answer.

"Yes," I said, and he kissed me. Slowly at first, tentatively, until

I kissed him back, and then he pressed against me. I could feel his body pressing against me, and it felt strong, insistent.

"I was kind of hoping you'd let me share your sleeping bag," he murmured into my ear. I pulled away.

"I hope you don't think I'm easy—I mean, after the tent thing," I said.

He rolled his eyes. "Believe me, I don't think you're easy at all." He drew me back into his arms.

I pulled away again. "And I hope you're not in a relationship," I added. "I don't want to be the other woman."

"Single," he said, pulling me close again. "Heterosexual, good health. Likes to walk on the beach, hold hands in the moonlight, and solvent. Anything else?"

"No," I whispered, and let him kiss me again and again.

⁂

First kisses are like opening a door and stepping through, into a new country with a different landscape and a different language. His arms, his lips felt different from those of anyone before, his body moved in a different rhythm from the one I was familiar with. All different, surprising my body with its newness. There was a resonance between us that made me feel alive; the world was suddenly full of promise.

We lay together, and he stroked my hair, and slowly caressed my body. Slow, slow, like we had infinity to be together. Slow. He moved his fingers across me, then his lips, then took my hand and ran it across his own body, letting the slowness build into demands. He covered my face with a thousand little kisses, like butterflies, telling me that I was beautiful, beautiful; then he braced himself above me, resting on his hands, and looked so intently into my eyes that I thought he could see my soul.

"Are you ready for me?" he asked.

"Yes." I moved against him. "Oh yes."

He pressed into me with urgency, with strength and tenderness.

The universe crashed around us. Stars imploded and pulled us together, whirling, burning white, rising into a small sharp point of light and desire and release.

I spent a wonderful night with Thomas Princeton Pennington.

Was it Revenge Sex? Consolation Sex? Rebound Sex? I didn't know, but I had never felt anything like it.

◦   ◦   ◦

We did a donut run together in the morning and brought our goodies back to the house and ate them together, sitting across the table, the table that was all mine, in a kitchen that was all mine. Maybe it had been Neutralizing Sex, because I felt very much that my home was mine, that I had a piece of myself back. We drank our coffee and ate jelly donuts, which I thought were especially good that morning, and we talked while Grace slunk under his chair and punctuated our conversation with occasional growls.

"How do I get on her good side?" Tom asked, after he accidentally moved his foot and she grabbed the toe of his shoe.

"She can be bought off with Liver YumYums," I said, crawling under the table to detach her. "Bring her a box and she is all yours." I chucked her into the backyard.

"So—are you and Matt able to work together?" Tom asked when I returned to my coffee. "Because I don't want to put any more strain on you than you are already under."

"It's no problem at all," I said. My strategy was to visit the sanctuary in the morning, and let Matt come in the afternoon. "We're both very professional."

"And have you picked out a baby name yet?" he asked.

I gasped and dropped my donut. "It's not up to me," I exclaimed. "That's between Matt and Holly."

He took my hand. "I meant the baby elephant."

"Oh. Right," I said, quickly casting through my mind. "I might have a few ideas. Maybe 'Dorothea,' after my grandmother."

"Very pretty," he said.

"Or not," I continued, now thinking of how my mother reacted. "I'm—not sure yet."

The morning flew. I started steeling myself for his departure. I didn't want to fool myself for one minute into thinking that Thomas Pennington was going to remain interested in me. He explained that he was leaving for England in a few days, where he had a board-of-directors meeting for one of his companies. He would stay at his apartment in London and then go on to Belgium for a week of business, before visiting his twenty-three-year-old son, who was finishing law school at Tom's alma mater, the Université Catholique de Louvain. Thomas Princeton Pennington was a very busy man.

"You must spend a lot of time traveling," I said. "It sounds like fun."

"You should get to England someday," he said. "They've got horses everywhere. It's a national preoccupation, like baseball here."

Get to England. Not, I would love to take you to England with me. But that was okay. I smiled at him and bit into my jelly donut. I had horses to work and an elephant to train, and a living to earn. "Do they have jelly donuts?" I asked, giving him a sly smile.

"They have spotted dick," he said very solemnly.

I choked on my donut. "Is that a medical condition?"

"It's a dessert," he said. "Honestly."

I saw him check his watch, and I took my cue. "I have to get to the sanctuary," I said.

"I have to get back to the city," he said.

We stood up, almost simultaneously, and he took me into his arms and kissed me again.

"I'll call you after I get to England," he said.

"You don't have to," I said. "I know how busy you are."

"I *will* call you," he said, and I wanted to believe him. I almost believed him. He gently wiped a bit of jelly from the tip of my nose with his thumb.

"We'll be in touch," he said, as I walked him to the door.

"Safe journey," I said.

He gave me another kiss good-bye and left. I let Grace in from the yard, and together we watched Tom's car drive away down the road.

"I hope you like him," I said to Grace. She licked the tips of my fingers and blinked her big round googie eyes at me a few times.

The hunter-green Bentley disappeared around the corner, and I shut the door. It had been very good between us. Tom hadn't murmured anything about love to me, and I hadn't murmured anything back. We hadn't made one promise between us. I didn't know where it was going to lead, if anywhere, and I don't think he knew, either. It was just the two of us, needing something from the night, from each other, and being able to give it.

And even if it was only one night of No-Strings-Attached Sex, that was okay. At least it was honest.

Chapter Thirty

I'M NOT really a big weeper. Really, I'm not. I don't fall apart and get all teary-eyed during the heartrending scenes in movies. I never cry reading sad books. I don't cry at funerals, or when someone tells me a heartbreaking story. I hold things very close. My brothers used to pin me down when we were kids and give me noogies on my head, but they never got me to cry. "Tight Ass" became their nickname for me. Of course, I had nicknames for them as well: Reese the Beast and, my older brother, Jerome the Gnome. But I never cried. I didn't even cry when Homer died. That's why the past few weeks had been very out of character for me. I was constantly surprising myself with all the crying I was doing, and now I was sniffling because Tom left.

I splashed cold water on my face so my eyes wouldn't be red, and I was ready to leave for work when the phone rang. I lunged for it, hoping, I don't know, that maybe it was Tom calling to tell me he was going to come back and take me away with him. I could even have supplied him with the white horse, although Mousi might have some objections to being asked to actually work for a change.

It was my lawyer. I really did not want to hear from my lawyer, because I always sounded snuffled up when he called and hated sounding weak and helplessly heartbroken over Matt. Again.

"Bubeleh, I have some bad news and I have some very bad news," he said. "Which do you want first?"

"What kind of choice is that?" I asked.

"I'm sorry to have to put it that way," he replied, "but sometimes shit happens and you have to know about it. Are you ready?"

"No," I said.

"Listen carefully anyway," he said, "and try not to get all confused with what I'm going to tell you. I did a little detective work about your finances, and found out that Matt signed half his practice over to Dr. Scarletta, sometime in the past year. That means very little for you to negotiate over."

The breath was knocked out of me. My legs turned into electric eels, tingling but not willing to support me. The kitchen faded in and out of my vision, and I heard oceanic waves crashing against my ears. I slid from the chair and down onto the floor, which had become my emotional haven of late. At least I still owned my floor.

"I am sitting on the floor," I said to him. "I can't sink any lower than this, so I'm going to hang up now."

"Wait," he said, "I'm sorry, but there's more. He also took out an equity loan against your house. Took out quite a bit, almost completely up to market value, and now his lawyer is proposing for him to sell it so he can get out from under the debts."

In a flash, I realized that was why Matt had generously offered to pay the expenses. The house had been mortgaged right up to its chimney. I was certain I had heard it wrong. And certain I had heard it right. The floor began revolving backward now in a dizzying spin, and I put my hand over my mouth for a moment, because it would have been tacky to retch into the phone. I counted to five and took deep breaths. There was a definite quake in the floor just before it opened up and swallowed me. Then I stopped breathing. Could I breathe? I was panicking, and gasping for air. Was that considered breathing?

"Are you okay?" my lawyer asked. I couldn't answer. He waited a polite amount of time before calling my name again.

"Can he do that?" I finally managed. "My name is on the mortgage."

"Well, someone illegally signed your name. Probably his lady friend. That's why he said he didn't want to sell the house. It would have opened up a whole can of worms."

Worms again. Matt and Holly-Felony had managed to worm me right out of my own home, without my even being aware of it.

"Why?" I gasped.

"What can I say?" My lawyer paused. "He did it. He obviously planned to get all the assets before he divorced you. Weekend breast barges."

"Breast what?" I was getting lost in words again.

"I said we can press charges," he said. *"Prosecute.* You'll have to do it through the district attorney to make him pay up, and it can get pretty messy."

"Oh God," I said.

"And expensive," he added. "But we do have a case. Just say the word and I'll get things started."

He spoke some more, but all I heard was a mash of meaningless words. I heard "gilded bracelet canary foot" somewhere in there, and "snow fort coffeemaker." And maybe "pretzel bender." It didn't matter what he was saying. I had been betrayed. Matt had lied about Holly just being a quick fling. They had been working very hard to steal my home from me.

I hung up the phone and lay right there on the floor, in front of the kitchen sink, in the kitchen that had belonged to me and Matt and then only to me, and now, apparently, mostly to Matt. And maybe Holly. Holly-Vulture. I couldn't bear even to look around. Everything felt tainted. Grace came over to give me a few sympathetic kisses and then settled next to me to lick the tears from my face.

After a while, my legs fell asleep, and I got up. I needed to go somewhere, but not the barn, not the barn. I wouldn't be able to walk through the barn and touch the doors, and stand in the feed room that I had designed, and look at my horses standing in their stalls, because I knew it wasn't going to be my barn for much longer. I walked to the back door and pulled it open to get some fresh air. Conversano whinnied, and I realized that he must have spotted me. Horses make very good watch dogs.

My life was going to change, I knew. I was standing on the very edge of the cliff and looking at a pile of rocks below, and the long fall down wasn't going to be pretty. I shut the door, ignoring Conversano's calls. Then I got into my car and drove off.

∘   ∘   ∘

Margo rumbled to me as soon as I walked in. Though she pushed the baby to her other side, and flapped her ears at me, this time it seemed the flaps were less, well, flappy. I blew my nose, but she didn't seem to care about red eyes and runny noses. She just turned and faced her fruit basket. She was definitely one pragmatic elephant. I had to force myself to be calm, to forget what was going on in my life, because elephants pick up on high drama and can become agitated. I took a deep breath and stuffed my tissue into my pocket. Then I grabbed a banana from the basket and held it through the bars.

"Hello," I said, then corrected myself. "Look here," I commanded.

She fastened one eye on me. I waved the banana. "Look *here*," I repeated. She ignored me. Apparently, I wasn't even banana-worthy today.

"Margo," I commanded again. "Look here."

She hesitated, checked on her baby, then took a few steps toward my upraised hand. It was a pleasant surprise that she was responding to me at all. She was so quiet every time I was with her. Depressed, Richie said. And why wouldn't she be? She had lost everything that made up her life.

"Come on," I said, then corrected myself again. "Look *here.*" She looked at me. "Hey, be glad you still have your baby," I said. "At least you have your baby."

She took a step toward me.

"Good girl," I said. "Come on. Do it for me. I'm probably the one person in the world who really understands you."

She took another step, and I waited, holding out the banana. I waited for a long time. Then, slowly, slowly, she extended her trunk, ran it up my arm, and touched my shoulder, before continuing upward. The two muscles at the tip of her trunk touched my face, moving to my nose, my lips, and then up to my wet eyes. Maybe they do notice things like that after all. I cautiously took the tip of her trunk and blew gently into her nostrils. She left it against my lips for a moment, and looked very thoughtful. Then she moved it back down my arm, and very carefully took the fruit from my hand.

I caught my breath. Margo had taken a piece of fruit from me! I had become more than a representative from a particularly obnoxious and predatory species. I was a source of something good. I had commanded the attention of an elephant. I picked up an apple and repeated my command. She responded again, with slow, clumsy grace. I looked up into her intelligent face and knew what I had to do.

I had to show her that I trusted her, too. I had to take things one step further. Trust for trust. I walked to the front of her cage and tugged at the heavy chain wrapped around the door. Maybe I was being stupid, but I didn't care. I had to go in to her. The gate swung open and I walked in, closing it behind me, then leaned against it with the fruit basket in my arms.

She turned to me again. We were alone. She wasn't chained or sedated. She was alert, aware of me. We were only a few feet away from each other, a wild elephant and me. I could feel my breath coming hard. She was so tall I had to press back against the bars to see her whole magnificent body, her shoulders, her sad, dignified face. She took a step forward. I could feel a low rumble carry through the air. A vibration, and I froze. I didn't dare look at her baby, or move a muscle. I just stood. She stretched her trunk toward me. She knew I had made myself very vulnerable to her. How stupid of me. I was nothing, compared with her size. She could lift me and throw me as easily as she could throw a piece of fruit across the floor. She could press me against the bars and squeeze the life out of me far more efficiently than Matt, for all his machinations, ever could. She stepped closer and reached toward me. I took a deep breath and let her trunk press over me. She touched my face and sniffed at my hair, lifting a piece of it. She touched my sweater as if trying to figure out the texture. The rumbling was pronounced now.

"Look here," I said, my voice squeaking from nerves, and I held out another banana. She was either going to take it or kill me. At one time I wouldn't have cared which, but now I realized it mattered. Then I thought what a stupid place I was in, to come to this kind of realization. I waited, and my hand shook as I held it out in front of me. She made a low sound, and took it from my hand.

"Good girl," I praised her, my heart thumping with relief. "Good girl."

I heard a sound, and knew Richie had come into the barn. I didn't dare turn around. He stopped moving behind me. I reached into the basket again, and she continued to take the fruit from me, piece by piece, until the basket was empty.

"Get out," Richie said in a deadly still voice. *"Get out now."*

And I slowly, slowly backed out of the enclosure and pulled the chain across the gate. Margo looked for more fruit, then trumpeted.

"You broke the rules." Richie said, his face severe and flushed with anger. "That was a stupid, stupid crazy thing to do."

"I know," I said. "I'm sorry."

"Don't ever do that again without someone here," he said.

"But she's taking bananas from me," I said. "I think I'm really making progress."

"Oh, Neelie," he said, and let out a long, long sigh and tilted his head to the side. When someone lets out a long sigh and looks at you at an angle, you're about to get bad news. I braced myself.

"I've been working with her," he said. "That's why I knew she would take a banana from you when Tom was here that day. I didn't want you to fail in front of him and Matt. I want this elephant to stay here."

"Oh," I said. Then I burst into more tears. What do they say about tears? A bucket a day keeps the doctor away? "You mean I didn't really teach her to take a banana?"

"Hey," he said, "why are you crying? I wanted to show Tom some progress before Faye came to evaluate her."

"Faye?"

"The elephant trainer from that big elephant sanctuary in Tennessee," Richie explained. "Tom called her to fly up here and give you a hand. She's coming tomorrow."

"Faye?"

"He didn't want you to get hurt before your learning curve kicked in."

I felt my color rise. I was not going to share Margo with anyone.

"I can do it by myself," I said, feeling my voice tighten. "I already blew in her nose."

"Don't be silly," he said softly. "Let Faye show you how to manage her. Otherwise, Tom mentioned, he might have to send her to Tennessee. And I don't want to lose my elephant."

"You can't let him do that," I said hoarsely. "I won't let anyone take our elephant from us!"

"I agree. I love her, too." Richie gave me an affectionate pinch on the cheek and headed for the barn door. "I've wanted an elephant my whole life. So be nice to Faye."

I watched him for a minute, then took a deep, shaky breath. "Richie?" I called.

He turned around. "Yeah?"

"Thank you," I said. "You know, for the banana trick."

"Yep." He saluted me with two fingers. "Just call me Chiquita."

Chapter Thirty-one

FAYE THE Elephant Girl was short and to the point. Her brown hair was cropped close to her head, she wore no makeup, spoke in economical sentences. She came dressed in jeans and a tank top. Low-maintenance—she was all about the elephants.

She arrived from the airport by cab, punctually at nine, and was going to stay with Richie and Jackie while she trained me in the ways of handling pachyderms.

"Faye," she said, giving me a quick squeeze of a handshake.

"Neelie," I said.

She stood back and studied me. "You should know I already told Tom I don't think the elephant belongs here," she said. "You shouldn't have even gone to Africa, but my schedule was too crowded for me to make the trip. I'm only doing this as a big favor to him."

"Favor?" I repeated.

She gave me a curt nod and stood with her arms folded. "I don't care if you are some big-shot horse trainer," she said dismissively after looking me up and down. "Elephants can kill. I'm a graduate of the Exotic Animal Training and Management Program at Moorpark College, and I'm still very, very careful. I told Tom to send her down to us in Tennessee as soon as her health got stabilized, but he said he'd promised Richie he would keep her here. I think you're both too inexperienced."

"I see," I said.

"This is not a horse."

"I noticed," I said. "But I'm willing to learn."

"And I worked alongside an expert for seven years," she said.

I looked her up and down, too. "Then we better get started," I said.

* * *

She brought her suitcases into Richie's house and came back out, carrying a long thin stick with a white flag attached to the end of it.

"Target stick," she said, holding it up.

"Do I wave the white flag while she's coming at me or after I'm under her?" I joked. She didn't laugh. That didn't bode well, I thought. It's one thing to be dedicated, it's another thing to be grim about it. I followed along as she marched off to the barn without another word.

"Name?" she asked as she slid the barn door open.

"Neelie," I replied.

"Elephant," she snapped.

"Margo."

"It's all about respect," she said, and walked inside the barn. "You have to establish leadership or they will ignore you."

Pretty much like horses, I thought.

"You have to think like an elephant," she continued, standing outside the enclosure and watching Margo suck down the last of her bananas. "Get into their heads."

I understood that, too.

"African elephants are hot-blooded—more impetuous than Asian elephants." She was opening the cage door now. Margo had turned around to assess this intrusion. "And there are no accidents. Only stupid handling mistakes."

"Like with horses," I said. Faye didn't respond. She waved the white flag around.

"Use her name frequently," she said.

"Margo," I said again.

Faye ignored me and pulled a metal clicker from her pocket. "Clicker," she said. "You link it with a reward."

"I already know how to do that," I mumbled.

"Margo!" she said loudly. Margo looked Faye up and down and went back to her hay. I smiled inwardly. Elephants are great equalizers.

.   .   .

The first thing Faye did when she introduced herself to the baby was take her trunk and blow gently into her nostrils. Then she handed the baby's little trunk to me and I took a turn.

"She'll remember us forever now," she said. "Now we can all be good friends forever." I liked the idea that we would be linked together forever.

Faye worked hard over the next three weeks. She showed me how to wait until Margo approximated what I wanted from her, then to press the clicker, even though it might be only a portion of what I was hoping for, then, immediately, to reward her with a piece of fruit. She showed me how to touch the target stick to Margo's feet and click and treat. How to click every time Margo lifted her trunk, even if it was random, and link it immediately with the words "lift trunk" and a treat. It was called shaping, this molding of behavior into something we wanted. And gradually Margo was getting socialized. At times, I thought she looked almost cheerful.

Faye didn't say much, but that was just fine with me: I don't listen much. We worked well together. She had a good instinct around animals, and grudgingly told me that I did, too. She had a sweet tooth and appreciated my morning donuts. She never changed her clothes, not once in the first two weeks she was with us. One night, after a long, hard day, I found she could drink all the local barflies under the table. But she preferred the company of elephants to anyone else.

Almost anyone.

"What's the story with the vet?" she asked me one morning. "Richie won't talk about him."

"Matt?" I asked.

She nodded. "Married?"

I thought for a moment, then figured, what the hell, let her give Holly-Humpkins a run for her money. "No," I said. "Single."

"Nice," she said.

She didn't say much after that, but she did start changing her clothes on a regular basis. I think she may even have washed her hair a time or two.

"How's it going with Matt?" I asked her one day, while we were teaching Margo's baby to fetch.

She shrugged. "I think his life's a mess. He lives in a motel. Sometimes he's hard to reach."

"Emotionally?"

"Yah, well, that, too, but I meant his phone."

"If you ever need to get in touch with him," I said, "you can always get him through the other vet, Dr. Scarletta. They stay in touch all the time. She should be able to give him the message." I gave her Holly's cell number.

"She won't mind?"

"Nah," I said. "Call her anytime."

"Great," she said. "I'm not into anything long-term, but he sure fills out his jeans. He looks like a good lay."

I didn't care anymore. I had given up on Matt. I wanted him to screw everyone in the world. All I wanted to do now was hurt Holly.

*   *   *

One day Faye and I were outside, watching mother and daughter play in the muddy pond just after we had given them a beauty session of massages with warmed coconut oil. Margo had progressed, presenting her foot on command, lifting her trunk. And letting us play with her daughter. We fed her handfuls of carrots as her reward after a successful training session.

"I'm leaving in two days," Faye said quietly as we watched Margo spray mud all over her baby.

"Oh?" My heart skipped a beat. My future with Margo was going to be based on her report to Tom.

"But I think you're going to be okay with them," Faye said, and gave me a quick pat on the shoulder.

I turned to study her face. She barely cracked a smile. I almost wanted to blow in her nose.

*   *   *

I greeted Faye on our last morning with a celebratory box of donuts. Maybe it was more bribatory, because she was going to give Tom her opinion on my expertise when he got back from Europe.

We met in front of Margo's cage.

"Go in with her," Faye commanded. I opened the lock and went in. Alone.

"Ask for her foot," Faye said from outside.

"Margo, lift foot," I said. Margo looked at Faye and she looked at me and yawned. Then she dropped a pile of dung.

"Margo, lift foot," I said, in my best master-of-the-universe voice.

Margo rumbled and lifted her foot. I gave her an apple.

*   *   *

My graduation ceremony consisted of Faye's presenting me with the target stick and clicker.

"She needs to respect you more," she said. "Work on it. And try to get her to like you."

I took the target stick like I had won an Oscar, and clutched it to my chest. "Thank you," I gushed. "And I think she will really, really like me."

We both turned to look at Margo. "Right now, she likes me best," Faye said. "I just hope she doesn't miss me too much."

"Will that be a problem?" I asked.

She shrugged. "They form attachments, you know? And then sometimes refuse to work for anyone else. We'll see."

We turned to face Margo. She was eating her graduation treat, a large watermelon. She had broken it apart by stepping on it with her big front foot and now was lifting chunks into her mouth. She looked happy, if elephants could look happy The rips in her skin, the slashes, the torn ear were all healing. Maybe her heart was, too.

"And take good care of that baby," Faye said. I thought I detected a tiny waver in her voice.

"I will," I promised. "Tom even said I could name her."

"Pick something dignified," Faye said, then snorted. "I hate when people get all sweet."

"Don't worry about me," I said. "I haven't a drop of sweet left in me."

Chapter Thirty-two

TELEGRAPH, TELEPHONE, tell a horseman. All I had to do was put the word out among my horsy friends, and within a week I had leads on a nice little pony. I first checked it out on my own and then took Alana and her girls.

It was a medium-size pony, a brown-and-white pinto with a thatch of color-coordinated brown-and-white mane and a tangled, particolored nest of a tail, which I thought would make perfect projects for Alana's daughters. They could spend endless hours bathing him and brushing him and fluffing all that hair, and tying it up in hot-pink bows. He was a gentle old gelding, and he was up for adoption because he belonged to a family with three kids who had grown up and gone off to college. He had been their first pony, and now was "sadly outgrown," as ponies are called when they are no longer useful.

His name was Tony, Tony the Pony, and he was almost as old as Alana and me.

"Thirty-five years old?" Alana exclaimed when I told her about Tony. "Do you think he remembers the Reagan years?"

"He probably remembers the Hoover years," I said, "but that's exactly what you want for a first horse."

He was well broke, was trained to pull a little cart, was safe and mannerly, and could probably even make hot chocolate for the girls when they were done riding for the day. I took them to his barn to meet him, and it was love at first sight, all around.

The pony's owner, Mrs. Hammock, was thrilled to have her pony find a good home.

"With the kids gone, there's no point in having a house with a barn," she confided to us. "I'm actually planning to moo in the near future."

"Moo?" I asked.

"Moo?" she asked me.

"Move," Alana whispered in my ear. Pony Lady took a check from Alana and went into her house. The deal was done.

"I'll pick your pony up with my trailer and bring him to my barn," I told Alana, "but I might not be able to keep him for long. I'm probably going to be mooing myself."

She gave me the squint eyes. "You talked me into this pony," she said. "So, whither you goest, he goest with you."

"Very biblical," I said, "but I might not get another barn."

"Your living room will do just fine," she said. "I'm not fussy."

*   *   *

Finding the pony seemed to be the last good thing I was able to pull off. After he was happily settled in my barn, I developed a reverse King Midas touch. Everything I touched turned to crap.

Delaney was getting more difficult, and had now taken to spooking at his breakfast. Conversano was not thrilled to see me anymore since I'd started saddle-breaking him, and he thought he could avoid me by hiding behind the trees in his paddock. And Isis's owner complained incessantly during her lessons.

"Can't I do something more than just sit here?" she wailed, when I made her sit for long periods of time on her horse, just doing nothing. She seemed to have already forgotten that, only a few weeks before, she had been begging me to get her horse to stand still.

Other areas of my life weren't faring much better. Reese was calling and suggesting that he move back in and give me a hand with things, my mother was calling and suggesting that I let Reese move back in and give me a hand with things. My lawyer was calling every few days warning me to get my ducks in a row. Apparently, they were just one more species of animal that was not under my control.

And Faye's words had become prophetic, because Margo

started being naughty within a few days of her leaving. She became cranky and temperamental, and had cultivated a mean curve ball with the apples she was tossing back at me.

I was getting discouraged. Any attempt on my part to further her socialization was met with resistance. I could see that she had gotten depressed after Faye left. Sometimes she grudgingly accepted a piece of fruit, but more than once my "lift foot" command was met with a loud trumpet of indignation and a rush at me. And more than once I slipped out of her pen just in time. Sometimes I got hit with the piece of fruit, like an unpopular performer in a vaudeville show.

If she were a horse, I would have had her trained within the week to lift her feet, move sideways, walk next to me, and maybe even throw in a salute or two. But she was an elephant, and you just can't discipline an elephant. I did the white-flag routine again and again, and she turned her back on me. When you are an eight-thousand-pound elephant, a small white hankie tickling the side of your foot does not make a huge impression. She ate her bananas and apples and carrots, but I could see they weren't motivating her anymore. She wanted Faye. So did I.

I needed to find something more inspiring.

I was on an exhausting treadmill of waking up while it was still dark to give my horses breakfast, do my donut run on the way to the sanctuary, work all morning with Margo, run back to my barn to put my horses out for the day, run back to the sanctuary to help Richie put Margo out for the day, and then back home to train horses and students. I was beginning to develop a great respect for the work ethic of hamsters who ran all day on their wheels.

"You need to find a way to motivate her," Richie informed me as we ducked yet another barrage of fruit.

"I don't understand it," I said. "She used to love her apples and bananas."

"That's when she was starving," Richie pointed out. "Now she gets two big helpings a day. It's not that special."

I switched to watermelons. She loved crushing them under her feet and feeding herself big juicy pieces, but watching her step on watermelons was alarming. I kept picturing my head under those big gray platters. And though the melons did placate her for a while, it was impractical to carry two or three of them around in my pocket for immediate reinforcement. There had to be something else that would tickle her palate and renew her interest in her training.

"Have I told you about my Midas-touch theory?" I complained to Alana one night. "Everything I touch becomes doo-doo. Things just can't get worse."

"Be careful what you say," she warned me. "Those doo-doo gods are always listening in."

       *   *   *

A few mornings later, I was feeding Margo a handful of peanuts. She liked them enough, but was ignoring my command to pick up her feet. Richie was standing next to me and watching us with a serious expression.

"It's important she respect you," he said. "Faye said that accidents happen from a basic lack of respect. And if you can't get her to work with you, she'll have to go on protected contact." Protected contact was when elephants are kept away from their handlers. They are always fed and worked from behind a barrier.

"I know," I replied, touching the white flag to her big gray feet. They remained firmly planted while she watched her daughter play with the peanuts.

"Well, I hope you come up with something soon," Richie cautioned me.

"I will," I promised.

"Okay," he said quietly, "because, if you can't, she's going to be a resident of Tennessee, and I will die from heartbreak."

The doo-doo gods were locked and loaded.

       *   *   *

That night, Pony Lady called. "I hope Tony is getting on well," she said. "And I just wanted to let you know that my house is for sale. No point maintaining it if the kids are gone. Thought I'd let the word get around. You know that old saying, telegram, telemarketer, tell a horseman."

Tell a horseman. Tell an elephant girl. I suppose it's all the same. And for the first time, I thought that if someone would only tell me what to do I would really, really listen.

Chapter Thirty-three

WHEN YOU'VE seen one dawn, you've seen them all.

Actually, that's not really true.

Dawn breaking over the plains of Zimbabwe was breathtaking. A rose-colored sky, streaked with orange and gold that finally gave up to a burning cerulean blue, set off by high, brilliant white tufts of clouds. The daylight in Africa looks different. Like it streamed straight from the sun, each particle of light burning, keen, without any interference from earth at all.

Dawn breaking over my barn was gray-blue, with tentative slivers of pink that tried to insinuate their way across the horizon before the foggy air muted them into submission. Maybe it was just because of the way I felt. I quickly fed the horses, gave them fresh water and hay and a promise that I would be back in a few hours to turn them out.

My two coffees and a bag of jelly donuts were already waiting for me. I was in such a routine by now, the owner of the shop had things ready by the time I walked in. I supposed he had been up since dawn himself.

I drove with my usual hurricane speed to the sanctuary, where Richie and Margo were waiting. Well, at least Richie was waiting. I had gotten him hooked on jellies by now, and after we finished our coffee and several donuts, we were ready to start the day.

The baby was being playful. She trotted around the enclosure, sampling the fruit, grabbing at my stick with her little trunk, and squealing like a badly played saxophone.

I gave her things to touch, and she grabbed them with her trunk like a toddler picking up a toy, comically clumsy. Sometimes she sniffed at my clothing. Elephants have a scent organ in their mouths, like horses do, and I loved watching her explore by sniffing things and then sticking the tip of her trunk into her mouth to capture the scent. I even let her sniff the last of the jelly donuts that I was holding.

"So what should I tell Tom?" Richie asked while I played with the baby.

"Tom's in Switzerland," I replied, now rubbing the baby's trunk with a soft towel.

"Actually, he called me late last night," Richie said. "He's back, and he's coming up here in a day or two."

I tried not to react, but I felt a wrench. Why hadn't Tom called me? And right away realized that it was absurd to believe I was important enough to him that he would.

Then I made a mistake. I wrapped my arms around the baby and hugged her. Margo spun around and rushed me, bellowing at the top of her lungs. When you are four feet from a very angry elephant, it's not only impressive, it's imperative that you remove yourself from the immediate vicinity. I jumped away and darted for the gate, dropping the jelly donut that I was holding.

"This isn't working," Richie said to me once I was safely outside. "I'm going to be frank with you—"

"Not now," I said, walking toward the barn doors to leave. "Not now." I couldn't bear another delivery from the doo-doo gods.

◦　　◾　　◦

The phone was ringing as I was letting myself into my house. I ignored it and bent over to pet Grace. I had African music playing loudly on the stereo, but I could still hear the ringing.

"Did you have a nice day?" I asked Grace in a forced happy-voice, an octave too high. She wriggled her square, formal-looking, little black-and-white body to indicate that her day had gone quite well, thank you. Especially pertaining to the garbage that I had left safely in the pail under the sink and that was now artistically strewn across the kitchen floor.

"I'd better clean this up," I said to her, studiously ignoring the phone. After all, it was only going to be more bad news. I went for the broom. Another ring.

"Gracie," I said as I began to sweep up the remains of my last night's dinner, "you need another hobby."

She wagged her tail in agreement. The phone clicked off, and the answering machine picked up.

"I'm going to give you supper," I said to her, hoping to drown out the bad news that was sure to be recording any moment.

"Neelie, it's Tom. I've been trying to get you, but your line's been busy or there's no answer. I plan—"

I leapt across the room, grabbed for the phone and stereo at the same time, and lowered the volume on a CD of Thomas Mapfumo. "Hello?"

"I'm so glad I caught you," he said. "I've been trying to get you for days. As soon as I knew when I was returning."

"You have?" I said.

"Absolutely," he said. "And I left half a dozen messages on your mobile phone." I took my cell phone out of my pocket and turned it on. There were seven messages.

"Wow," I said. "You're right."

"Why do you carry a mobile phone if you never turn it on?" he asked.

"I like the way it feels," I said. "Like I could reach out and touch someone if I wanted to."

"And the point of keeping it turned off is—?" he asked.

"I don't usually want to," I replied.

"How's it working for you?"

I had to admit, it wasn't. Somehow the bad news always leaked in, like rain through a broken roof. It was the good stuff that I was missing.

"You're right," I said. "It doesn't work at all."

"Well, I would like to reach out and touch *you.*" He laughed. "Is there a possibility of my seeing you?"

"I would like that," I said.

"I'm putting together my schedule, but the morning after to-morrow?"

"Terrific," I said. When we hung up, I gave Grace a big hug. "Have a party," I said, pointing to the trash pail. "Help yourself any-time."

· · ·

I barely slept that night, then raced through another dawn, an-other round of chores, another round of garbled answering-machine messages from my lawyer that sounded like "eagles kidnap the let-tuce," and "statutory Eskimo pies." I pushed it out of my mind and raced off to the sanctuary. Richie was waiting for me.

"Thank you," he said, as I handed him his morning jelly and cof-fee. "I suppose you know that Tom is coming up here tomorrow?"

"I know," I said, careful to keep my voice normal.

Richie studied me for a moment. "Are you worried?"

We let ourselves into the enclosure, where Margo was finishing the last of her breakfast. Her baby trotted up to us and tugged at my arm with her trunk. "A little," I answered him. "I don't know what Faye told him."

"Well, she might have told him the baby is more socialized and Margo is definitely more responsive," Richie said, then added, "just not to you."

· · ·

I worked with Margo some more that day, while Richie watched. She needed to learn to open her mouth on command now, so that she could be given medicine or have her teeth checked, and I was tickling her lips with the target stick. She pushed it away with her trunk and turned her back on me, lifting her tail and dropping a pungent commentary on my training techniques. I walked to the other side to get to her lips again. She shifted her weight and turned around once again to show me her tail.

"Well, I got her trained if she needs a rectal exam," I said to Richie.

"Speaking of assholes," Richie said, "Matt mentioned that Holly had the baby. Did you know? It was a month premature."

I didn't know. How could I know? My heart thudded to a stop. I did a quick calculation. Holly had called me in April—this was August. She must have gotten pregnant during Christmas.

I dropped my arms to my sides and shook my head. "I have to sell the house because of them." I said.

"I'm sorry." Richie put his arm around my shoulder. "Matt's been a friend of mine for a long time," he said, "and I don't know what's come over him."

"Greed?" I said.

"He doesn't love her," he said. "You have to know that."

"It doesn't matter to me anymore," I said. "You have to know that, too."

*   *   *

I worked my horses later that day, and when I got back into the house, there were two more messages. A dinner invitation from my mother, who I knew was going to give her all to cheer me up, and another one from my lawyer.

"Bubbee, call me," he said. "I must talk to you this week."

He wanted to talk to me about lining up my ducks, I knew. I couldn't avoid it anymore. These were very tough ducks to line up. I couldn't bring myself to start prosecuting Matt, yet I was going to lose my house. *Carnival of the Animals,* which could have been a great title for my life, was playing on the stereo. Light was fading from the sky outside my windows, and I stepped out the back door and watched as dusk transformed the barn into something shapeless and indistinguishable from the smoky sky behind it.

Dusk, dawn, dusk. I took a deep breath and realized that I had better take my lawyer's advice and get my ducks marching along, because, before I knew it, I wouldn't have either dawn or dusk breaking over my barn to watch anymore.

Chapter Thirty-four

PATIENCE IS one of my better qualities. I will hang in there long after everyone else has packed up their toys and gone home.

I waited a long time for Tom to come to the sanctuary the next morning and made a thousand excuses for why he didn't. Maybe he was hung up on some world-shaking business decision, I thought. Maybe he forgot to write me into his calendar. I worked with an indifferent Margo, and chatted with Richie, and tried not to keep looking over my shoulder every ten minutes for the sight of Tom walking through the barn doors. The morning passed into afternoon, and I knew Matt was going to be pulling up the driveway any minute, and still I waited. I wanted to see Tom very much.

He didn't come. He didn't call.

I know patience is a virtue, but this time it was a drawback. I finally flung the rest of my jelly donuts into Margo's treat pail, gave Richie a quick good-bye peck on the cheek, and left, hoping I had enough time left to avoid Matt. I didn't. He pulled into the parking lot just as I was walking toward my car. I kept walking, looking straight ahead, and tried to ignore him, even as he followed me a few steps.

"Neelie," he called out softly. I opened my car door.

"Neelie." I turned around and stared at him. He looked drawn and a bit disheveled. Maybe a bit haunted. I got into my car and slammed the door, turned the car on and pulled away, leaving him standing there, his shoulders sagging, his arms hanging at his sides.

He didn't look like a happy new father.

"Tom is a very busy man, you know," I told Delaney, as I checked my cell phone for the third time before mounting him. No messages. I took him into the riding ring, and we struck off into a nice rolling canter. I congratulated myself on having been so patient with him. Delaney was respecting me now, riding very well, and I was basking in a little self-congratulatory pride when he gave a loud snort and bolted, throwing me hard into the sand. I sat there, my head between my knees, to catch my breath. A sharp pain was slicing across my chest, and my lungs felt like they were filled with sandy ring-footing.

"Good God, Neelie, are you all right? That was quite a fall."

I looked up to see Tom's face, filled with concern. He extended a hand and helped me to my feet.

"I'm fine," I managed to gasp out. And I was, as long as I remained folded in half. "How long have you been here?"

"I got here just in time to see you come flying off that thing," he said. "That thing" was now bucking and leaping around the ring like an escapee from an equine mental institution.

"Not one of our better moments," I mumbled, and tried to straighten up again. This time, a searing pain tightened my ribs into a knot, and I had to let Tom help me hobble to a nearby fence.

"Why don't you rest for a minute?" Tom said. "I'll go catch him."

I leaned against the fence, bent like a paper clip, and concentrated on trying to breathe without whistling.

Tom grabbed Delaney by his bridle and marched him into the barn. I followed slowly and then eased myself down, to sit on a bale of hay.

"I'm sorry about this morning," Tom said, efficiently unbuckling the girth and removing the saddle from Delaney's back. "I had a last-minute meeting in the city. I raced up here as soon as I was able. I got to the sanctuary just after you left." He hung the saddle over a stall door and knelt down in front of me. "Hey." He looked very worried. "Are you sure you're okay? I can drive you to the hospital."

"I'm—okay." I had to break up my answer into short, painful

wheezes. "And I should—really be—getting back—on him—so that he doesn't—think—he can end—a training session—like that."

"No, you're not," Tom said. He took off the bridle, slipped a halter over Delaney's head and led him into a stall.

"You—know how—to handle—a horse?" I had to hold my sides to support me enough to form words.

"I ride," he said, and then planted himself in front of me with his arms folded. I know that when people fold their arms, and stand in front of you, rocking back and forth on their heels, it means they are going to give you a piece of advice.

"May I give you a piece of advice?" he asked.

I coughed and nodded my head yes.

"It's something I learned early in business," he said. "When you smell defeat, cut your losses and get out."

"I don't smell—defeat," I gasped. "I smell—a training problem."

"I think you're wrong, and my advice is to send this horse packing," he said. "You're going to call that horse's owner and say that you can't ride it anymore." He lifted me to my feet.

"He's my—income," I protested.

"How about if I pay you not to ride him?"

I flushed with embarrassment. "I can't—do that. It could start a—whole economic trend. You'll wind up—having to pay stores—to not deliver pizza, or car dealerships—to not drop off—a new car every week."

He wasn't amused. Instead, his face took on a sternness that disconcerted me. "That horse is going to kill you."

"I'll call a vet," I hedged. "Maybe there's—something we overlooked."

"I don't care if he gets PMS, he's too dangerous," Tom said, taking both my hands in his. His eyes were a serious gray-green, like the middle of the ocean, with the same unfathomable depth to them. "Now, promise me you won't ride him."

I looked down at my shoes. I didn't like to think that Delaney might be just another entry in my quickly accumulating inventory of defeats.

"Hey," he said. "Do it for me. I don't want anything to happen to you."

But, then again, my ribs were throbbing with extreme pain. I had to make a choice, and Tom was waiting for my answer. Death or Tom. Death or Tom. "Okay," I said reluctantly. "I promise I'll call a vet and see what he says."

•   •   •

We had dinner at a local rib house, in honor of the flamboyant colors that were beginning to emerge across my chest. Tom had no more advice, but he did have a few apologies.

"I'm really sorry about not showing up this morning," he said, "I hope you don't think I was blowing you off."

"I couldn't wait—"

"I figured," he said, and smiled. "Matt."

"I hate him," I said.

"Unproductive emotion," he said. "Don't waste time on it."

•   •   •

We were halfway through a good bottle of wine when he leaned back and cleared his throat.

"You know, I spoke to Faye last night."

My heart leapt at his words. "I hope she gave me a good report card."

"She did, but she's worried that you might not be ready." He swirled the wine around in his glass and watched it for a minute. "Especially to take on the baby."

"Oh no!" I jumped, then clutched my side. "Please don't send Margo and the baby away."

His lips made a straight line. "I'm an impatient man, I admit," he started. "And I want things done. The baby is the one who needs to be socialized early, so that she'll be safe to work around. We'll never be able to completely trust Margo, no matter how much you work with her, so the baby is the main focus here."

I knew that. It would be good just to bring the danger level in

Margo's interactions down a notch or two, so that the baby was more accessible, because the baby's future was at stake.

"That's why I thought Tennessee would be the best place," he ventured.

"No," I said. "Please give me some time. I'm a good trainer." Then I remembered what he had just witnessed. "Don't go by what you saw today." My fingers unconsciously sought out my ribs, and I winced at my own touch. "Besides," I added truthfully, "I love them."

He laughed, then asked, "Are you really all that emotionally involved with them? I mean, you haven't even named the baby yet."

"But I have," I said. "I have. I named her Abbie. After my mother."

                ⚬   ⚬   ⚬

I didn't have to ask Tom to stay. We got back to my house, and as soon as we stepped inside, mindful of my bruised ribs, he gently pulled me to him and kissed me. Gracie snapped at our heels while Ladysmith Black Mambazo blasted loudly in the background, their sweet harmonies blending into a deafening rendition of "Homeless." I had been playing "Homeless" relentlessly, every day, since that call from my lawyer.

"Do you want me to stay?" Tom said into my ear.

"Please," I said.

"Then would you mind if I turned this off?" He moved away from me and turned the volume down.

"I need the music," I said, walking over and reaching for the volume knob.

"No, you don't," he said, taking my hand and holding it. "You need to turn off the music so you can listen to what's going on in your life. It's time."

He flipped the switch and took me again into his arms.

                ⚬   ⚬   ⚬

We made love carefully. Tom tempered his passion with concern for my injuries.

"I feel like I'm tiptoeing around a mine field," he said, stroking my bruised body cautiously. "I've never made love to a rainbow before."

But he kissed me a million times, before taking my hand and showing me how to caress him. We fell together naturally, legs over legs, arms entangled, the fresh, thrilling feel of bare skin. When we fell apart, he ran his fingers lightly across my face and neck.

"I can't make promises right now, Neelie," he began.

I put my fingers across his lips. "I know," I said. "I can't, either."

"And I tend to want everything my way."

"That wouldn't bother me, unless I wanted something *my* way," I countered.

"And I have very little patience."

I rolled over and looked at him. Gray-green eyes like the brush of African grasses. I was growing to care about him so very much. "Patience is the one thing I have," I said. "I have enough for both of us."

Chapter Thirty-five

DR. KARL SIMMONS couldn't have behaved more awkwardly. He got out of his truck, already blushing. He was an old friend of Matt's, a good equine vet from the next county, and, just as I had promised Tom, I called him for a final checkup on Delaney.

"How are you doing, Neelie?" he asked, then busied himself before I could answer.

"The horse is over here," I said. I had Delaney already waiting in the barn, on the cross-ties.

"Let's get right down to it," Karl said, avoiding my eyes. He ran his hands down the horse's legs, examined the shoeing, stood back to check the alignment of Delaney's spine. Then he put drops in Delaney's eyes and, while waiting for them to take effect, ran his hands across the horse's back, pressing here and there to check for a possible reaction to pinched nerves. He flexed Delaney's back legs, holding them up for what seemed like an eternity, before having me trot him off, to see if there were hock problems. Everything was normal. He returned to Delaney's eyes.

"Hmmm," he said, his face pressing close to Delaney's face, eye to eye with the horse, shining a penlight deep into the eye chamber. "Hmmm."

"What?"

He rolled the light from side to side, and looked again.

"There appears to be some kind of lens abnormality, and it looks more complicated than anything I've ever seen before," he said, talking into the side of Delaney's head. "I'm not an eye man—it's beyond my expertise. I think you should call Dr. Reston—the equine ophthalmologist."

"Floaters?"

He put his penlight back in his pocket and made a face. "I think it's a lot worse than that." He hurriedly packed up his equipment. "I'll give him a call for you, if you want."

"Thanks. Would you like a cup of coffee or something?" I offered.

"Uh, no," he said, turning toward his truck.

"So—I guess you know about Matt and me," I said, in a let's-get-this-over-with tone of voice.

"Uh, yeah." He stood for a moment, looking at his shoes with a sad face. "I kind of knew it last Christmas, when he brought her to that big Christmas party at the Parkers'."

A chill went through me. The Christmas party was a full four months before Holly's first phone call to me. We hadn't gone because Matt had called me early in the evening and described, in horrible detail, a dog mangled in a car accident that needed emergency attention. I had been dressed up and waiting for him to come home.

"I guess I'll go by myself," I had said to him.

"The weather's supposed to be crappy," he had replied. "If I were you, I'd play it safe." And, grateful that I had such a concerned husband, I stayed home. I stayed home and Holly got pregnant as a Christmas gift.

"In fact," Karl said, "I took Matt aside. Asked where you were. He said—actually—that you two were separated."

"Well, we weren't together at the party." I made a feeble joke. "So he wasn't entirely lying."

"Right," Karl said, but I don't think he got it.

○   ○   ○

I called Delaney's owner, and she authorized the ophthalmologist. He came two days later.

Dr. Reston was in his sixties, lanky and soft-spoken. He had a wonderful reputation as a specialist in animal eye diseases, and was a very busy man who didn't usually make barn calls; most of his patients—equine, canine, and feline—were brought to his surgery. I was glad he could come, but I think that maybe Karl prevailed upon him a little. They arrived one right after the other, and Dr. Reston immediately gave Delaney a mild sedative, put atropine in his eyes, and then whipped out an elaborate ophthalmoscope.

"Do you see it?" Karl asked him, leaning over his shoulder.

Dr. Reston said nothing. He examined both eyes, taking his time, moving back and forth between them.

"It looks like a congenital coloboma of the zonules," Dr. Reston said.

"Wow," said Karl. "I've never seen that."

"Very rare," said Dr. Reston. "I've only seen it maybe two or three times before myself."

"Could you repeat that?" I said, trying to suppress a giggle, "because I thought you said Colombian zombies."

Dr. Reston smiled and repeated himself. He really had said it was a coloboma of the zonules. And it was incurable. Delaney was going blind.

"He'll never be a reliable ride," said Dr. Reston. "Too bad. He's a nice-looking animal."

"What do you recommend?" I asked.

"There's nothing medicine can do for him." He shrugged. "And I don't like to tell clients what to do in terms of keeping the horse alive." I watched him pack up his medical equipment and turn to leave. "You know, sometimes it's not the medical problem," he said, looking back thoughtfully at Delaney, "so much as their reaction to it. I've seen blind horses cope very well. If he was calmer, he could be turned out in a small, safe pasture somewhere for the rest of his life. But he panics. And that makes him very dangerous. He can't even see you enough to not run into you."

"It won't be my decision," I said. "You know—whether to keep him"—I could barely say the word—"alive."

"Probably not," he said, "unless you plan to adopt him." He walked outside the barn.

"I can't afford to feed a blind, crazy horse," I said, following him.

"Most people can't," he agreed, climbing into his truck and pulling away with a wave. "I'm very sorry. Good luck with him."

Karl remained behind.

"Hey," I said, and gave a little laugh. "Who would have suspected Colombia even gets zombies?"

"Listen." Karl put his hand on my shoulder. "I'm sorry—about Matt. We all knew something was up when he left his equine practice and decided to concentrate on small animals and buy all that fancy equipment. I heard near a million dollars' worth. Whew!" He sucked his breath in with disbelief. My mind reeled at the amount.

"We knew it was because Holly was pressuring him," he continued. "We all knew there was something going on. He was a good equine vet." He stopped, embarrassed that he might have said too much. I nodded, acting as though I wasn't going to run into the house right after he left and use up another box of tissues. "I felt he had kind of lost his way, you know, when I saw him at the Christmas party," he added, "when he told me about his big plans."

"Yep," I lied, "that's what did it for me, too."

Karl patted me on the shoulder again and then gave Delaney an identical pat. "Lucky this isn't your horse," he said, "because he's basically finished."

"Lucky," I agreed, and watched him pull out of the driveway.

•   •   •

I stood in the barn for a while, with my arm draped across Delaney's neck. One mystery was solved. Delaney just saw things coming at him out of nowhere, and it terrified him. I had a fairly good idea of what his fate was going to be. His owner was a good person and would give him a humane end. He was eating his hay now, unaware that his future had just taken a sharp left turn. It was good that animals didn't have a sense of their own mortality, I thought, it saved them a lot of therapy bills. Or maybe they really do know when their end is near, and they just accept it with grace. Something we humans still need to learn.

Delaney picked his head up and put it over the top of his stall door to sniff my hands for carrots. I ran my fingers absentmindedly through his forelock and rubbed his head and thought about Matt and a million dollars' worth of vet equipment. I couldn't imagine him making a business decision like that. Without ever discussing one word with me. He had a busy practice, but nowhere that busy. What could he have been thinking? One mystery solved, another beginning. Delaney gently licked my hand.

"Poor Delaney," I said. "I know what it's like, when things come out of nowhere."

And I stayed in the barn with him for a long time.

Chapter Thirty-six

"REESE SAYS you have a young man to bring to family dinner Friday night?" It was my mother, making plans to make me happy.

"I don't have a young man," I said. Tom wasn't young, and he wasn't mine.

"You don't have to worry," my mother said soothingly. "I know how hurt you are over Matt, but you have a right to be happy. If this young man makes you happy, then I'm happy. I just want you to be happy."

There it was again, the "happy" word. I really didn't want to have dinner with the family, because I was only going to let everyone down on the happiness front.

"I won't be able to come to dinner," I said. "I have horses to ride."

"You don't ride horses in the dark," my mother pointed out.

"Okay," I conceded. "I'll come to dinner, but under two—make that three conditions."

"Conditions?" my mother repeated.

"Conditions," I said firmly. "Ready?"

"I suppose," my mother said. "I've never made dinner under conditions before."

"Well, one condition is, we are not going to talk about Matt, or my marriage to Matt," I said.

"Okay," she said. "I guess I can agree to both of those."

"That was one condition," I said.

"I heard two," my mother replied.

"It was one."

"Oh, all right, and the second condition?"

"I will be coming alone, and there will be no questions about whether I have a man in my life or not."

"Don't mothers have any rights to advance information?"

"No. And the third condition is, you will not keep heaping my plate with food and telling me how thin I look."

"Who's going to criticize you if not your own mother?" she asked.

"And, fourthly, can it just be us? You and me and Dad and maybe Reese? I just would like it less—public."

My mother sighed. "You have more conditions than the Weather Channel."

"Well?"

"I've already invited Jerry and Kate," my mother said, referring to my brother Jerome the Gnome and his wife, Kate the Relentlessly Happy Homemaker. "And Reese is bringing his girlfriend."

"Reese has a girlfriend?" I asked in surprise. "He never told me he was seeing anyone."

"He didn't want to make you feel bad because he was happy while you were unhappy," my mother replied.

"So he thinks that I would be happier if I thought he was un-happy?"

"Please," my mother said, "let's not get into it."

        *   *   *

Jerry, my happy architect brother, and his wife, Kate, attended with their twins, two very happy, very bright, very precocious four-year-old girls. Jerome designs commercial buildings, and Kate used to model swimwear. They flashed me sadly compassionate smiles all throughout the meal and, well coached by my overachieving mother, refrained from asking any personal questions at all, even as to how I liked the weather. I was trying hard not to be such a stubbornly tragic figure, and made jokes and really tried to listen to the conversation. Reese introduced the new interest in his life, Maribelle. Or Tinker bell. Maybe Doorebelle. Okay, so I wasn't paying that much attention, but I couldn't help noticing they sat so close it looked like they were suffering from a bad case of static cling.

My mother made a roast beef and new potatoes with dill, and made dinner rolls, as well as two other kinds of breads, honey-glazed carrots, noodle casserole, corn soufflé, and, in case she missed a food group, lots of salad, the last of which was all Kate ate, because she was never sure if her agent was going to put in an emergency call and beg her to climb back into a bikini again immediately, even though she's forty-one, with two kids, and probably a tad past prime time for swimwear ads.

Jerry and Kate waxed proudly about their children, practically holding a PowerPoint presentation of their nursery-school report cards from the past year, then had each twin do twenty examples of long division followed by several song-and-dance numbers fresh from their ballet and singing classes, a demonstration of Tai Chi from their martial-arts class, a quick exhibition of their finger paint- ings, and, the grand finale, a recitation of prime numbers that started with two and took us through dessert.

We sat in the dining room. I watched my father being courte- ous, almost courtly, pulling out my mother's chair before she sat down and patting her arm, and raving over her cooking. He acted like the devoted and doting husband that I always remembered. He gave his usual toast to everyone's continuing good health and happi- ness. He refilled my mother's wineglass twice and complimented both her looks and the lightness of her dinner rolls. I watched him, and I had a flash. Why hadn't I been aware of it before? HE WAS SEEING SOMEONE. There was an undercurrent that I could al- most feel, that undercurrent of tension that lives below the surface of hidden infidelity. I felt it as strongly as I did the subsonic rum- blings of Margo when I came into the barn in the morning, and I couldn't look at him.

"Have some more food," my mother urged me, then realized she had just violated condition number three. "Sorry."

"Thanks, but I couldn't eat another bite," I said, pushing my plate away.

"Nonsense," said my father, piling three large slices of meat onto my plate. "Meat is good for you. It builds character."

"Really," I said, "I couldn't—"

My mother shook her head. "That's because you fill up on donuts all day," she said. I heard Kate gasp. My mother then foisted another huge helping onto Reese, who is always too goodhearted to say no.

There were piles of leftovers after dinner that my mother wrapped and, at my father's insistence, sent home with me.

"I want to see some meat on those bones of yours," my father said, pinching my arm like he was evaluating me for breeding stock.

I thanked them as I took the ten-pound bag and put it near my coat. Leftovers. So much food.

As soon as we finished our coffee, Clarabelle jumped up to help with the dishes in that overly ambitious girlfriend-trying-to-impress-the-family routine. Reese carried the piles of dishes to the kitchen, and she washed them carefully, because my mother likes her dishes sterile enough for surgery. I was stuck in the kitchen, loading all the newly washed dishes into the dishwasher for round two on their journey toward supreme sanitation.

"You'd think we were going to manufacture microchips," I grumbled as I stuffed the washed glassware into the dishwasher.

Jerry and Kate took a pass on the domestic work, since they, of course, had to get their kids home to bed so they would have the energy for their photography, French, and calligraphy classes after nursery school the next day, all of which practically guaranteed that they would continue to grow up supremely—happy.

    •   ▪   •

"So—Reese tells me that you ride horses," Whateverbelle said, taking a pile of dishes from my brother and plunging them into a suds-filled sink, after which she attempted to scrub off their yellow-rosebud pattern.

"Um," I replied, grabbing a washed stack from her and fitting them neatly around the dishwasher rack.

"He said you ride English," she said.

"I don't discuss horses when I'm off duty," I joked, grabbing another stack and putting them in the way my mother likes, with all of them facing forward like kids in a classroom.

"Reese tells me you used to compete, too," she said. "So did I. I rode Western for years." She paused. "Gymkhana. I love horses. I still have my old competition horse."

"Great," I said, now checking to make sure the points of the knives were facing downward.

"He said you stopped competing."

Why did she care? I wondered. Where does it say that you have to make small talk and pretend you care about someone just because you're in the same kitchen with her and she wants to marry your brother?

"Reese says that you gave it all up, even though you were really good."

"Long time ago," I said, shrugging it off. "I don't do it anymore."

But she was relentless, and then I knew where she was going with it. I eyed the knives I had placed so carefully and wondered, if I just turned one facing back up and pushed her . . .

"I felt so bad," she said, now handing me some already sparkling glassware. "I mean, when he told me about the accident."

I flashed Reese a how-could-you look while she kept talking. He tiptoed out of the kitchen. "I mean," she said, "it sounded like a horrible thing to go through."

I didn't answer her. Where was my music? I needed music. How was I going to stop her?

She sighed and gave me a comforting squeeze of the shoulder with a wet hand. "You were so young. I can imagine how awful it must have been for you, to see your coach get killed like that. And by your own horse."

Chapter Thirty-seven

THE TRUTH was, I really had never forgotten that Captain Chandelle-Meiers had been killed along with Homer. I just hadn't cared at the time. He deserved to die, I had thought shamelessly. He deserved it. I didn't care that he had most likely left a Madame Chandelle-Meiers back home in Switzerland, making wheels of cheese with the help of their Alpine-blond children. He had taken my horse from me, and I was filled with seventeen-year-old rage. My only concern had been my horse.

I sat up in the kitchen long after I got home from my mother's, with Beethoven playing loudly—I needed the strength and power of Beethoven—while I ignored the apologetic messages that Reese was leaving on the answering machine.

The plastic shopping bag of leftovers was still on the floor next to my coat, and Grace was very interested in its contents. She was sniffing it carefully and whining, and I didn't get up from the table until she started taking matters into her own hands, by pulling out the little silver-foil-wrapped torpedoes that my mother had packed.

I picked up a package labeled "rst. bf." and opened it to give her a few slivers, then shoved the rest of the bag into my refrigerator. An embarrassment of riches, I thought, considering that I had returned from a country, a mere several thousand miles away, where leftovers were an unheard-of problem.

I lay awake in bed for the rest of the night, with Grace and Alley Cat tucked one under each armpit, and the covers pulled up to my chin, and Beethoven still da-da-da-dumming on the stereo. I thought about dinner and my father and Blabberbelle.

Was it possible that I was wrong about my father? I really had no grounds for my suspicions, except that I was, well, suspicious, and that might have been more of a result of Matt than reality. The phone rang again, and I got out of bed to listen, hoping that maybe this time it would be Tom.

It was Reese. He was sorry again. He had only been telling Cutiebelle about the family, and didn't think that she would latch on to the horse thing. Sorry. Sorry.

I was sorry, too. I was sorry that I was such a pain in the ass to be around.

•   •   •

"It's not like I ever forgot," I was telling Margo while she ate her breakfast the next morning. "I never really forgot."

I was outside her enclosure, sipping coffee and eating a jelly donut. I had asked Richie to let me feed her every morning so that she would learn to focus on me, but right now she was only focusing on her elephant chow. I talked to her anyway, as though she were listening. Abbie—the baby—was picking up little bouquets of hay and throwing them at me. I pushed the rest of their breakfast, a pail of fruits and vegetables, through the little trap door in the cage.

"Margo," I commanded, "look here." She looked at the fruits instead, picking them over like an old grandmother, pinching and squeezing and selecting the best ones to eat first.

"I remember everything about Homer," I said to her, and sat down next to the bars. "You know, you never forget things like that." Then I felt a stupid giggle rise up inside of me. How foolish it was to talk to an elephant about not forgetting.

I leaned my head back and sifted through time. I remember my mother hurrying me away from the riding ring right after the accident, but not before I saw two figures lying there, like fallen statues in the pale sand. A dark-brown horse, the stirrups askew, with the very proper Captain Chandelle-Meiers, halfway out of the saddle, still holding the reins most correctly in his two fists, his head pressing into the sand at a terrible angle. Someone escorted my mother and me to a room on the second floor of the barn. We were ushered into a beautiful mahogany-paneled office that matched the nineteenth-century architecture of the barn below us. I sat in a leather chair with brass hobnails and ran my fingers up and down the bumpy nail heads and stared at the pictures on the wall. Olympic horses. They had all passed through this barn. This beautiful barn with its Belgian-block aisles and brass fittings on polished dark wood stalls, where the horses were literally bedded up to their knees in straw. Homer had been assigned a corner stall, huge, airy, a brass ball on each side of the stall door, like an entrance for royalty.

I heard an ambulance siren. And someone came into the office to tell my mother to take me home.

*   *   *

I felt something in my pocket. Abbie had managed to put her little trunk through the bars and take out a tissue. I pulled it gently from her grasp, and she gave an indignant squeal. Margo pressed instantly at the bars, giving me a warning bark, ready to protect her baby.

"Look," I said to her, "I would never hurt your baby. She's my baby, too, you know."

She shook her head up and down as if to tell me that she was just doing her job, and that this was what you did when you were grown up. You became responsible. The world no longer revolved around you, it had to revolve around the things you most cared about.

And I realized I was all grown up, too. It was time to rethink that afternoon. With the filter of Zimbabwe to look through, the filter of people dying for nothing, of animals dying for nothing, I grew ashamed that I hadn't cared that Captain Chandelle-Meiers had died. For me. A man just doing his job. A man who had been trying to help me. I had felt no compassion for him, and now I was filled with shame.

*   *   *

I felt a push at my arm and, before I could react, Margo had pulled the jelly donut out of my hand. I jumped to my feet in time to see her pop the donut into her mouth. Then she reached toward me with her trunk again, swinging it up and down, pressing it along my arm, searching.

"Hey," I complained. "That was my breakfast." She barked at me.

I may as well get some work done, I thought, since this was the rare occasion when she was actually paying attention to me. I picked up a few pieces of fruit I had left and grabbed the target stick that was propped nearby. I touched her ankle.

"Margo, lift foot," I said. She eyed me up and down. I could see she was calculating the cost-to-benefit ratio of obeying me and possibly getting another banana.

"Come on, Margo," I said. "Please. Please." I knew there was nothing in the elephant-training manual about the effectiveness of begging, but I was getting desperate. Tennessee wasn't very far off.

"Margo, lift foot." I tickled her foot with the flag. She swung her trunk through the bars and examined my hands. I could feel her warm breath, feel the moist, muscular tip roving over my fingers. Then she turned around, indifferent.

I stood there wondering what to do. Like with horses, there had to be a key to winning her trust. I was overlooking something. Maybe I needed to listen harder, needed to pay more attention to the things that mattered to her. She rumbled at her baby, then looked at me and lifted her tail to deposit her usual end-of-training commentary, a big, steaming pile of dung.

"I'll see you tomorrow," I promised. "We will definitely finish this conversation tomorrow."

*   *   *

I was at loose ends once I got back to my barn. With Delaney out of training, and Isis now on the road to achieving karmic oneness with her rider, I had nothing much to do. I needed to earn some more money. I felt bored, lonely, restless. Vacant. Thinking about my last afternoon with Homer had left me with an odd, disoriented feeling.

Conversano nickered to me, and I thought maybe I would throw a saddle on his back and edge him a little further along in his training. Though he was good enough for competition, I didn't care about that. Mousi reached over his fence and pursed his lips together, stretching them out like they were made of rubber, begging for a treat, and I absentmindedly ran my fingers over his face.

I needed more horses to train, I thought. More rearers, buckers, bolters, nappers. More horses that fell over when you tightened their girth, ran backward when you mounted them. More wheezers, head-shakers, man-haters, lady-killers, child-maimers, more biters, kickers, balkers, stoppers, rollers, stall-walkers . . .

No, I didn't.

I ran my fingers along the bruised patch of ribs that was still tender on my right side, courtesy of Delaney, and wondered why we don't get nine lives like cats. Maybe we do—the Buddhists believe we do, except they believe it's sequential and after death, and we have to come back to life again and again. And then I thought, Someday, if I keep riding problem horses, I could wind up like Captain Chandelle-Meiers, trying to fix a training problem and dying for it. And then I'll have to come back in my next life and learn to ride all over again.

It wasn't worth it.

I went back into the house and called Reese. He was relieved to hear from me.

"Hey," he said, "I'm sorry. I didn't think she would bring it up. It was just—"

"It's okay," I said. "And I'm sorry, too. You were right, and I'm going to try and grow up."

We talked for a while. He really loved this girl, he said. She was an associate math professor in the same college, and she was a good person, and she liked horses. I was happy for Reese and listened to everything he said. Really listened. After we hung up, I thought about our conversation. I thought about his girlfriend and how happy he sounded. I knew that she was probably going to be my new sister-in-law. I was happy for Reese. I was happy for her. I was happy that she was going to be part of my family.

Marielle. Her name was Marielle.

"**Y**OU CAN'T unring a bell," Alana was saying.

I had just finished giving her two little girls their first riding lesson on Tony the Pony, and it had gone very well. The girls were too intimidated to ask Tony to do much, and Tony was too lazy to volunteer anything but a very slow walk. Each girl spent ten minutes on a lunge line, a sort of long dog leash, attached to Tony's bridle, which allowed him to walk a big circle around me while I controlled him. Alana spent the entire lesson alternating between peeking through her fingers and beaming with pride.

We were now relaxing over hot chocolate; the girls were planted in front of a video, and I was telling Alana how awful I felt about Captain Chandelle-Meiers.

"You can't unring a bell," she repeated. "What's done is done. It wasn't your fault, and it's over. You need to move on."

"But how?" I asked. "How do I do it?"

"Do that lucid-dreaming thing I taught you," she suggested. "Put yourself back into that afternoon, and give him a proper good-bye. Tell Homer good-bye. Then move on with your life."

I thought about it for a moment. "I don't know if I can face losing him again," I said. "I don't know if I can go through all that by myself."

"You don't have to be alone." She touched my hand. "Take the Captain with you."

I went to bed that night filled with trepidation, wondering if I really wanted to relive that afternoon. Then I thought how I would hug Homer's neck and kiss him one million times before I let him go.

If I could let him go.

I needed a game plan. I would try to reconstruct him, I thought, refabricate him. Start by remembering what he looked like, felt like to ride. I knew it wasn't going to be as easy as reconstituting orange juice, and, despite a few pre-launch suggestions from Alana, I hadn't a clue on how to begin.

I put on a CD of Wagner—*Tannhäuser,* which I thought was appropriate, because it was about someone who was safe and comfortable and left it all to find answers that would settle his heart and spirit. I lay in bed and listened to the music, the soaring notes, the soft bells tolling, and clutched Grace to my chest and let myself drift back to the day I lost Homer. It was sunny; I remembered a strong breeze, and being afraid that the wind would make him nervous. I wore a sweater over my white competition shirt, and a tiny gold pin of a horse doing a piaffe, pinned to the white stock tie around my throat. My mother had given me the pin as a birthday gift. I wondered where it had gone over the years.

I felt sleepy now, my eyes started closing of their own accord, and I found myself at Gladstone. The riding ring was ahead of me, and the grass turned into a velvet crush under my boots as I walked slowly toward it, afraid of what I would find there, afraid that Homer would be there, and afraid that he wouldn't.

Suddenly I saw him, in the ring, on the ground, lying very still. His big bay eggplant-shaped body was still wearing my saddle. I drew nearer. His legs were frozen in a trot that was never to be executed. His eyes were closed and his mouth was slightly open, showing a set of teeth that met in a triangle of age.

I climbed into the ring and hesitated, before walking to him very carefully, just in case he was sleeping, just in case he would spring to his feet and kick out, like he did after a good roll in the dirt. But he lay very still, and I sat down next to his head and picked it up and put it on my lap. It weighed nothing. My fingers brushed the soft nap of his face, brushed away the flies that were buzzing in disrespect around his mouth and eyes.

"Homer?" I whispered his name. He didn't move. I clucked to him, like I always did when I was astride and wanted him to pick up the pace. He still didn't move.

This isn't right, I thought. My brilliant Homer, the largeness of him humbled onto the ground; it wasn't fitting that he should be so still.

"What should I do?" I called out.

"The horse must respect his rider!" I turned my head to see Captain Chandelle-Meiers standing next to the fence rail, his arms folded. "Make him rise," he commanded.

"You're dead," I said to him.

He agreed. "But you must still ask your horse to listen to you. A good horse obeys his rider."

I laid my head down on Homer's neck and twirled his forelock with my fingers, twisting the black hair into a stiff curl, rubbing his long, noble face. He had been a very good horse.

"I don't want to remember him like this," I announced, my tears making wet splotches on his neck.

"Of course not," said Captain Chandelle-Meiers. "You must get him up."

I rose to my feet and stared down at the expanse of his brown body, his black legs, his black tail fanned over the dusty ring like the fringe on a shawl.

"Homer," I said to him. "Up."

He didn't move. Somehow I had to get him to his feet.

I willed myself to think of the horseness of him, his smell, his warmth, the feel of his rolling gaits beneath me. "Please, get up," I said, but to no avail. I turned to the Captain. "I can't do it."

"Come again, come again," Captain Chandelle-Meiers urged impatiently. "We don't have so much time to waste."

I concentrated harder. "Homer," I called. "Up!" I clapped my hands.

I felt something in the air next to me. A stir, a thickening of molecules. Then nothing.

"Homer!"

I tried to remember the way he felt underneath me, the slippery hair, the roundness of his back, the sharpness of his withers. "Homer!" I called out his name again and again.

I turned to Captain Chandelle-Meiers. "He's not listening," I said.

He threw me a pair of roweled spurs. I ran my thumb over the tiny teeth. "I can't use these," I said.

"They will not harm him," he said, "if you use them with the lightest leg. They are made just to tickle his side. To keep him light and sensitive."

"Oh," I said. "I never knew that." I bent down and buckled them over my shoes. I took a step toward him.

Something nudged my shoulder and I turned around.

"Homer," I shrieked, and threw my arms around his neck. He felt solid and soft, familiar and strangely different, all at once. His eyes shone with life. I pressed my face against his neck and held it there for a long time.

I took the saddle from his back and removed his bridle, then looked around for a halter and lead line. It was such a simple plan—why hadn't I thought of it before? *I could have him back!* I would lead him straight out of my dream and into my backyard, and put him in the empty stall I had in my barn. And this time I would be very careful about who was riding him.

Captain Chandelle-Meiers was beside me now, crisp and military. "You can't do that, you know," he said. "The horse must remain here."

"No," I said. "I'm taking him home."

"You must do what's right," he said. "He doesn't belong with you anymore. You must always do what is right for the animal."

I dropped my hands from Homer.

The Captain nodded his head in approval.

"Good," he said. "Good."

"You can't stay, either, you know," I said. "You've been with me for too long."

"Of course," he said. "I belong with the horse." He placed his hands on Homer's neck and swung himself up onto Homer's bare back.

"He doesn't have to obey anyone anymore," I reminded him. "He doesn't have to perform anymore."

"He will be as free as he wants," he promised me. "He is a wonderful horse. We will ride the clouds."

"Okay," I said, and stepped away. I let him go. Reluctantly, I let him go. They circled me in a beautiful rolling canter, then rose up into a blue sky that made my eyes ache, Homer's essence, his soul, cantering until he was out of sight.

I felt something happening inside of me. A flutter, the barest feeling that I had taken a first step toward something, but I didn't know what. I just knew that I was finally free to take it.

And then I suddenly saw Africa laid out before my eyes, a quilt of gold and rose and dust, of the savanna with its tall, wispy pale-yellow paintbrush grasses, of gray-green bush, and red flowers, and lavender birds. There was a trumpeting of elephants bidding Homer good-bye. A glorious trumpeting. Here. It was here where my first step had to take me. Somehow I knew that it was here.

I awoke to a drenched pillow and the "Pilgrims' Chorus" welcoming me home.

Chapter Thirty-nine

DELANEY STAYED with me for another two weeks, until his owner decided to have him put to sleep. He got more dangerous to handle with each passing day, and I knew she was making the right choice.

I felt bad, and told her what Dr. Reston had said about how sometimes it's not the problem that's the problem, so much as one's reaction to it. I suggested that she might even want to try a different trainer, perhaps someone who could train him to understand what was happening to him and teach him not to react so violently. Someone who owned a suit of armor and had the reflexes of, say, an Olympic speed-skater. But she had already purchased another horse for her daughter and really couldn't afford to board one that was going to need a course in Braille in order to find his oats. She was doing the right thing, of course. His life would have been misery.

In the end, she came to my barn with the vet while I waited inside my house, hiding in the bathroom with a box of jelly donuts and a box of tissues, trying not to cry. I couldn't bear to see another dead horse, but you always have to do the right thing.

Tom was right when he said he smelled defeat. He didn't even have to sniff that hard.

*   *   *

There wasn't much left for me to do that afternoon besides starting to pack. My lawyer had informed me a week before that Matt was eating cheap tarantula steaks, which doesn't sound all that improbable after you've spent a night eating worm appetizers, but he was really saying that Matt was in deep financial straits and couldn't make payments on both the mortgage and the huge equity loan. The bottom line was that the house would need to be sold or we would lose it and have less than nothing. He went on to inform me that it was imperative that I connect it to red pig snorts. Maybe he meant protect my credit report, but what difference did it make? I didn't care about listening. The house had to be sold. He finished by saying I needed a radical integration of chicken bulbs.

I'm still working on that one.

I filled a few cartons with stuff from my bedroom, thinking I would work my way downstairs. I put a small carton aside for Grace, and sent her off to fetch her toys and put them in her box. After an hour or two, I was restless. Grace was sleeping in a carton of my winter clothes, her toys heaped all around her, and Alley Cat was hiding under the bed, nervous about the disarray. A quick check of my watch told me that Richie would be putting Margo in for the day, and I thought I would help him. Matt didn't go to the sanctuary in the afternoons anymore, since Margo was healed enough to be reduced to a once-a-week checkup, so I was safe.

My cell phone rang as I was driving to the sanctuary. I flipped on the car microphone. Matt was on the other end.

"Don't hang up," he said. "I need to talk to you."

"You are really pathetic," I said. "Don't call me anymore."

"Give me a chance," he said.

I snort-laughed into the microphone. "Let me guess. Does Holly need my underwear now? Because she got just about everything else."

"Please let me see you," he said. "I can explain everything."

"I would need about a million explanations," I yelled back into the mike. "One for every dollar that you—"

"NO! Wait! I—" He sounded flustered, desperate. "Please let me talk to you in person."

"Talk to the hand," I said, then realized that he couldn't see me holding my hand up in front of the microphone.

"Neelie, please," he said in a pitiful voice. "Snogfest wimple doom. Lariat pencil hats. I really mean it."

I pulled the mike from the phone and threw it out the window.

*   *   *

Margo and her baby were just going back into the barn from their afternoon play date outside when I arrived. Margo marched along, with great dignity even though she was caked with mud, and her daughter was holding on to her tail, like a child holding on to her mother's hand. A procession of elephants, comical yet stately, marching into the barn, blaring their trumpets to herald their arrival.

I helped Richie swing the heavy doors shut behind them, and Margo dug immediately into her chow. She swept up a trunkful of pellets with a graceful scoop, dropped them into her mouth, and was about to go back for another helping when she stopped and turned her head toward me, as if she had just thought of something.

"Hello, Margo," I greeted her.

She took a few steps toward me and pressed her trunk through the bars and swept it along my arm. Up to my shoulder. Down to my hand. She sniffed me thoroughly, as though searching for something. I picked up a banana from her basket and handed it to her. She took it and then dropped it. Apparently that wasn't what she was looking for. I tried again with an apple. No. I tried to understand what she wanted. She touched my hand again, and I took a gentle hold of the tip of her trunk. She rumbled at me.

"What, Margo?" I asked softly. She rumbled again and ran her trunk down my arm, then down my leg. It's an odd sensation, to get felt up by an elephant, but I remained immobile. Another trumpet, and she slammed her trunk into me in a fit of pique, knocking me across the room. I landed sitting, much to Richie's amusement.

"You know, I thought about giving up horse training," I said, checking myself over for injuries, "so that I wouldn't get dumped anymore."

"You have to admit," he said, giving me a hand up, "this is a more exotic way to get dumped."

"After Matt, this is amateur stuff," I said.

He made a face. "Yes, well," he said, "Matt. There is something very wrong going on with Matt."

"You just noticed?" I said. "You know what they say about making your bed and lying in it."

"Actually, from what he's told me, I think he's lying alone."

We were interrupted by Margo, who had reached through the bars again toward my hands, rumbling with impatience. There was something she wanted from me, and I wished I knew what it was.

"The lady is definitely trying to tell you something," Richie said.

She touched me again, pressing her trunk up and down my arm, snuffling hard like the hose on a vacuum. Suddenly I understood her. It was so obvious now.

Then I laughed out loud.

"What?" Richie asked.

"You'll see," I said to Richie. "I know exactly what she wants."

Chapter Forty

"I'll take two dozen jelly donuts, please," I told the donut man the next morning.

"How you stay so skinny?" he asked in a Pakistani accent. "Every day you eat donut! Donut! Donut! Donut! Now more donut!"

"It's the new donut diet," I said.

A very overweight woman behind me tapped me on the shoulder. "Can you please tell me how it works?" she asked.

I nodded. "Just take one bite and feed the rest to your elephant," I said. "Works like a charm."

* * *

I couldn't wait to show Margo the donuts. First, like a conscientious mother, I let her finish her breakfast of hay and vegetables mixed with her elephant chow. Good nutrition should always come before junk food.

Then I opened a donut box and showed her its contents.

"Margo," I commanded. "Look here."

She looked. I bounced the donuts around a bit in an effort to tantalize her. She responded immediately with an excited ear-splitting trumpet.

I held out a donut. She stuck her trunk through the bars and took it gently from my hand, grunting with appreciation.

"Margo, look here." I tickled her foot with the target stick. "Lift foot." She didn't hesitate. She lifted her foot like a Radio City Music Hall Rockette. I held out her reward, a second donut. After that, I had her. A few jellies and she was obeying my every command, and literally eating out of the palm of my hand.

*   *   *

Within a few days, I had a standing order for three dozen jelly donuts and two large coffees, just waiting for me to pick up every morning. The fat lady from earlier in the week was sitting at a table with a big pile of donuts on a paper plate. She gave me a wave as I passed by.

"It's not working yet," she called out, "but I have to say, this is the best diet I've ever been on."

*   *   *

Every morning now, Margo greeted me with her trunk held aloft through the bars, waiting for her fix. I was handing donuts out like the Red Cross as I put her through her repertoire. She lifted her feet, opened her mouth, and moved sideways, all with a tap of the stick.

Though Faye would have been proud of me, I had yet to show our progress to Richie. I had just finished working when Richie emerged from the cool morning outside, greeting us with a cheery salute.

"Did Margo finish her breakfast?" he called over. "It's time to play."

"She ate every bit," I said proudly.

He grabbed his coffee, then noticed the three empty donut boxes. He lifted their lids. "Wow, aren't you getting quite a sweet tooth," he said. "Three dozen donuts and not one left for me."

"Margo ate them," I explained. "I've been using them to train her. She loves donuts."

"Ah yes," he said, laughing. "They must remind her of all those donut trees in Africa!"

"All I know is, I've developed a new respect for the power of sugar."

"Well, if donuts work, donuts it is." Then his face took on a very serious expression. "There's just one thing you need to remember from now on," he said, sternly shaking his finger at me.

My heart skipped a beat. "What?"

"My commission is one raspberry jelly every morning."

*   *   *

We opened the gates to her enclosure and gently prodded Margo outside. She marched through the barn doors, little Abbie attached to her tail. Richie and I followed them. Suddenly Margo became animated and swung around, letting out a rackety trumpet. It took me a split second to realize that she was heading directly at me.

"Watch out!" Richie yelled.

I ducked out of her way as fast as I could, but not before she swung her trunk and knocked me over. Then she stood over me and patted me down like a police detective. No donuts. Satisfied, she marched to her mud pond.

"Jesus," said Richie, helping me up, "that could have had a bad ending. Are you okay?"

"I'm fine," I said. "Just practicing for my next career as a bowling pin." I made a joke of it, but I had been scared down to the soles of my feet.

We watched Margo blow mud all over her baby. The baby, who normally sprayed water back, accepted her mud bath quietly, then closed her eyes to doze.

"Do you think she's been acting a little funny lately?" Richie asked.

"I noticed she's sleeping a lot," I said, "but I'm not sure what normal is for such a baby."

"I'm not sure, either," he said, looking worried. "I think I'll call Matt. I don't like taking chances." Then he stopped himself. "You'll probably have to be here to help, you know."

"I can't," I said. "What happens if he starts talking about how happy he is about his baby, and—"

He put his hand on my arm. "We'll just starting talking about ours," he said gently. "And ours is bigger."

*   *   *

By the next day, it was obvious that Abbie was very sick. She had a cough and a green runny nose and was lying down in the hay, her trunk stretched limply in front of her, her eyes half closed. She lost interest in nursing. Matt was summoned immediately, and Richie asked me to help Matt as he did the necessary tests. Margo was put into leg bracelets, though even when wearing them she could be protective and dangerous. I had several emergency boxes of donuts at the ready.

Richie helped support the baby's head while Matt conducted a thorough examination, taking samples of her blood and a culture from her trunk. He handled her so tenderly that I suddenly pictured him holding his baby, holding Holly, caressing her. I bit my lip and looked away.

"You can hand me my instruments," Matt instructed me. His face and voice were very neutral. We both knew that the welfare of our charges came first and, without any discussion, had independently decided that we were going to be very professional about things.

"Please pass me the culture tube," he asked politely, as he steadied Abbie's head and swabbed the inside of her trunk.

I handed him the bottle of culture medium so that he could put the swab back inside for the lab. He missed the opening and the swab fell to the ground. "Come on, come on," he said impatiently. "Another one."

I tried to slip a second one from its case, but it was stuck.

"Another tube," he thundered. "I can't keep holding her head up forever."

"I'm hurrying," I said, trying to slide the lid off. Now the tube flew from my hand and fell to the floor. Matt snatched it off the floor and efficiently snapped it open with one hand. The swab popped right out.

"How was I supposed to know there was a secret way to open it?" I defended myself.

"Maybe if you watched what I was doing a little more closely you might have picked up on it," he said in a nasty voice.

"If I were the type to watch everything you were doing, we wouldn't be in the mess we're in," I retorted.

"Touché," he said. "Big, fucking touché."

*   *   *

We had a diagnosis within two days. It was pneumonia, most likely due to her weakened immune system. She couldn't have nursed much in her first few days of life, because of Margo's dehydration and terrible injuries, and so hadn't receive the necessary antibodies. She was a very sick little elephant, and we were fighting for her life. Matt came to check on her condition almost round the clock. He spent hours consulting with Billy DuPreez on the phone, as well as with the vet from a renowned baby-elephant rescue in Kenya, and even got Tom to buy a very expensive state-of-the-art special triple antibiotic and fly it up from Texas in his private jet.

*   *   *

It was decided that Richie would take care of Abbie during the day, since he was at the sanctuary anyway, and I would take care of Abbie at night. Margo was kept in bracelets to protect us—now I understood their importance—while we worked on her baby.

Every night I sat on a hay bale, close to Abbie's head, to feed her a gruel made from warm oatmeal mixed with puréed fruits and coconut milk.

And though it was awkward to work within a foot of each other, Matt and I persevered. Except for giving him some physical assistance, I just ignored him. I sang songs to Abbie, and massaged her ears, and made sure she was kept covered.

"Music, always music," Matt muttered to me only once, but more of a statement of fact than criticism. I didn't answer him, I just continued singing "Bridge over Troubled Water," which I thought she might especially like.

Matt kept her hydrated with saline solution, and gave her strong antibiotics, but other than daily medical reports we still barely spoke. We worked side by side, sometimes elbow to elbow, without letting our eyes meet or speaking one word more than necessary, though a few times he paused and cleared his throat and turned around to look at me as though he wanted very much to say something. And I wanted very much to hear something. I didn't know what—another apology? his profound regrets? We just left a stiff, polite silence between us.

Sometimes it's what you don't say that counts.

Chapter Forty-one

A WEEK became two weeks, and Abbie remained very sick. Her fever rose, and her breathing became labored. She coughed deeply, her sides heaving from the effort, and then she would drop down into her nest of hay, exhausted.

Tom called me every few days, always preceding his request for a progress report with apologies for not being able to get away. He had business all over the world, and called me from his jet, from his hotel room, from restaurants, from every continent, before and after meetings, at the oddest hours.

"Richie tells me you've been working day and night on her," he said as I spoke to him on my cell phone, early one morning. I had just left Abbie half an hour earlier, and I was pulling into my driveway. "I want you to know that I appreciate it. You've gone above and beyond the call."

"I don't want to lose her," I said.

"And how's it going with Matt?"

"We're both being very professional," I said. Loosely translated, that meant that we'd gotten into one major blowout and several minor fender-benders.

"I just got into New York late last night," Tom said, to my surprise. "Do you need a break? I could fly Faye up from Tennessee and we could spend a few days together. I have a little cottage in Bretagne. It's beautiful this time of year."

"I have to pack up my own little cottage," I said. "I'm selling it." I had avoided telling him about the house because I didn't want his pity.

"Why?" he asked.

"It's a Matt thing," I said.

"Don't do anything until we talk," he replied. "How about if I take you to dinner tonight?"

"I'll be sitting on elephant duty," I said, then realized it wasn't quite what I meant. "Sorry—I didn't mean 'dooty.' I meant 'shift,' 'shift of duty.' Does that sound better, or am I getting delirious?"

"I'll bring dinner and come to the barn," he said. "You sound like you need a good meal."

             *   *   *

I grabbed the next phone call without checking the caller ID.

"Wow—you're actually answering your phone now?" Matt said.

"I didn't know it was you," I said nastily. "I have to be available if Richie needs me."

"Well, I was wondering if you'd have dinner with me before you head up to the sanctuary," he said. "I have to go there tonight, to check on Abbie. Maybe we could have an early dinner and sit down and talk. Please?"

"No."

"How about if we get together sometime this week?"

"Not interested," I said. "For some odd reason, I'll be very busy packing up the home that I lost."

"That's one of the things I want to talk about," he said. "I want to talk about doing something—to make it up to you."

"Oh, I just couldn't accept one more thing," I said in extra-saccharine tones. "Not after all you've done for me so far."

"Are you being sarcastic?" he asked.

"No," I replied. "I'm being hateful and angry."

             *   *   *

He called back five more times that day, begging me to talk to him. After the sixth call, I managed to hone my hang-up skills to where it took me less than a second to disconnect, by pressing the phone's on and off buttons nearly simultaneously.

"Talk to me, talk to me, talk to me." He left several desperate, pathetic messages on my answering machine. I pressed "delete all," wishing it could somehow include both him and Holly. Then I got myself ready for my night shift with Abbie.

But Matt took things a step further.

I was about to leave for the sanctuary, later that afternoon, and opened my front door to find Matt standing there, his finger just about to press the doorbell. He looked awful. There were black circles under his eyes, and an expression of profound sadness on his face.

"What are you doing here?" I asked.

"Please, let's talk." He held both hands up as if to fend off my anger. "Can I come in?" He leaned forward to peek inside. There was a one-hundred-decibel rendition of "Graceland" playing in the background.

"Wow," he said. "You still blast music!"

"It's no longer any of your business what I do." I yanked the door closed behind me and pulled out my keys, ready to lock it.

Matt cupped his hand over the keys. "I need to talk to you," he said. "And I can't talk in front of the elephants."

"They don't speak English," I said. "They won't care."

"It's just that we can't seem to talk without arguing, and I don't want us to get into it in front of them and get them all agitated."

"We have nothing to talk about," I said, yanking the keys out from under his hand and locking the door with a crisp snap.

"There are some things you have to know," he began, but I started down the porch steps. He tried to block my path.

"Go away," I said, angrily pushing him aside.

"I still love you," he said. "You used to be a therapist. You have to know—things sometimes aren't what they appear—"

A flash of fury tore through me like the white bolts of light that had torn across the African skies, so overwhelming that it burned everything inside of me. I hated Matt. I hated what he had done. I hated his deception, his carelessness, his declarations of love. I hated the look of him.

I had to turn away from him. So searing was my anger, it could have ignited the house behind me, it could have turned my tears to puffs of steam.

"I never want to see you again," I said through clenched teeth. "I wish there was another vet Richie could call. I hate working with you." I stamped off to my car. He stood there on the porch, his shoulders drooping.

"I hope she was worth it," I called back to him while getting into my truck. "I hope losing me, losing the house, losing everything—I hope it was all worth it."

"It wasn't," I heard him say, as I was pulling the truck door shut. "If you care to know—it absolutely wasn't."

＊　＊　＊

Matt followed me to the sanctuary, wordlessly checked on the baby, and left just as Tom was turning into the driveway. It was like an English comedy, with doors opening and closing and people sailing in and out with perfect timing.

"How's our baby?" Tom asked. He had come into the enclosure with me. I turned to explain Abbie's treatment, but he put his arms around me. There was no one to witness his sweet kiss except Margo, and she was busy eating her dinner. Abbie was asleep, on a big pile of hay, under her favorite yellow-and-blue plaid blanket.

Tom held me close, smelling of mint and wild grasses, and I buried my face in his shoulder and closed my eyes.

"I wish our schedules gave us more leeway," he said into my hair. "I think about you all the time."

"You do?" I looked up into a face filled with kindness and concern. "Thank you." I traced his scar with the tip of my finger and then leaned toward him and kissed it. I ran my fingers through his silver hair, and thought how sweet it felt to be near him again.

"I miss you," he whispered, and kissed me again. Margo looked over her shoulder at us and rumbled. We broke apart. Tom knelt down next to Abbie.

"She's still sick," I said. "Still has a fever."

He took a gentle pinch of skin from her ear. "Not dehydrated," he said. "So the IVs are doing their job. But I know how touch-and-go these things can be."

I knelt next to him. "We're trying so hard."

"You're doing great, Neelie."

I started to cry.

"Hey." He stood up. "Wait till you see what I brought."

He left the barn for a moment and returned, producing a shopping bag filled with covered aluminum containers, a bottle of wine, a linen tablecloth, and real knives and forks. We opened the tablecloth over several bales of hay and set the food out. Shrimp scampi and salad and good bread. He had even brought china plates.

"So—what's going on?" he asked, pouring us wine as though we were sitting in a very fine restaurant. "Why are you moving?"

I told him about Matt and the house. He looked very grave.

"Do you have a good lawyer?" he asked.

I shrugged. "How do you know until the shooting stops and you see who's left standing?"

He leaned back against the bars. "Let me get you a lawyer," he said. "And let me buy the house."

I grimaced. "I can't."

He folded his arms and scowled. I'd never seen him look like that, fierce, his features seeming to sharpen. "It's a good business decision. The market's strong for these little houses, it would be nothing for me—just another investment."

These little houses. I had to remember who was speaking. He caught my look.

"What's wrong?" he asked.

"What happens if I can never afford to buy it back?" I asked. "Then you become not only my employer, you become my landlord. I can't have all that between us. It makes things too complicated."

"Don't be so stubborn," he replied. "We can cross that bridge when we get to it."

"No," I said. "I like to cross my bridges now."

He reached out and caressed my face. "Neelie, you can pay me back when you get on your feet." he asked. "What's the rush?"

I shrugged. "I guess it's because I want to make sure I can put up a bridge when I need it."

⁂

It was time to take care of Abbie. Tom watched me heat the coconut milk and stir in the oatmeal and puréed fruit. I poured it all into a bottle and gently pushed it between Abbie's lips, coaxing her to take a sip, singing my song to her.

"Looks like you're an enamel server yourself," he said.

"Thank you," I said, "I'm very flattered to be considered one."

"And you know what, Neelie?" he said, giving me another kiss, this one on the top of my head.

"What?" I asked, balancing the bottle against Abbie's lips.

"I think you would have made a very good mother."

Chapter Forty-two

I WAS in a quantum state of mind. Quantum superposition, it's called, when matter is neither here nor there, when it is neither alive nor dead, neither a particle nor energy, perpetually fluctuating between two conditions of existence, its very essence called into question.

I was a horse trainer who didn't train horses. A therapist who offered no therapy. I wasn't homeless, but I would soon have no house, no barn, no money. I spent my nights awake, and my days in a blurred state of half-light, dozing and working, and napping and dreaming.

I had a lover who never said he loved me, and an ex-husband who swore he did but treated me otherwise. I heard things that were never spoken, and seldom heard the things that were.

It was all going to come to no good, I thought miserably. Like the flame from a match, everything I worked for was going to disappear in a flash and a wisp of smoke, leaving nothing behind but the smell of defeat. If Tom only knew how far his words carried.

I dreaded the days, filled with strangers poking about my beloved house, opening closets, checking the state of hygiene in my bathroom, standing next to my bed and mentally measuring the room for drapes, and always, always finding the tiny pee spot that stained the corner of the living-room rug, where Grace had once had an accident as a puppy. I hated their glancing at the nursery with my lovely painted ponies and sparkly halters, and then growing suddenly quiet and sympathetic when they saw how empty the room was. I hated their peering through the kitchen window, out at the barn, and wondering what another house was doing in the back.

"It's a barn," my helpful agent would explain. "But of course you can always turn it into a cabana and backfill the riding ring and put a swimming pool in."

Sometimes she suggested they turn my barn into a little cottage for their mother-in-law. I would smile inwardly at that, wondering whose mother was going to get the nice stall on the end, the one conveniently located near the cement wash-area.

"Bring *horse* people," I told her more than once. "Bring people who can appreciate the barn and the riding ring."

"I will bring whoever comes into my office and can meet your price," she said arrogantly. "You don't have a lot of room for bargaining."

•   °   °

I may have dreaded the days, but I looked forward to my nights with Abbie. She was my anchor. When I rubbed the black fur that sprouted though her wrinkly gray skin, making her resemble a moth-eaten toy, she rumbled with appreciation. I massaged her ears and sang to her, and I felt real. I felt grounded.

And I would think, This is why I would like to rescue elephants. Because I can become their oasis in the great tangle of pain and cruelty that circumstance tied to their lives. I could unravel some of it. And, in what was quickly becoming my own tetherless, free-falling state of nothingness, they gave me a place to land.

°   °   °

Though I had turned down his generous offer to buy my house, Tom was persistent. He was waiting for me a few days later, sitting on my front porch, when I got home from the sanctuary.

"Shouldn't you be merging and conquering?" I asked him as I led him through a living room stacked with cartons.

"Listen," he said. "I have a proposition."

Grace lunged for the cuff of his pants.

"Let's sit down and talk business," he said, taking my arm and marching me over to the table, dragging along Grace, who was still hanging off one leg. He sat down and folded his hands like he was at a board meeting, and gestured for me to sit down. I removed Grace, popped her into the bathroom, and returned.

"I appreciate your offer," I said. "But I'm just barely making ends meet. I don't have any horses to train, and only the income from my students and what I make at the sanctuary is keeping me from stealing Margo's fruit—"

He held his hand up. "I wasn't planning to ask you for rent."

"I don't take charity."

"How about if you consider it part of a housing package I give you for working for me," he said. "Just until you get on your feet."

"That wouldn't be fair to you," I said. "You already pay me a salary."

"Consider it a bonus," he said, "for your extra hours. Or I can raise your pay."

"Don't," I said, embarrassed.

"Consider it a birthday gift. Consider it a—"

"I consider it out of the question," I said quietly, standing up. "Please don't ever mention it again."

*   *   *

"What is wrong with you?" Alana shrieked at me. "How could you say no to someone like Tom?" We were leading Tony the Pony back to his stall after another afternoon of lessons. He and the girls had graduated to a walk that was just barely faster than funereal, while Alana had graduated to peeking through the fingers of only one hand to watch them. Tony jumped at the sound of Alana's voice.

"I don't know," I said miserably. "I don't want to be dependent on him." Tony stood patiently as I took off his bridle and put his halter on him. "I can't be a kept woman."

"He wasn't going to keep *you*, you idiot," she said. "He was going to keep the house. *For* you."

"But what happens when we break up?" I said, now removing Tony's saddle from his back.

"I thought you said you weren't even officially together," Alana pointed out. She removed his fleece-wool saddle pad and held it aloft. "Where do you put Tony's sweater?"

"That's a saddle pad," I said, taking it from her and draping it over the saddle to be put away. "It's only every once in a while that Tom and I are together. I don't want to take advantage of him."

"You aren't taking advantage if he's *offering* it to you," Alana said with her usual run of logic. "Allowing him to be kind will make him feel good, so, in a way, you're doing it for him. Just say thank you and graciously accept."

"I can't," I said. "I'm too cranky to be gracious."

"Do it for poor Tony," Alana said, petting his neck. "Or he won't have a place to hang his hat."

"Tony doesn't have a hat to hang," I said. I put Tony in his stall and gave Alana a little hug. "Thanks for caring, but I don't want Tom to think of me as this needy person that he has to rescue. It's not a good basis for any kind of relationship. You, as a therapist, ought to know that."

"I, as a therapist, know that you are denying him the pleasure of being kind," she said. "Of doing a good deed. Don't be so stubborn. Things could turn into downhill fish sticks if you don't get a fluffer."

⚬　　⚬　　⚬

She was wrong about the fish sticks. I did get another offer. Actually, two.

The first one was from my mother.

"Your father and I have talked it over, and we are ready to buy the house and turn it over to you," she said.

"Thank you, Mom," I said, "that is the sweetest thing, but I can't let you do that."

"I'm your mother," she said. "I can't bear the idea of you sleeping in the street."

"I won't sleep in the street," I said. "I promise."

"Then where will you go?" she asked. "We already turned your room into my craft studio."

I laughed. "Don't worry, I won't come home. I don't ever plan on being one of those kid returnees."

"I wasn't worried about that," she said. "You could always have the basement. Your father could move the washer and dryer over a few feet for a bed. That's what parents are—"

"Your laundry is safe from invasion," I said. "But I love you for offering."

*   *   *

The second offer was from Reese.

"Marielle and I are planning to get married this year," he said over the phone. "I was thinking how your house would be perfect." He paused, then asked gently, "Do you mind if I bring her over to see it?"

"Not at all," I said.

He came over with her that same afternoon. Marielle really wasn't so bad, I decided. She was pretty, with a straightforward manner, warm brown eyes, high cheekbones, and an ever-present smile. I could see she was very much in love with my brother, and actually reduced his goofy factor by at least one-half. And, like a true horseperson, she wanted to see the barn first of all.

She examined the construction of the stall doors, and the quality of the latches. She closed the shutters to see how tight they fit over the windows to keep out the cold winter chill. She exclaimed over the triple insulation in the ceiling and the extra-strong flooring in the hayloft. She marched around the riding ring to check out the footing.

After an hour or two, we returned to the house.

"Look." Reese showed her around the kitchen. "Viking range. Neelie always cooked great meals for family get-togethers."

"That's when we were all happy," I muttered.

"We're still happy," Reese said, and gave Marielle a peck on the cheek. "At least I am."

He stepped over to my refrigerator. "And look here," he said, "huge new refrigerator, side-by-side doors." He swung the doors open to reveal a jar of mayonnaise and a can of tuna. "And a big freezer," he added, swinging the freezer door open. Inside was a neat stack of the foil-wrapped leftovers my mother had sent home with me.

Marielle gave him a little nod, then turned to me. "I hope you don't mind us."

"No," I said. "I'd rather it be you and Reese than anybody else."

"I do love your barn," she said. "Those stalls looked so roomy. Twelve by twelve?"

"Yep."

"Awesome," she said.

"And granite counters," Reese interjected, rubbing his hands over their smooth surface.

"I love the way you have the tack room reachable from the middle of the barn, and the hayloft with the double-wide pull-down staircase," Marielle continued. "Great design."

"Thank you," I said.

"So," Reese said, "what do you think?"

"And the shelves outside each stall for brushes and stuff—so convenient," Marielle enthused. "It's a terrific barn."

"The house," Reese said. "I meant the house."

"Great," she answered him, then turned back to me. "You know, I wouldn't mind if you kept your horses here with us after we moved in," she said shyly. "You could even give lessons, if you wanted."

"Thank you."

Reese put his arm around my shoulder. "I could talk to my landlord. You could probably have my apartment. And he loves dogs, so it would be okay for Grace."

I stared at them. They were trying so hard. I didn't want to sell my house at all, but somehow selling it to Reese didn't seem as painful. And Reese did have a very nice apartment. Five large, comfortable rooms—I could just consider it a kind of swap.

Marielle touched my arm. "I was even thinking maybe you could find me a horse to ride again."

"I don't know anything about gymkhana horses," I said.

"I didn't mean for gymkhana." Marielle's eyes were sparkling with an idea. "I still have my old horse, if I wanted to do that. I was thinking I might learn some of that fancy-pants riding that you do. I mean, if that's okay with you."

I looked at both of them as they fluctuated between states of happiness and love-struck wonder, thrilled at their future together. How could I possibly say no? I didn't want to move, I didn't want to leave my house. But quantum states are like that. You can only stay suspended in the ether for so long before you have to form a bond with something in order to continue existing. I couldn't be a one-dimensional particle for the rest of my life; I needed to find a home.

"I'll call my agent first thing in the morning," I said to them. "And tell her the house is sold."

Chapter Forty-three

IT IS an ironic universe that creates both the tiniest and the largest of creatures and then pits them against each other in a fragile arena of flesh and blood, where they must struggle until the death of one allows the other to survive.

Poor Abbie. The infinitesimally small bacteria were mounting a relentless war, and the pneumonia was staking its claim in her weakened lungs. It was all we could do just to help her maintain the small margin of life she had left. Matt checked on her every night, I hand-fed her, Richie massaged her and worked on her every day. We were a determined and grim bunch.

The irony wasn't lost on me. That Holly and I had been in a struggle, too. For Matt. For my home. For whatever had been important to me in my life. Unlike Abbie and her bacteria, Holly and I were equals in size, in strength, in determination, but though I fancied I had morals and ethics on my side, it was a struggle I apparently had lost.

Almost a month had passed, and I had spent every night with Abbie. I sang my songs to her and rubbed her ears and told her about the beautiful and troubled country that she had come from, knowing that she could never return to it. I told her about the gold plains and reeds, about wild birds that sat in the strangest-looking trees, how the sun shimmered through the bush during the day, leaving black dapples against the dried-out earth, and about the haunting calls that rang through the night. And I was certain she was listening.

I worked with Margo early in the mornings, reinforcing what she knew and even expanding her repertoire. She fully accepted my presence in the stall now and allowed me to stay close to her baby without rumbling her usual warnings. She had learned to trust me, although I still kept her bracelets on for my safety while I took care of Abbie.

I sat up every night, in the barn, watching over Abbie as she fought to breathe. I sang songs very softly to her as I fed her, and then remained quiet when I was finished, in order to let the two animals rest. I had never allowed myself such quiet. My initial panic at the stillness gave way to anxiety, to discomfort, and finally to a sort of uneasy compromise with the night. I made myself concentrate on Margo's deep breaths, on Abbie's shallow rasps. I forced myself to listen to their rumblings and squeaks, to the sounds of hay being chewed, to small animals rattling in the walls, the rain clattering against the metal roof. I listened to owls call outside and stomachs rumble inside, and the wind blow around the corners of the barn, and I wondered how I had missed so much of it before this. In the end, I made peace with all of it. I could hear my own breath, and my own thoughts, and finally, finally, I was all right with the stillness.

I spent all night either sleeping on a cot or checking on Abbie. Every morning I awoke to feed Margo before I left for home. My alarm clock was an elephant rumbling loudly for breakfast, after which Richie would wheel open the big barn doors, unlock the enclosure, and help me march Margo out into the warm summer sun. Abbie followed, with our assistance; Billy DuPreez had told Matt it was important that Abbie spend time in the sun. Richie and I would support her wobbly walk and weakened body with cotton ropes until we reached the sunny patch of ground that we had covered with straw. Abbie would drop down and nap there, next to Margo. Every morning, before I left, I would sponge Abbie down with cool water, and rub Vaseline on the tip of her trunk, so that it wouldn't get chafed raw by the mucus that poured from it. Every day I listened with a stethoscope to the rales in her lungs, not really sure what I was hearing, but hoping that it wouldn't suddenly change into something more ominous.

One night, as I fed her, and told her stories of Makuti, she squeaked and barked and touched my face with her trunk.

"I know," I said to her. "You're a very brave little ellie."

She pulled the bottle from my hand and held it out to me. "Thank you," I said, and plugged it back into her mouth, "but you need it more than I do."

The barn door creaked behind me, and I looked up. It was Matt. He managed to come every evening, after his practice closed for the day, to check on her. We usually acknowledged each other with a stony nod and then worked together without a word, doing what needed to be done, after which Matt would leave without much more than a curt good night. He was a very good vet, I knew that. He was fighting very hard to save Abbie, I knew that, too. And though I hated and resented him, I respected his skill and dedication. His absolute commitment to animals was one of the things that I had loved about him.

Tonight, he took the stethoscope I had left outside the enclosure and listened to Abbie's lungs. There was no expression on his face as he passed it along her side, then between her front legs. Next would be her temperature.

He held the thermometer up to the light and checked the digital readout before inserting it under her tail. I watched without comment, as I did every night. He waited a few minutes before checking it.

"Hmm," he said to himself, furrowing his brow and resetting the thermometer for another try.

"What?" I asked him, but he didn't answer. He pursed his lips and took her temperature again. I looked away. If her temperature went any higher, I knew that it was the end, that the bacteria had won. The tiniest of the animal kingdom—were they animals?—Matt had called them pathogens—and they would have defeated her. Defeated us. These one-celled, minute, weak particles of life, these parasites that need flesh and blood to exist, could wind up winning the battle. I just couldn't watch Matt as he looked at the thermometer for the third time.

"Free beaver smoke," he uttered.

I was staring at the far wall so I wouldn't see the numbers, but his words still filtered into my brain. I startled. "What?" I asked. "What did you just say?"

He was still kneeling over Abbie, and he looked up at me with tears in his eyes. "Oh, Neelie," he said hoarsely, "her fever broke. It's totally normal. I really think she's going to come out of this."

It took me a full minute to absorb his words.

She was going to live. She was going to be all right. My elephant child.

Tears of joy flowed down my face. I dropped to my knees and laid my head on hers and ran my hands over her face and wept.

"You saved her," I said to Matt. "You did it."

He took a slow, deep breath. "You did, too," he said. "I never saw anyone work so hard over an animal."

We looked down at Abbie. She was sleeping, taking long, regular breaths, her sides rising and falling in perfect rhythm.

"Thank you," I said to Matt.

He put his hand on my shoulder and I left it there, and he looked at me with such hunger that I had to look down at Abbie again.

"I wanted to save her," he said, "for you. Because it was so important to you."

"Thank you," I said again.

"Please—" he started, then he dropped to his knees and buried his face in his hands. His tears streamed through his fingers and left splotches on his trousers. I watched him cry. I watched the tears run through his hands and down his arms. I tried to summon my anger. "Please," he said. "Please talk to me again."

I took a deep breath. "Okay," I said. "Okay."

I would let him tell me what he wanted to tell me. I would listen to him; I owed him at least that. And it was only because, in another of the universe's little ironies, in what could be the punch line for some twisted cosmic joke, Matt had finally given me a baby.

Chapter Forty-four

Diners make the best confessionals. The food is never good enough to be the focus of attention, the booths provide enough intimacy for talking, yet just enough public display to keep the conversation from getting too emotional. There is no starched waiter to fuss over you if you don't finish your meal, just an indifferent waitress who usually and correctly assumes you didn't eat because the food was awful. There is just enough murmuring in the background to mask declarations, apologies, denials, and explanations, as well as fill in those deadly excruciating silences that can inhibit a juicy tête-à-tête.

Plus you can order just about anything you want.

Matt and I decided to meet at the local diner.

He started with a hamburger and profuse apologies, the former of which he smothered in hot sauce. I started out like my Caesar salad—cool, crisp—then ultimately wilted into a blobby mess.

"It's been hell for me," he said slowly. He stacked his French fries like Yule logs before covering them with a liberal sprinkling of salt. He always stacks his food in neat piles when he is nervous.

"It hasn't been a picnic for me, either," I said, spearing an unappetizing, desiccated anchovy and laying it carefully across my napkin like an offering to the diner gods.

A little vein throbbed across his left temple. It's his tension vein, and it always puts in an appearance when things are getting emotionally difficult for him. I poked around at my salad, wondering where this was all going.

"First," he said, "I want you to know that I really am sorry. I never meant to hurt you."

I nodded. I had heard all that before. I was waiting for something new. Something that made it worthwhile to sit in an ancient aqua-and-red diner, on a ripped plastic seat that had duct tape holding it together, and eat crummy Caesar salad.

"I wanted to build up my practice, make a lot of money," he started. "For you."

I dropped my second anchovy. "Don't tell me you screwed around for me," I enunciated in deadly tones, making sure to keep my voice low. There's only so much background noise a diner can produce, and I didn't want to compete with the lottery Quick Draw monitors to become the evening's entertainment.

"Listen to me," he said, holding up a hand. "Please, let me explain."

"Go ahead," I said, crunching my way through the croutons strewn across the top of my salad. You can't mess up croutons too much.

"I don't even know how to start." He took a deep breath. "I guess it was because I wanted to have a big practice." He thought about his statement. "No, actually, Holly wanted a big practice."

Yeah, I thought, of course it had to start with Holly-Grabitall.

"She came from this huge practice in Colorado, big surgery, four surgeons, full-time radiologist, huge," he said wearily. "She kept telling me how we could do the same if only I had the guts. The ambition."

"Guts," I said encouragingly. "Okay."

"We could be big, she said." He picked up a French fry, lost in thought.

"Big?" I repeated.

"Yeah." He ate the fry. Then another. I watched him and thought that, at this rate, we were going to be sitting here until the breakfast specials.

"It was the money," he said softly. "She had this whole plan worked out. I would take out a second mortgage and another loan and make her a partner for orchestrating the whole idea . . ." His voice was filled with pain. "She was so sure of things. She was so enthusiastic."

I could see her, blonde and vivacious, with all that outdoor Colorado c'mon-guys-let's-ski-the-big-one enthusiasm.

He dropped his head. I lost him again. I picked at my salad. Was anything worth eating this salad?

"I thought I would keep it all a secret, and then, after we built the new building—"

"New building?" I interrupted, shocked at his words. "What new building? What was wrong with the old one?"

"Wasn't big enough," he said. "I was going to tell you all about it. When we were finished. To surprise you. We were going to add on this whole . . . _wing_ . . ." His voice cracked again. "I wanted you to be able to train horses, maybe open up an equestrian center, big indoor arena, with all the money we were going to make." He dropped his head in his hands and gave a brief, broken sigh.

It brought the waitress back to our table. "Is everything all right?" She looked concerned that perhaps something might not be exactly appetizing about a dried-out burger with burnt onions, cold greasy fries, old coffee, and a droopy Caesar salad with anchovies that looked like leftover bait from a fishing contest.

"Everything's fine," I reassured her. Matt never looked up.

"Does he want a refill on his coffee?" the waitress asked me.

"He's fine," I said to her, and she left. "Go on," I cued Matt. "Indoor arena."

"Yeah," he said. "Holly had these amazing plans. Investors, and movie-star clients that she was talking to all the time—"

"There are no movie stars around here," I said.

"We were going to have a pet limo from the city. Take in boarding—a pet hotel, very posh. Offer them a week in the country. Like Pet Camp." He gave me a "Wasn't that the craziest thing you've ever heard?" embarrassed grin.

"Pretty ambitious," I said.

"So I went ahead," he said. "I got myself in deeper and deeper—with the money and all."

"So you did," I said.

"And then we signed the contracts, and ordered all the equipment . . ." His eyes got a faraway look. He was seeing himself signing contracts.

"Yeah?" I encouraged, trying to bring him back to the diner.

"And—then I found out about Holly. Her secret." His voice dropped. His eyes looked dead. "And then it all made sense."

My heart skipped. Like knots tied in the dark, secrets always come undone. "What about her?" I asked.

He looked around, as though he were looking for someone to help him. He accidentally caught the waitress's eye, and she came bustling over again.

"Dessert?" she asked.

"No," I said. She gave me a look and I tried to appease her. "But I'll have more coffee." We waited for her to fill our cups with stale coffee.

"Holly?" I asked Matt after she was through. "What did you find out about Holly?" I wanted to know Holly's secret. Maybe he was going to say that Holly was an evil sorceress, or at least a vampire. That she hadn't come from Colorado at all, that she had come from some cave deep in the bowels of Transylvania, and that she bit him on the neck when he wasn't looking, sucked out his blood along with his common sense, and that he had been under a spell ever since.

"She's—she's—bipolar," he said. "What they used to call manic-depressive. That's why her marriage broke up. That's why she lost her job in Colorado . . ." His eyes filled and he fought for control by minutely examining his burger. He took it apart and stacked it neatly on his plate, bun on one side, burnt onions on the other, gray burger in the middle. He cut it into four quadrants with his knife and fork. And then stacked them atop each other like poker chips. "She goes off the deep end because she's not compliant," he said, his voice dark and empty now. "She won't stay on her medications. She gets manic, out of control." He leaned back in his seat, defeated. "She just created this whole fantasy about how we were going to pull it all off, and I got caught up in it." He stopped and looked surprised that such a thing could have happened. "I got lost in it with her. I _believed_ her. She told me that she was talking to these movie stars all the time!"

"Wow," I said, "did she get any autographs?"

He gave me a weak smile. "She told me how we needed to build things quickly because they were so interested in her ideas. Spend money to make money, she said."

"I might have understood the money part," I said evenly. "Maybe. If you had come to me. But that doesn't answer how she got pregnant."

I waited a long time for him to answer. To explain it to me. I didn't want to picture them together, but I couldn't help myself. I saw him taking Holly into his arms and pressing her into bed. Or maybe under the Christmas tree. I didn't want to picture it, but it was there, in front of me, superimposed over the pale-green romaine lettuce.

"We had a brief affair," he said very softly. "She was so full of energy and enthusiasm, and wild and"—he looked away from me, his face flushed—"exciting. She never slept, she never ate. It was like she lived on sunlight. She was so dazzling. So magnetic—so—everything. And then"—he stopped here and I thought I heard a sob, a quick catch of voice and breath together—"she crashed." He looked away. His eyes were filling. I couldn't watch. I just sat back in my seat and stared at my coffee cup.

So that was it. That was it. Holly was crazy. Holly was a manic vortex of insanity, spun out of control, like a centrifuge, her force pushing Matt away from me, away from his own good judgment and into the outer rims of the fantastical. But what had he been doing, dancing around the edge of it so willingly?

"You didn't have to sleep with her," I said. "And you could have told me about the money."

"Ah, Neelie," he said. His eyes were rimmed with red now, and he was barely able to look at me. He restacked his French fries into a rough log cabin. "You don't always listen." A few fries fell over; he carefully restacked them "I wanted to tell you a million times, and wanted you to help me find a way out of it, but you"—his eyes finally met mine; hazel eyes, clouded with pain—"you never hear me."

I was going to stand up and shout, "Don't blame this thing on me!" I was going to be indignant and righteous. I was going to call him a liar and stalk off in a huff. But, truth be told, he was right. I don't listen. I hadn't been there for him, and he had fallen. Instead of arguing with him, I sat mute from guilt, realizing he had stumbled and fallen and I hadn't been there at all.

He cleared his throat. "So—this is what I want to say." He sat erect with purpose. "I will pay you back monthly, whatever amount your lawyer says, until you get everything you're entitled to."

I sat back, still thinking, *I don't listen.* He was right. Then I realized he hadn't really so much apologized for the money thing as he had somehow made it partly my fault. And he hadn't apologized for getting Holly pregnant. Somehow that was Holly's fault. I looked into his eyes. They didn't seem sad to me so much as weak. Or maybe I had been the weak link. I looked for the answers in his eyes.

He shifted in his seat, trying, I knew, to figure out my steady gaze. Trying to figure out my silence. "I'll keep the practice going," he said. "Holly is too unstable to work anymore, so I'm interviewing for a partner. Things are going pretty decent again, and I'll pay you back."

"Okay," I said, nodding my head. Then I thought of something. "What about the baby?" I asked. "How is Holly taking care of— what's the baby's name?"

"Isabella." He looked inexorably sad. "Holly doesn't want her. Never did. And she's too sick to take care of her. She split. I don't even know where she is. Her parents are kind of filling in. But they don't want to."

"Why not?" I asked.

"They're in their late seventies. Her father has Parkinson's. It's too much for them. They want to retire to Arizona." He paused, then gave me a significant look. "I was thinking—"

And I knew what he was going to say, my mind practically reciting it along with him, as he spoke: "I was thinking that maybe you would forgive me somehow and we could get back, and we could raise her together."

I poked at my food while my mind split itself into two opposing voices. This was not how I wanted a baby. The baby is an innocent victim. But this wasn't how I wanted a baby. It's a little girl. Elephants adopt other elephants' babies. I am not an elephant.

I could barely look at him.

"Think it over, Neelie," he said. "Please think it over before you give me an answer."

Chapter Forty-five

I DON'T know why I did it, slept with Matt again, but I knew I was going to, as soon as we walked out of the diner. He had turned to say good-bye, and we suddenly embraced, and he kissed me, and I let him, and then, like a lost puppy, he simply followed me home.

Grace was beside herself with joy. Her black-and-white body flew into his arms as soon as he walked through the door, and she covered his face with a hundred bad-breath kisses.

"She missed you," I said.

He kissed her back, then looked over at me. "And you?"

I shrugged. "I guess I missed you, too," I said.

He held out his arms to me, and we embraced, and I let him lead me upstairs.

＊　　＊　　＊

It felt like home, to be in Matt's arms again. Like putting on your comfy sweats after a long day of dress-up. Like a deep breath after a long run. It was familiar and sweet, and comforting, and I didn't let myself think about anything at all except how he felt. I just responded to his hands and his lips and the sound of his words telling me how much he missed me and how much he loved me and how much he wanted me. We moved together, in a familiar chore-ography, like we hadn't been apart all those months.

＊　　＊　　＊

When it was over, he was where he had always belonged, next to me, lying on his side of the bed, asking me if I loved him. Yes, I said, and I supposed I did. The heart keeps things locked up in funny compartments, and we can't always empty them. He asked if I forgave him, and I thought, at some point, I might even be able to do that. But I didn't tell him that. I didn't say anything. And he took my hand and put it across his body and held it there, until we fell asleep.

Morning came, and it was almost painfully ordinary. We got up together like we were both on autopilot, and brushed our teeth and showered and got dressed.

"Please think about what I asked you," he said. "Please."

I didn't answer him, and we left the house together. He went to work, and I did my donut run. I marveled at how routine it felt. How almost perfectly right. How it could be like this again.

All I had to do was say yes.

But I was in too much of a rush to dwell on it for too long. I had to get up to the sanctuary to see Abbie, my wonderful Abbie, who was going to be all right, thanks forever to Matt. Then I had to come home and finish packing up the house, thanks again to Matt.

                    ●   ●   ●

"It was Pity Sex," said Alana when she had come with her girls for their riding lesson later that week. "You were being generous. I know I told you to be generous, but the problem is, you wound up being generous with the wrong man. I meant Tom."

"It might have been Sex for Old Time's Sake," I said. "And now Matt thinks he can come back into my life."

Her girls had just finished riding Tony the Pony and were brushing his thick brown-and-white coat before I turned him back out in his paddock. It was my last lesson with them as the owner of my barn. My last afternoon of being able to look out at the horses while I served hot chocolate in my kitchen.

"Creative," Alana said as she watched me heat the cocoa and milk in the oven, in an aluminum fish-stick tray, since I had packed up all my pots and pans and dishes. "I never would have thought to make hot chocolate like that."

"Tell me what to do about Matt," I repeated. "And that poor motherless baby."

"Interesting hint of haddock," she said, sniffing her chocolate, then directing her attention back to me. "It all depends on what you want out of life."

"What should I want?" I asked.

She took a tentative sip of her drink, then continued talking. "If you take Matt back, with his baby, you know you will always have Holly somewhere in your life, forever."

"I know," I said. "I feel sorry for Matt and the baby." I poured Alana more hot chocolate. "And I'm trying very hard to summon sympathy for poor, sad Holly-Mental."

She touched my hand. "You can have all the sympathy in the world," she said. "Just don't feel like you have to wrap your life around it."

*   *   *

Since Reese had been saving his money from the age of eight, he was able to pay cash, and a week later, the paperwork was complete. Matt and I sat next to each other, across from Reese and Marielle, and exchanged signatures and checks and enough paperwork to boost the logging industry for the next millennium. The house was sold, and it was time for me to move.

*   *   *

I dreaded moving day. I wished I could have hidden out at the sanctuary and skipped the grunt-labor part and then just blithely gone home to my new apartment, but I had to direct traffic, all the removing of cartons and moving of furniture and erasing of memories as I bid my house good-bye.

Reese generously offered to help. I rented a U-Haul, and it got loaded by the grace, muscle, and brawn of several of Reese's college students. I paid them in cheeseburgers and pizza, which was all I could afford, and I even threw in a bonus of several boxes of donuts, although I was certain that Reese had added to their take with some actual currency. I left some of my furniture behind—with Reese and

Marielle's excited approval—a sort of start-up gift to the happy couple, who were very . . . well, happy.

After the truck left, I walked through the house one last time as its official ex-mother, to reassure it that it was going to be all right.

"Reese will take very good care of you," I said to the bare and solemn-looking walls and staring, unblinking windows. Then I extracted a promise that it would take good care of Reese. That its furnace would not go out on cold nights, that the septic system would remain pure and flowing and not get spiteful and stop up some morning when Reese and Marielle were running late and rushing to get to work. Both those disasters had occurred during my reign, and after several large checks to a local plumber and a stern lecture to the pipes, Matt and I had restored the balance of power to ourselves. I wanted to make sure it remained that way for Reese and Marielle.

I said good-bye to Mousi and Conversano. I had sort of given Mousi to Marielle. After a few lessons on him, she adored him, and I knew she would be a good mother to him. She moved Rocky, her retired gymkhana horse, a few days earlier, to his new stall in the barn, where he struck up an immediate friendship with Mousi. They were trading war stories over a pile of hay when I went out to say good-bye. I promised Conversano that I would find him a good home, and I gave Tony the Pony an extra hug. They would be fine, I knew. Marielle would be taking good care of them in exchange for lessons.

I also advised Reese and Marielle to burn white candles in every corner of each room to cleanse away any negative energy left over from Matt and me. I wanted them to start with a clean slate. That last suggestion was courtesy of Alana, who also recommended smudge sticks.

"It's Native American," she explained. "It's so that your brother won't get contaminated with your bad luck."

Like a New Age Mr. Clean, I had to light the smudge sticks and wave them around the house, putting the final, smoky touches on bringing in good fortune. I bought a dozen sticks, for good measure, and they smelled like sage and wild grass and reminded me of Tom and Africa. When I was finished, I walked through the house one last time before giving Reese the key and leaving.

*   *   *

Fortunately I didn't have to perform the same rituals in my new apartment, since Reese had always been happy there. Happy. Happy. Happy. I walked through the rooms after the U-Haul was unloaded and unpacked my coffeepot and a mug. A few minutes later, I was sitting in my new kitchen, sipping coffee and taking stock of things. It was a good apartment, I decided. It was only ten minutes more to the sanctuary, and five minutes from a spanking-new donut shop.

Alley Cat hid under my bed for a week, and Grace and I whimpered together under the covers for several nights, but we soon adjusted.

The apartment had new silences, new noises, but they had no memories attached to them. None at all. I lay in bed and listened to the wind rattling the shutters outside and the windows creaking, and thought about Tom, and wished I didn't feel so alone.

Chapter Forty-six

LIKE IT was a patient in the ICU, I managed to get my apartment hooked up on life support within the week. Electricity was transferred into my name, phone lines, cable, Internet, mail delivery, all the vitals were plugged in and running.

Since I had permission to use the backyard, Grace had a place to play, plus there was cracked white plastic furniture for me to sit on, so I could admire the view of a neighbor's cluttered property. I had a refrigerator with an icemaker that, when prodded, spat ice across the kitchen like the character in *The Exorcist,* a stove that had two settings, off and incinerate, and a bathroom window that neither opened nor shut, letting the breezes blow the curtains apart, which I'm sure provided great amusement for the locals.

I also had a new snake plant, courtesy of my mother. And a lot of raisin bread. The latter a bonus, because she had tried to drop off her usual dozen loaves at Loaves to the World and her archrival, Evelyn Slater, had beaten her to it, by dropping off a dozen pumpkin breads earlier that morning.

"Evelyn Slater knows our regulars like my raisin bread," my mother complained as she plunked an overstuffed white shopping bag onto the kitchen table. "But everyone filled up on *her* pumpkin bread and went home. So I had extra."

"Mom," I asked, after peeking into the bag, "what am I to do with a dozen loaves of raisin bread?"

"But you always liked my raisin bread," she said, watching me stack it on the table.

She had come for lunch, which she had packed into the shopping bag, along with the plant and the breads. Next, I removed the plant from the bag.

"You know I don't do well with plants," I said by way of thanking her. I set the snake plant down in a corner somewhere.

"That's because you put them in dark corners," she chided, picking it up and moving it to a patch of light under a living-room window. "And don't forget to water it. The last plant I gave you turned dark brown."

"Isn't dark brown the new green?" I asked as I unpacked a very nice lunch of crab-and-pasta salad and Key-lime pie.

She gave me an exasperated look. "Next time, I'm bringing you a cactus. I don't think you can kill cactus."

"There won't be a next time," I said. "I am never moving again."

She reached out and caressed my face with long, tapered fingers that always ended in beautifully manicured nails. I had always envied her nails, since mine were stumpy and shaped like garden spades, which I'm sure, was directly attributable to all the barn work I did.

"Things will get better, darling," she said. "You'll have your own home again."

I shrugged and tried not to get teary.

"Let me look around and see what you've done to the place." She wandered off through the rooms.

"All I did was fill it with cartons," I called after her. "Not much of a decorating effort."

"Well, I think it's a very nice apartment," she declared, joining me again in the kitchen and pulling out a chair to sit down for lunch.

"Stop trying to cheer me up," I said to her. "Reese has been living here for four years, and you always told him you thought it was dingy."

"But you've done nice things with it." She took a plate of salad from me. "It's very nice now."

"All I did was hang a pair of curtains in the kitchen," I said.

"But they're nice curtains," she said.

•   •   •

Alana brought me a housewarming gift, too: a set of Homer Simpson oven mitts, and a picture of her two girls with Tony the Pony, framed in cherrywood and gold, which I immediately set out on a side table to admire at my leisure.

Alana looked around the apartment. "Nice apartment," she said, while I made coffee.

"Nice," I agreed.

"Is your landlord nice?"

"Nice." I said.

"That's nice." She took the coffee from me. I burst into tears.

"What's wrong?" she asked.

"I don't want nice," I said. "I want to go home."

•   •   •

A few days later, Tom called me on my new phone number. "Are you still angry with me?" he asked as soon as I picked up the phone. I could hear amusement in his voice.

"When was I angry?" I asked.

"When I offered to buy your house for you?"

"I wasn't angry, I was just upset," I said. "I was at loose ends with myself, but everything is all tied back together. It's all moot now, where I live."

"Things are never moot," he said. "Just when it looks the worst, something will come along and pull you up by your mootstraps."

I laughed. "I'm sorry for my attitude. I really should have thanked you a hundred times for your kind offer."

"Moot," he said. "A hundred times would have been ninety-nine times more than enough. Is it okay if I come see you?"

"A hundred times yes," I said.

•   •   •

He brought me a dozen roses. They were a beautiful shade of dark pink, edged with red; their colors glowed, and they filled the kitchen with a dizzying sweetness. I buried my face in them and took a deep, luxurious breath.

"I love them," I said. "They're so beautiful." I poured out the last inch of orange juice from a carton in the refrigerator and filled it with water, and put them in. "I haven't unpacked yet," I apologized. "But I think citrus is supposed to be good for everything."

He walked around the apartment, then stood in the doorway to the kitchen with his hands on his hips and his head tilted. "It's half the size of your old house," he announced.

"But it's still nice," I replied. "Right?"

"No," he said. "I'm not crazy about it."

"Oh," I said, "but everyone else seems to like it."

He crossed the room and took me into his arms. I felt safe, like I was surrounded by a wall that would keep the world out. I rested my head against his shoulder. "You can be stubborn, Neelie," he said, running his fingers through my hair. "Please let me fix things for you."

"I don't want charity." I said into his shoulder.

"What's the point of having a rich boyfriend," he said, "if you won't let him do anything for you?"

I pulled back with surprise. "I have a boyfriend?"

"You could," he said, "if you allowed it."

There are boyfriends and there are boyfriends. I hadn't even been to his apartment. House? Condo? Palace? The only things we had shared so far had been his tent, two elephants, several dinners, and my bed. It hadn't been anywhere near a traditional relationship.

"How would that work?" I asked.

"For starters," he said, "I take you home to meet my family, and then you take me home to meet yours. We do a few things together, and if we like it, we decide if we want to do more things together."

I looked up into his eyes; his gaze was steady and penetrating. I wanted to say yes. I wanted to tell him that I thought I was falling in love with him. That I wanted to be with him. I looked away. "I'm afraid—" I started.

Tom interrupted me. "Let me kick things off. We can start by having you meet my mother," he said. "Just say yes. She's eighty-six, and I think you'll like her. She loves horses. You can talk horses all night with her. She knows a lot of big names in the horse industry."

"I'm already intimidated."

"She'll like you," he said. "You're smart and down-to-earth and funny and beautiful. She doesn't like pretense. Just be yourself. And then you can take me to meet your family. How does that sound?"

"Do you like bread?" I asked.

*   *   *

We went for dinner and a movie, and returned to my apartment. I caught Grace mid-launch, just as she was ready to plant her teeth into Tom's ankles.

"She must be feeling better," I enthused. "This is the first time she's bitten anyone in my new apartment."

"Glad my ankles are so therapeutic," he called after me as I headed for the bathroom to incarcerate her.

"This must be so boring for you," I apologized, coming back to the living room. "I mean, you go all around the world, and then you come here and we do such ordinary things."

"I think about you all the time," he said. "I can't wait to be with you and do more ordinary things." Then he drew an envelope from his pocket. "Open it." A mysterious smile played across his lips. "I have a few plans that may not be so ordinary."

I opened it. There was a little piece of paper inside with a cartoon airplane drawn in and a note that read, "We are going to Bretagne. Pick a date."

I had to catch my breath. France. With Tom. "I don't know what to say."

"Abbie is doing okay, and you need a break," he said. "Say yes."

"But—"

"Say yes." He held his arms out to me, and I flew into them. "We'll take things one step at a time," he murmured into my ear. "I promise."

"One step—"

"Only one step," he said firmly. "I promise. So—what do you think?"

"Nice," I said.

Chapter Forty-seven

THE ORIGINAL Margo was almost as imposing as the elephant Margo. We were in her Park Avenue apartment, two floors down from Tom's penthouse, where we had gone first so I could be inoculated against culture shock. His apartment was huge. And stunning. We stayed for only a moment, to pick up some wine Tom had ordered, but it gave me enough of a heads-up to brace me for his mother's home.

"I'm nervous," I whispered to Tom as we took the elevator. Though I had gotten much better, I knew my ears still betrayed me when I got nervous. My plan was to concentrate very hard and understand every word out of Mrs. Pennington's mouth. I wanted to win over Margo Pennington as badly as I had wanted to win over Margo Pachyderm.

"You'll do fine." He smiled at me. "Just do what comes naturally."

"I'm not sure that's such a great idea," I replied.

*　　*　　*

Margo Pennington was certainly just as gray as the Margo I knew, and almost as wrinkled, though she had Tom's gray-green eyes and very straight posture. Tom made the introductions, and though I almost expected her to banana-slap my hand, she shook it warmly.

"I understand you were off on an adventure with my son," Margo Pennington declared, leading us into a large, elegant living room filled with antiques.

"Yes. I'd never been to Zimbabwe before," I replied.

"It must have been very novel for you," she said warmly. "Did you meatball creature?"

I hadn't been there more than five seconds and my nerves were already betraying me. I looked over at Tom for help, then realized there was no way he could know what kind of help to offer. I took a shot at an answer.

"Actually," I said, "we ate worms."

She gave me a slightly puzzled look and sat down on a delicate ivory brocade sofa, gesturing for me to sit down, too. "He's Tom right arm," she added. "Ferry green coated. Don't you think?"

My mind was racing through dictionaries—English, rhyming, and foreign. I threw in the thesaurus and several encyclopedias for good measure.

"Ah yes, Grisha," Tom said. "I try not to take his devotion for granted."

"Grisha was very helpful," I managed to add, making a mental note for later conversation that "meatball creature" equaled "Grisha."

"And Thomas tells me that you realized that there was a calf left behind," his mother continued. "How did the possum feather your nose?"

I plunged on. "I just knew it," I said, "that Margo—sorry, the elephant—had a baby."

I couldn't look at Tom.

"My namesake," said Margo Pennington with great humor. She leaned toward me and lowered her voice in a gesture of confidentiality. "I know Tom named that elephant after me. I know all about it. I'm not happy that he did, but he tells me that your mother took your naming the baby after her quite gracefully!" She gave Tom a fond look. I gave Tom a bewildered look. I hadn't told my mother about Abbie. He raised his eyebrows, in an effort to send me a message. I said nothing.

"Well, they say elephants *are* wonderful mothers," his mother continued. "So I'll take it as flattery. Bean shoes?"

"Of course," I murmured. My plan was to continue doing neutral-speak, commenting on nothing, agreeing to everything.

Now we were being served hors d'oeuvres and wine. "Cook

makes wonderful little things," said Mrs. Pennington. "Care to fry a hat today?"

"Hat?" I asked.

"Pâté," said Tom.

"Thank you." I took a small point of toast with pâté.

"And how about aghast divine?" She reached out toward the tray. Was I supposed to be aghast at something? I put my hand at my throat as though I could be aghast, but said nothing, in case I shouldn't be.

"I think Neelie could use a glass of wine," Tom said, getting up to pour one. "Yes?"

"Thank you," I said, now hoping to have a sudden, silent heart attack and instantaneous death, instead of the slow, gruesome one I was now experiencing.

I spent another twenty minutes courting disaster as we discussed coconut trimmings and rodeo roses and blue lamp pencils, until, much to my relief, dinner was finally served.

If the hors d'oeuvres were a mine field, dinner was a target range. I was asked if I was tempted to knit doily palm trees, if my cat guns were firing, if turtles ate corn chips. My answers were no, no, and maybe.

"Are you busy with turkey?" Mrs. Pennington asked, while we were eating a lovely dinner of boeuf bourguignon.

"Turkey?" I repeated, quickly scanning the table.

"Oh! Would you prefer turkey?" his mother asked. "I could find out if we have any."

"No, no," I said. "I love this." I gestured to my dinner.

"I thought you mentioned turkey," she replied with a little laugh.

"I thought *you* mentioned turkey," I said. "I'm sorry."

"Ah!" She nodded. "I asked if you were working."

"Just working with—uh—Mar—the elephant—and some riding students right now," I said. "But I have a master's in social work. I was a therapist. I used to have my own practice."

"Marvelous," she said. "No wonder you're so simpatico. And you gave it all guppies?"

"Yes." I pressed on, even though I didn't quite understand her question. "Marriage counseling, problem solving, life strategies." Everything I was failing at, I realized miserably.

"Neelie prefers working with animals because she has a wonderful gift to give them." Tom took my hand. "She has a uniquely intuitive knowledge of what they need, and she knows how to reach out to them. She understands their language."

Yeah, I thought, that special intuitive gift that leaves me totally in the dark when it comes to human language.

"And you ride, too." His mother smiled and looked over at me with approval. "There's nothing lovelier than a beautiful horse."

I sighed happily. Here was something I could talk about. And I did. I told her about Mousi and Conversano, and how I trained horses, and she told me about her first pony, and the last hunt she had ridden in, only two years previously. And I thought, Horses are great equalizers.

—   —   —

The evening passed, and I actually enjoyed myself. After coffee and dessert, his mother gave me a warm embrace good-bye and a little kiss on my cheek.

"You are always welcome here," she said graciously. "I haven't had such fun conversation in a long time. You know, horses are always going to be tropics of pollywogs."

"They are," I replied. "They certainly are."

—   —   —

"I'm sorry, I'm sorry, I must have sounded like an idiot," I agonized to Tom in the car as he drove me home.

"Well, you gave some interesting responses," he said. "Mother was certainly intrigued."

"I'll do better the next time," I promised, already dreading it.

"I know you will," Tom said. "I have two married sisters and tons of nieces and nephews, and my son, so you'll have lots of opportunities. Of course, they're probably all going to be waiting for my mother's report."

"Ah yes, the Mother's Report," I said. "The one that's titled 'How I Met the Village Idiot.'"

"My mother loved you," Tom reassured me. "She knew you were very nervous, but she did ask me, when you went to the powder room, whether English was your first language."

*   *   *

"I ruined everything," I moaned over the phone the next day to Alana.

"Don't feel bad," she said. "You were nervous. Lots of people get flustered when they are nervous."

"Next time I'm going to use a ventriloquist," I said. "I don't think I got anything right."

"You got Tom," she said, laughing. "And that's all that matters."

Chapter Forty-eight

TOLSTOY WAS right when he said that happy families are all alike. I guess it's because they all have that certain open friendliness that invites people into their hearts.

Tom's mother had been warm and very gracious, and though I knew my own parents would reciprocate in kind, I kept postponing their meeting Tom, because just thinking about it put me in a panic. His mother was elegant and dignified; I couldn't imagine what he would make of my mother, who, though elegant and dignified in her own way, was sure to be filling his pockets with crumb buns. Then there was my father, Northeastern spokesman for the beef industry; Jerome and Kate, and their twin Einsteins; and Reese, ever ready with his tacky elephant jokes.

But, despite my procrastination, the opportunity for Tom to meet my family presented itself before long.

Reese and Marielle made a big announcement during a barbecue at my parents' house the next weekend. Though it was fall by now, my father barbecues straight into winter, in the firm belief that people sitting around and shivering make the food taste better. Kate and Jerry were there together, the twins were together, Reese and Marielle were together, my parents were together, I had come alone.

Reese summoned everyone around the grill to break the news. "We plan to get married in two weeks."

My mother, who had been helping my father flip steaks the size of Utah, sank into a patio chair. "You can't be serious," she gasped. "This is so sudden. There won't be any time to make plans."

"We don't want anything fancy," said Marielle. She gazed adoringly at Reese. "Just the families."

"You can't be serious," my mother repeated. She started fanning herself with a handful of big blue napkins that featured a smiling cow with "Come and Get It" printed on its side. "Everything will be booked."

"We'll use a justice of the peace, and then we'll have a nice dinner in a restaurant," said Marielle. "We want to save our money for more important things."

"You can't be serious," said my mother once more. "What's more important than getting married?"

"Now, Abbie," my father cautioned. "It's their choice. I personally wouldn't mind a nice steak house. There's nothing like a good piece of meat to start a marriage off on the right foot." He held up one of the steaks and nodded with satisfaction.

"Actually, I was hoping to spend our money on new paddock fencing instead of a big reception," Marielle explained.

"Who gets married in a restaurant?" Kate asked. She pulled the twins close to her, as though protecting them from the trauma of an untraditional wedding.

"We'd rather do some work on the new house," Reese said.

"And make a few repairs on the barn," Marielle added.

"What kind of priorities are those?" my father asked, now pressing Frisbee-sized mushrooms onto the steaks.

"What's wrong with my barn?" I asked.

Jerome turned to me. "Will Matt be coming?"

"Of course not," I retorted. "I'm not going to even tell him, because, as you might have noticed a few months back, we're not together anymore."

"But that's what weddings are for," Kate said, "to bring people together."

"Only people that want to be together," I said. My father handed Kate a plate with steak overlapping two inches all around.

"Here's your first piece," he said to her.

"You can't leave Matt out," Jerome continued. "He's still family."

"He's not family anymore," I said. "His lease is up."

Jerome kept at it. "He's the twins' uncle," he said. "They love him."

As if on cue, the twins started crying. "Where's Uncle Matt?" they wailed. "We want Uncle Matt."

"See what I mean?" Jerome handed them a "Come and Get It" napkin to mop their tears. "You can't just de-uncle them like that without warning."

"Yes, I can," I said. "That's what divorce does."

"There's nothing really wrong with the barn," Marielle said, struggling through her steak. "We just thought we'd add on a stall or two."

"Well, I won't have my child getting married in a restaurant," said my mother. "We can have the ceremony and a nice reception right here in the yard. In my rose garden."

She pointed out a corner of the yard. We all looked over at a barren patch of land, the roses long dead.

"Where are the roses?" Reese asked.

"We'll just buy some potted flowers from a nursery and have your father plant them," she replied.

"It sounds like too much work," Marielle said.

"She's right," said my father. "It is too much work. I vote for the steak house."

"No one mentioned a steak house," said Reese.

"My mother had a nice French restaurant picked out," said Marielle.

"I know just the right caterers from my work with Loaves to the World," said my mother. "Please let me handle it." She began writing things on a napkin.

"Divorce affects the whole family," Jerome pointed out to me. "Have you ever considered that?"

"I'm sorry it's been so hard on you," I snapped. "I didn't intend to be so thoughtless." My father handed me a steak-covered plate.

"Eat," he commanded. "Those steak houses can't compare to my cooking. We should just have a barbecue after the ceremony."

"So—what do you think about the reception my mother suggested?" Reese looked at Marielle.

"My mother will be disappointed," she said. "But I suppose the rose garden sounds okay. That is, if your mother can pull it together."

My mother was already manning the phone, ordering a tent and a large heater.

"I guess everything's settled," Reese announced.

"Not everything," Jerome said sullenly. "The twins are heartbroken." The twins in question were setting marshmallows on fire and throwing them at each other and shrieking.

Marielle gave Reese a beatific smile. "Your family," she said. "I love them."

*   *   *

We were in Tom's apartment. He had picked me up from the sanctuary the next day and brought me back to the city, and now I was following him through his enormous, sun-filled penthouse. It was beautifully decorated with Kilim rugs and designer furniture, and filled with pictures of famous movers and shakers from all around the world. I couldn't move or shake a baby rattle, and I felt woefully out of my league.

"Wait up," I called after him, "I'm not used to jogging through a house."

"It's just my home," he said, leading me into a cavernous kitchen.

"And the Atlantic Ocean is just a puddle," I said. "No wonder you hated my apartment."

"Sit right there." He planted me in a chair. "I'm making us dinner." He opened the door to a huge refrigerator and began rooting around.

"You cook?" I said, surprised that he had found the time to learn.

"Actually, no," he said, turning around and looking sheepish. "I reheat. My housekeeper made everything. I hope you don't mind."

He pulled out a few covered containers with written directions taped to them and began putting things in a commercial-size oven.

"I'm actually relieved," I said. "I was getting scared that you were too perfect."

"But I wouldn't mind if you tell your family that I'm perfect," he said.

I took a deep breath. "Actually, now that you brought up my family, my brother's getting married, and I would like you to come."

He stopped putting little white ceramic containers of food in the oven and turned around with a look of surprise. "I've been waiting for you to crack," he said. "Yes. I'd love to."

"Great," I said, getting up to help him with dinner. "You'll get to meet my family and watch it enlarge at the same time."

"I look forward to it," he said. He peered at a package of food. "What does 'sauté' mean? In French, it means 'to jump,' but I don't think she meant for me to jump up and down while I cook these appetizers."

"Where's a pan?" I asked. "I can do it."

We reheated dinner together, and then sat across the table from each other to eat. I tried to find a sense of coziness, but it was a little like cuddling up in Windsor Castle. Tom looked at me and smiled.

"To us," he said, holding up a forkful of *penne alla vodka*.

"To us," I repeated, clicking his fork with my own.

I watched as he ate and thought how happy I was feeling. How much I liked him. His sense of dignity and ethics and kindness. His gentleness, his strength. Truth to tell, maybe a little of it was the giddy sense that, of all the women in the world he could be with, he was with me. And I liked that underneath his trappings of wealth was a good, decent man. And, I thought, we did have something in common, because underneath my trappings of poverty was a good, decent woman.

"Are you happy?" he asked.

"Yes," I said.

And I thought, so what if my mother plied him with bread, she would welcome him to the family. So would my father, after plying him with Angus beef. And eventually Jerry and Reese would accept him, and the twins, too. And if I allowed myself to think it, maybe we would marry someday and have our own children, and add to the unique and complicated weave of my happy family.

And I realized maybe happy families aren't all alike. Maybe, since Tolstoy never met my family, he couldn't know that happy families are happy in their own peculiar ways.

Chapter Forty-nine

I WAS so proud of Abbie. She was my baby. I thought she was incredibly smart, incredibly adorable, and, like my twin nieces, precocious even. I couldn't wait for another family dinner so that I could outdo Kate and Jerry with an honor roll of all her accomplishments. I planned to wrap my life around her, set up a college fund for her, save money for her wedding day, and not let her date anyone until she was thirty and found just the right well-bred handsome Prince Charmephant.

"I don't want to hear another word about Abbie," Alana warned me. I had spent the whole of our lunch together describing her latest antics. "I have two adorable girls," she continued, "and I don't talk about them half as much as you do about that elephant."

She was going to help me shop for the perfect outfit—a dress that I could wear to Reese and Marielle's wedding and then to Bretagne, since we would be leaving for France right after. It had to have green in it, because Marielle had made me the lone bridesmaid and requested I wear something with green, and it had to be versatile—something that could withstand plane rides without wrinkling, keep me cool on warm days, warm on cool nights, suitable for hiking on French country roads, attending fancy dinners, or boating on the Seine, and open like a parachute to save me, should I fall off of the Eiffel Tower. My budget was that small.

"If I were you, I'd be rolling on the floor with *agita*. I don't think you're going to pull it off," Alana warned me as I pored over racks and racks of clothing. "I mean, a dress that will go to a wedding and spend two weeks in France without getting wrinkled or dirty?"

"What does one wear to the French countryside anyway?" I said. "I keep picturing lavender dirndls and little white aprons."

"I think that's Switzerland," she replied. She held up a simple sleeveless floor-length green velvet dress and its accompanying shawl. The shawl had a print of tiny lavender flowers against the requisite green background. "How about this?"

"Perfect," I said, taking the dress from her. "Wish I could solve all my problems that fast."

"What other problems could you possibly have?" Alana asked. "I mean, besides losing all your money, your husband, and your home?"

"I could lose my elephant, too," I said worriedly. "What happens if, while I'm away, Richie realizes that he doesn't need me for Abbie anymore?"

"Then you come back to the therapeutic world and open up your office again," Alana replied. "There seems to be an epidemic of dysfunction going around, and I have more potential clients than I can take on. I could send some to you. You have to think about getting back on your feet again financially. You really do."

A few months earlier, I would have immediately dismissed her offer, but she was right. "Maybe it's not such a bad idea," I said. "I mean, to have a backup plan."

"Get one started," Alana agreed. "And don't back out of it."

*   *   *

I had always considered myself genetically an outdoor person. I loved the feeling of sun and wind and fresh air on my skin, had always chafed at the restrictions of sitting in an office, watching the sky through a window. But if I was thinking of reopening my practice, I knew I would have to find space indoors. It's hard to counsel clients with the rain in your face and the wind blowing the papers off your desk. I needed to find an office.

I spent the week before we left for France combing through the rental section of the local newspaper to look for office space. It seemed that all of them were located in neat tan boxes that sat next to run-down shopping centers. Sometimes the boxes were gray.

I finally found one that was different. It was located in a quaint old Victorian house that had been converted into offices. And it was two doors down from a shoe store and an ice-cream store. I asked Alana to meet me in the parking lot and give me her opinion.

She eyed the stores. "Good location," she said. "I see there are several additional treatment centers available, from those great leaders in psychotherapy, Ferragamo and Baskin-Robbins."

"I like my clients to have a choice," I said.

*   *   *

A few minutes later, the landlord parked his car and led us into the house, and to a small first-floor office. It had one narrow window, which revealed only the dark-red brick of the building next door.

"This should work," said Alana, looking around. "You could get back on your feet in no time."

No sky, I thought, not even a glimpse of one. "Uh-huh," I said, vaguely.

She put her hands on her hips. "Maybe it's time to cut back on the elephants?"

"Elephants?" repeated the building owner.

"Elephant families stay together for their lifetime," I said to Alana. "Mother and daughters, and aunts. They keep family bonds. I can't just up and leave; family is very important to them."

"I know," she said, exasperated. "But you can fit the elephants into your evenings."

True, I could spend a few nights a week working with Abbie. And it was a very nice office, clean and freshly painted, with polished wooden floors. The owner watched me nervously.

"And don't forget," Alana added, "you can still do the horses. On the weekends. Elephants at night, horses on the weekends. Your life will be very full."

Now the building owner looked worried. "What kind of counseling did you say you did?"

"Yes, I think this office will do very nicely." Alana started pacing off the floor space to see if my desk and file cabinets would fit.

Suddenly I felt like elephant bracelets were closing around my ankles. I had to escape. I said nothing and walked quickly to the carpeted hallway outside the office. Alana followed me. So did the building owner. I thanked him and headed for my car in the parking lot.

"Just remember," the owner called after me. "No animals. I don't care how you counsel them. I ain't runnin' a circus."

        ○   ●   ●

I watched as Abbie kicked the soccer ball across the grass, squealed with delight, and ran after it. Margo was resting in the shade, a picture of contentment and peace. Peace. I studied Margo's face. The drawn brow was gone, she was in good weight, she didn't seem threatened by us anymore. She had her eyes half closed now, and flapped her ears every so often to move the flies away from her face. Though we had taken her away from her home and brought her to one that was alien to her, she looked content. So was Abbie. Richie would take good care of them both while I was away. I would miss them all, but, truthfully, I was a little afraid that they wouldn't miss me. That my job here was finished. That it was time I called the building owner and rented the office space. I still had the ad in my jacket pocket.

Abbie trotted over to me and wrapped her trunk around my body. She stood past my waist now, and I put my arms around her knobby little head, and rested my face on the top, and pressed a dozen kisses onto her gray wrinkles. She grunted in my ear and pressed against me. How could I give this up? I had never known such peace.

I put my hand in my pocket and crumpled the piece of paper.

Chapter Fifty

THERE IS nothing like a wedding to put you in a cautiously festive frame of mind. I mean, your whole family is standing around looking more attractive than you've seen them in years, wearing their best clothes, and on their best behavior. Laughter is tinkling like crystal, faces are radiant, and everyone is kissing and hugging. They are a study in domestic high spirits.

I had made my grand entrance to Reese's wedding with Tom on my arm, and though I was enjoying myself, I couldn't help feeling that disaster was just one comment away, that someone in my family would mortify me in front of him. That Aunt Lily was going to pat my stomach as usual and say, "Well?," that Uncle Ray was going ask me again why I gave up my "medical practice" to play the horses, that ninety-five-year-old Great-Aunt Hattie was going to drink too much champagne punch and stand on a chair and sing her signature party song, "Don't Let the Stars Get in Your Eyes," that all my relatives were going to start openly speculating on where Matt was and why.

Everything you would expect from such a happy, happy family.

Tom's appearance created a small stir. Jerome the Gnome recognized him right away from the cover of *Forbes* magazine and apparently put his concerns about my traumatizing the twins by divorce on the back burner. Tom bestowed upon me a respectability that Jerome thought I had previously lost when I closed my practice. Uncle Phil asked Tom to autograph his cocktail napkin and then mentioned selling it on eBay; my gorgeous twenty-two-year-old cousin, Jessica, got flirty and tried to sashay past Tom and fell out of her four-inch-high Jimmy Choos into the guacamole; Marielle's parents were struck bashful and just stood there, their mouths agape, until Marielle brought them something strong to drink.

We made our way over to the groom.

"Here's a question I've been dying to ask you," Reese announced, jovially pumping Tom's hand. "What do elephant use for tampons?"

"What?" Tom asked, momentarily taken aback.

"Sheep," said Reese, and then laughed loudly.

I grabbed Tom away and introduced him to the rest of my family.

"Matt, you sure got gray." Great-Aunt Hattie's twin, Great-Aunt Ethel, poked Tom in the chest with her forefinger. "You been worrying too much?"

Kate shook Tom's hand and immediately introduced the twins, who needed no prodding to launch into a prolonged demonstration of their newly honed spelling skills.

"Give us a word, Aunt Neelie," they begged, hanging on me like the baby baboons I had seen in Zimbabwe. "Any word." I spent the rest of the cocktail hour giving them words and sentences and paragraphs, all of which they dispatched with ease.

"Give us a word," they begged again and again. "Give us a word."

"Sound this one out," I finally said, and spelled "G-i-v-e m-e a b-r-e-a-k." They decoded it and obeyed.

I finally found my mother, fussing over the food and getting in the caterer's way. Now that she had gotten over not being asked to make the wedding cake, she felt compelled to monitor the freshness of the dinner rolls. I introduced her to Tom.

"It's my pleasure to meet the original Abbie," Tom said, kissing my mother's hand and doing a courtly little bow with his upper body.

She looked puzzled. "The *original* Abbie?"

I still hadn't told her.

Suddenly the light went on and she turned to me. "Neelie?" she began in measured tones. "Is there *another* Abbie?" She gave me the squint eye, waiting for an answer.

"It's an honor to have an elephant named for you," I said. "Tom even named one after his mother, and she was thrilled and flattered. Right, Tom?"

"Really?" my mother asked Tom.

"Oh yes. It's the latest society trend," Tom said. "Everyone is going to want it."

"Oh," said my mother, suddenly beaming. "Wait till I tell Evelyn Slater."

.   .   .

It was to be a simple ceremony held under a big white tent that had been erected especially for the occasion, in my parents' backyard. The weather was magnificently warm, Marielle looked radiant, and Reese couldn't take his eyes off her. She had chosen an elegant white off-the-shoulder Spanish-lace dress for herself, and a layered, ruffled purple dress for her pregnant sister, who was her maid of honor, and who unfortunately, when she wasn't blending in with the purple tablecloths, resembled an eggplant. There were festoons of white roses and lavender sprigs pinned to everything that was stationary, and corsages of white roses and purple lilies worn by everyone who wasn't.

We were now gathered outside the tent for the beginning of the ceremony. I was in the lead, as the official and only bridesmaid.

Marielle's mother was behind my parents. She cast a jaundiced eye over the backyard. "I wish Marielle had listened to me," she said to no one in particular. "A church ceremony and a nice sit-down dinner would have been more civilized."

"My rose garden is civilized," my mother responded.

"But where are the roses?" Marielle's mother looked around.

"They're dormant, but they're here in spirit," my mother replied.

"Getting married in a backyard is just a step up from getting married in the street," Marielle's father interjected.

"What difference does it make where?" asked my father, taking my mother's arm. "Married is married. It's still a big day."

"That's right," agreed my mother. "Their next big day will be their first child."

"Marielle's just a baby herself," Marielle's father retorted as he stepped into place next to his wife. "She has plenty of time."

My mother turned to him. "She isn't a baby at thirty," she stage-whispered. "Her clock is ticking, you know."

Marielle's mother leaned toward my mother. "It's her wedding day, Abbie, for goodness' sake," she hissed. "Clocks don't tick on your wedding day."

"Clocks don't take time off," my mother whispered back. The chamber quartet struck up the first chords of *Lohengrin*.

"Mother, the music is starting," I said, suddenly understanding why the bride's and groom's families are seated separately.

The music swelled across the lawn. Tom turned around expectantly in his seat and winked at me. The twins threw petals, and I led the march down the aisle.

.   .   .

Marielle and Reese recited their vows, their tremulous voices accompanied by soft music and the ominous buzzing from several varieties of stinging insects, who left their hibernation especially for the occasion.

Marielle's mother wept out loud; her father nervously told everyone sitting within ten feet how hard it was to lose their baby. My parents beamed with pride, and not without a little relief that Reese was finally settling down.

"At least she doesn't have to share her name with some elephant," my mother muttered during their first married kiss. "I'll bet she saves *her* mother's name for her *children*."

"I thought you'd be flattered that I named an elephant after you," I replied, sotto voce.

"Well, high society or not, elephants should have elephant names," she replied. "Like . . ." She paused to think.

"See what I mean?" I said. "It isn't easy to name an elephant."

"Well, I'd know one if I heard it," she said.

Uncle Ray tapped her from behind. "Abbie? What's this about elephants?"

"Neelie has an elephant," my mother answered.

"Well, this is what you get when you let your daughter quit medicine and gamble on horses," Uncle Ray said. "They always start small and then get addicted to the bigger stuff. Pity."

.   .   .

I knew they were going to be happy. They were so much in love. And all their words boiled down to one thing: That they were offering each other the traditional gifts of marriage. Promising to become a universe of two. Promising each other holidays and dinners together, and someone to worry if they got home too late on a rainy night, and 2.6 children in the garage. Promising to enhance each other's lives. Lives very similar to the one I once had—a hundred years ago, it seemed.

I took a deep breath and let it out slowly. I had been on that merry-go-round ride once, and I had been forced to get off when the horses stopped short. True, Matt was offering me a second ride. All I had to do was say yes and grab the brass ring, and everything would be restored. I would have a nice house, maybe a barn in the back. Definitely a swing set. And maybe someday Matt and I would even have a child of our own. I would be a therapist again. Look how the ride comes around and goes around, I thought. A ride without a beginning or end, just an endlessly repeating pattern of love and hurting and love and hurting. And then there was Tom, who was just asking me to enjoy the music.

I touched Tom's arm, and he smiled over at me. A new life, an old life. A new career made out of an old career. There was so much to consider. I closed my eyes.

It seems sometimes you don't have to get back on the merry-go-round for everything to go spinning around you.

Chapter Fifty-one

"WHAT DO you want, Neelie?" Tom asked me. "What do you want? How can I make you happy?"

We were in France, at Tom's château, on the outskirts of Vannes, in the northwestern region of Bretagne. We had flown to Charles de Gaulle Airport, just north of Paris, in Tom's corporate jet, a few days after Reese's wedding. We were met there by a driver and whisked away to Tom's estate, about a two-and-a-half-hour drive.

Vannes was a beautiful medieval town with the Cathédrale Saint-Pierre at its heart and a picturesque old harbor as its soul. High walls surrounded the old city, and small colorful shops and outdoor cafés invited hundreds of visitors. We drove through the town's tangle of streets and roadways that wove around dozens of gardens in glorious fall colors, and I had to close my eyes more than once, when it seemed we were on a collision course with indifferent pedestrians dashing in front of us, or other vehicles furiously speeding in and out of the traffic circles like a carnival ride.

"*Eh, touriste,*" said our driver with distaste.

 · · ·

Tom called it his country cottage, but as with his apartment, the name suffered from grave understatement. An ancient château, three stories of rose-granite walls covered in dark-green ivy, it sat high, overlooking the red stone cliffs that lined the coast of the Golfe du Morbihan. It sat like an elegant dowager, awaiting our arrival. We drove through great black iron gates, past meadows so thick you wanted to run barefoot, and dark, brooding woods that hovered beyond like protective parents. Blue thistle and lavender were still blooming everywhere, and their fragrance followed us around the circular gravel path. The scent of gardenia hung in the air like vapor.

To the side of the house stood a small stone barn, and I found myself drawn to it as soon as we got out of the car.

"Horses?" I asked, hopefully.

"Chickens," Tom said. "And, I think, one cow."

I opened a little wooden gate, stepped into a small tiled court-yard, and waded among a dozen or so small red-and-brown chickens, who clucked noisily at my intrusion and pecked at my shoes. I peeked over a blue wooden half-door into the dim barn. There was fresh hay strewn across the floor, and a large brown cow lying down in the middle of it. She stopped chewing her cud long enough to greet me with a low moo.

Tom came up behind me and rubbed his hands across my back.

"What's her name?" I asked him.

"I'll find out," he said. "She belongs to my caretaker."

She dropped her head to take in more hay.

"She has the right idea," said Tom. "Why don't we get something to eat as well?"

I followed him out of the courtyard to the house. Across the gravel path, onto a wide white-columned porch, and through a heavy, arched wooden front door. He led me through a large foyer of ancient plaster walls and hand-cut stone floors into a big cheerful kitchen, with black pots hanging from dark beams, and braided rugs, and chickens painted on the furniture. Estelle, the caretaker's wife and Tom's housekeeper, gave me a small curtsy and immediately set out platters of cheese and bread and fresh tomatoes and glasses of *pastis* and fussed over me until she was certain that I was beyond satiation. Then she said something to Tom, who nodded and translated.

"Estelle says you might want to wash up and rest a bit."

"That would be great." I thanked her, then followed him through enormous, bright rooms with soaring ceilings and tiled fireplaces and thick colorful rugs and overstuffed furniture covered with soft shawls. I felt very much at home right away.

Our suitcases had already been brought upstairs, to a sunny bedroom with tall leaded-pane windows lining one wall. I could see the gulf, iridescent green-blue, just beyond the gates.

"It's so beautiful," I breathed.

"We'll be sharing this room," Tom said. "Unless you mind. There are thirty rooms, fourteen bedrooms—you can have your pick."

Before I could answer, he had taken me into his arms and was covering my face and neck with a dozen kisses. I pulled him close to me. The scent of mint and wild grass and gardenia filled the room, and he slowly removed my clothes.

·   ·   ·

We napped the afternoon away, rolled against each other. I awoke to find him sitting on the bed, next to me, stroking my face and looking lost in thought. I reached up and touched his hand. Our eyes locked, and I saw him struggle to say something.

"Neelie," he said, then suddenly stood up. "I'll check on dinner."

I washed up in an old-fashioned bathroom with sunflower wallpaper, in the whitest, whitest porcelain claw-foot tub, after generously sprinkling the lavender salts that had been left for me into the steaming water. I slid down into the fragrant bubbles, up to my nose, in a reverie of comfort and wonder. This is what life with Tom could be like. Comfortable, endlessly carefree, full of flowers and color and peace. Peace? No, not peace. Love? Tom had never said he loved me. And this beauty, this luxury wasn't really my life.

I dried myself with one of the thick white towels piled on a small carved table and brushed my hair and let it lie loose on my shoulders, then put on jeans and a white tee and sandals and went down to dinner.

Tom's face lit up when I walked into the dining room. "You look like an angel," he said, and pulled out a chair for me, next to him.

We had oysters and the freshest fish I'd ever eaten. And marvelous grilled vegetables and fruits and Kir, a drink made from *crème de cassis* and Chablis, which didn't hit me until I left the table.

"Let's go outside," Tom suggested after we finished our dessert—strawberry-filled crêpes with crème fraîche. "It's a beautiful night." I felt besotted, spoiled.

We walked the grounds and listened to our steps echoing across the crunchy gravel. A barn owl called; an answer came from a nearby tree. Tom put his arm around my waist, and pulled a gardenia from a bush and gave it to me. I was afraid to speak. It was too perfect, but perfect has the burden to remain the same. It can never change. And it can be shattered like a piece of thin glass. I was afraid of perfect. The air was warm, though the wind that came up from the gulf had a strong edge to it. I shivered a little, and Tom stopped walking.

"Are you cold?" he asked, facing me and putting both arms around my waist. "Do you want to go back?"

"No."

"Not cold?" he asked, puzzled. "Or you don't want to go back?"

I looked toward the water. The smell of the sea was being carried on the wind, and washed across my face, ruffling my hair. I could hear the waves cresting against the rocks and retreating, only to return. I felt like an impostor. I had no right to any of this beauty. I was a guest. A guest. And in a week or two I would be home, worrying about losing Abbie or renting office space or thinking how lost I felt in my apartment.

"What is it?" he asked. "What do you need?"

I needed to find my balance. I wanted so much for us to stand there, in the warm night, in the cold wind, that smelled from late gardenias and the sea, and stand there forever. Forever wasn't possible, I knew that. My balance would come, as it came on a horse. A shift of weight and touch, of trial and error, until you sat perfectly even, perfectly fine, perfectly in control.

"Don't you want to share this with me?" he asked softly.

He hadn't said he loved me.

"We are sharing this," I said. "Right now. And I thank you for it."

"Oh," he said ruefully. "I see."

*   *   *

We spent the next week exploring Vannes itself. We ate in a wonderful restaurant on the rue des Halles, and bought blue-and-yellow pottery and leather bags and copper jewelry. We visited antique shops on the rue Saint-Gwénaël and watched the ancient craft of boatbuilding on the Ile aux Moines.

We drove to Belle-Île-en-Mer, an island of startling rock formations, and we walked along a coastline that rested on cliffs of rose and gray rock, while the surf below hammered away with Gallic confrontation. We biked into the village of La Vraie Croix, and bought bunches of white lilies and cheese and sausage and bread and a honey drink, *chouchen,* from local tradesmen whose attitudes were determinedly French, all short, with light-green eyes that matched the sea pounding near their doors. I smelled gardenias everywhere. And every word I heard sounded like a variation of "fwah fwah du bwah," which Tom easily translated, slipping in and out of French as one would through an open door.

It was enchanting, and I should have been enchanted. But I was restless, and Tom sensed it.

"Would you like to go to Paris?" he asked me suddenly. We were strolling along the coastline, several hundred feet from the château, watching small yachts sail by while we ate cheese and baguettes and sausage that had been wrapped in brown paper. "You can shop. It's only about two hours or so by train."

"I'm not really a shopper," I said to him. "But I would love for you to show me Paris."

We drove to Paris the next morning, and strolled through the streets, arm in arm, tripping over cracked sidewalks and eating lunch under ancient chestnut trees in the Tuileries Gardens. We strolled the Champs-Élysées at night, and I marveled at the Arc de Triomphe in the distance. We walked and ate all evening, the darkness revealing a glorious array of sparkling landmarks.

"Paris," Tom said, pronouncing it in French and waving one arm in great expanse as though he had personally arranged the glittering lights and unseasonably warm night just for my benefit, and I was appropriately dazzled.

But I couldn't shake the disquieting feeling that rolled up from my stomach and wrapped itself around my heart. I was quiet—too quiet, I knew, for Tom.

"Are you bored?" he asked. "Or preoccupied?"

"Not bored," I said, surprised that he would even think that. "Not at all."

"Then what is it?" he asked. "Because something's not right."

"I don't know," I said.

I didn't. I was restless. And distant, though I was thrilled with every minute that I spent by his side.

Maybe I was healing, I thought. Maybe things had to shift and resettle themselves before they would leave me. I didn't know.

We returned to his château. We had only a few days left, and late one afternoon, I wandered on my own to the road that ran along the coast. I climbed a narrow path with little wisps of yellow and lavender wildflowers poking through the crevices, and followed it up to the cliffs. Smooth rose-colored rocks, shimmering with mica, that looked out over a choppy turquoise sea.

I could see Tom's house from here. I sat down on a rock and looked back at the granite walls, sincere and solid, that rested within the fields and woods, at the weather-beaten stone barn, its one side covered with dark-green moss, at the weather vane on top of it, a black iron rooster that spun indecisively this way and that, back and forth, as the wind blowing up from the water ruffled past. It reminded me of the way I felt, spinning one way, then another, a little south, a little west. I would open my practice again—no—the breeze spoke—I would train horses.

The late sun slowly drifted into the water, turning the sky from azure to a brooding gray, and the ever-present wind whipped against my hair. I stood up to make my way back to the house.

"Glad you came back," Tom teased me at the door, then gave me a kiss and glass of *pastis*. "Get dressed," he said. "I have invited friends over for dinner."

·   ·   ·

They were a charming couple, Maryse and Gérard, old friends of his from New York, who came back to France on a regular basis to visit their families. Maryse had the most perfect complexion I had ever seen—flawless creamy-white skin—and deep-green eyes and chestnut hair. She and Gérard were perfectly matched in Gallic stature—or, rather, lack of it. They were lively and funny and apparently involved in some of Tom's charities as well as owning a diamond-import company from Africa. They spoke English with the French accent that I was getting accustomed to, and we enjoyed a good dinner along with good conversation. Until dessert.

"So, Thomas," Maryse asked, "what do you plan to do about the culling?"

Tom shrugged and ran his finger along the rim of his wineglass.

"What culling?" I asked.

"*Eh!*" Gérard exclaimed. "They are culling herds of elephants in Kruger National Park. We were in touch with your Grisha, but the sanctuary in Kenya cannot take any more. No one can take them!"

I sat up. My heart stuttered and started again. "Culling? You mean *killing?*" My voice broke.

"Stop." Tom took my hand, then turned to his friends. "We will do something about it, I promise. I have already been in touch with some friends in Kenya, and we're going to try and set up another sanctuary, maybe farther north."

"When?" I asked.

"I will be leaving for Africa right after I take you home to New York."

·   ·   ·

I don't remember saying good-bye to Maryse and Gérard. I don't remember preparing for bed. I do remember that we made love, and afterward neither one of us could sleep. I lay next to Tom, and he took my hand in his. His hand was strong and warm, and I ran my fingers across his broad knuckles.

"What is it, Neelie?" he asked, pulling me close to him. "Are you homesick? Are you ready to go home now?"

"No," I whispered. "I want to go to Africa."

Chapter Fifty-two

AFRICA IS a state of mind as well as a continent. We left Bretagne for Kenya two days later. And though I had never been there, as soon as I stepped off the plane at Jomo Kenyatta Airport in Nairobi, a peculiar déjà-vu settled over me. The air tasted familiar, the humidity that draped over us, the gray sky overhung with clouds—it was all strange and familiar at the same time, as if it had somehow settled into my bones long ago and I had come home.

Tom breezed us through customs, then told me to wait in the airport and promised to return soon.

The airport was old and clean, but had little seating, so I stood, leaning against a wall. There was a broken TV on a stand over my head, buzzing a pattern of white lines, and I watched them waver horizontally, then vertically, then horizontally. People milled everywhere. Some looked to be tourists "making" safaris, loaded down with cameras and the faux pith helmets and tan clothing they fancied one should wear to Kenya. Some were businesspeople, dressed in light suits; some were meeting relatives, rushing into arms and weeping. I waited. There were sleep cabins at the far end for rent, forty dollars for eight hours, and I watched several people pay for keys to use them. I watched people bustle in and out of the duty-free shops, until I grew bored. The television was still buzzing.

"Madame Sterling, it is my honor to see you repeat yourself."

I whirled around to see Grisha, with Tom, several feet away, coming toward me. Or, rather, a cloud of cigarette smoke moving toward me, with Grisha at its epicenter.

"Grisha!" I ran to him and gave him a hug. "I missed you."

He returned my hug, flushing with embarrassment, then kissed me once on each cheek. "Madame Sterling comes for more ellies?"

"Yes," I said. "And Madame Sterling is no longer Madame. Please just call me Neelie."

He took a long drag on his cigarette, squinting his eyes against the smoke. "Grisha is not electrocuted by this," he said.

I was puzzled for a moment, then realized what he meant. "I didn't think you'd be shocked," I said. "Our problems were pretty apparent."

"Ah!" Grisha nodded with understanding. "So—now you are a parent?"

"No, no—" I started, but Tom interrupted.

"We don't want to lose daylight," he said. "We'd better get going."

We hurried across the broken pavement of the parking area. It was small, and crowded with taxis and heavy equipment, and obviously in the middle of reconstruction. We walked for what seemed a mile until Grisha led us to a waiting Land Rover, pretty much like the safari jeep we had in Harare.

"So Mademoiselle comes to serve enamels," Grisha remarked, opening the door to the Rover and helping me in.

"I can't wait," I said. "To save them or serve them. I don't care which."

"Did you hire security?" Tom asked Grisha as he sat himself next to me.

"Yes, we make pickup outside Nairobi. They come from Makindu, much recommended," Grisha answered him, taking his place at the wheel. He gave Tom a sheaf of paper. "Good men."

Tom surveyed its contents. "They seem a bit off the road," he said.

"Everything is off road outside of Nairobi," said Grisha, "because there is no road."

"Okay. After we pick them up, we need to go farther southwest about eighty miles, to the reserve in Masai Mara," Tom instructed as Grisha started up the Rover. "Just watch these roads. I understand most of them have washed out."

"*Da,*" Grisha agreed. "Driving here is like jumping from plane."

Tom took my hand. "You want ellies, you are going to get ellies," he said. "All the ellies you can handle."

.   .   .

The Rover bounced along the scrambling six-lane Uhuru High-way through the city of Nairobi. Grisha drove at breakneck speed, weaving around potholes, and trucks belching diesel fumes, and *matatus*—minibuses—that would suddenly jerk to a stop in front of us, without warning, in order to discharge passengers every few min-utes, before racing rambunctiously to the next stop. An hour and a half later, we were in the town of Narok. It was definitely courting the tourist trade, with souvenir shops everywhere, and street ped-dlers selling beadwork and Maasai shields.

Grisha selected one of the several small native restaurants, and I gladly got out of the Rover to stretch my legs and eat something. He ordered samosas, a fried dough wrapped around sausage or po-tato, and after we ate our fill, he ordered dessert, which, for a change of pace, turned out to be fried dough, but sweetened, called *mendazas.* We enjoyed them with very strong, very good coffee. I used the *choo,* which was native for "loo," which was British slang for *toilette,* which was French for "bathroom," then waited with Tom while Grisha left to pick up the security men.

"Are they police?" I asked Tom.

"Better," he replied. "They're Maasai."

.   .   .

Grisha returned about half an hour later, with the Rover and four Maasai tribesmen, tall, solemn, slim as bamboo, sitting stiffly in their red robes, their short hunting spears tucked into elaborately beaded belts. They greeted me with great courtesy as I got into the Rover and then resettled themselves, two in the front, two in back.

"*Jambo,*" they said in Kiswahili.

"Hello," I said.

"The proper reply is *hatumjambo,*" Tom said to me.

I bowed my head slightly. *"Hatumjambo,"* I said. They seemed pleased.

"Unatoka wapi?" one of the men said to me. I looked over to Tom.

"He asks where you are from," he said.

"United States," I replied.

"Mzuri." They nodded.

" 'Nice.' They like that," Tom translated.

Then one of them said something in Kiswahili to Tom, who gestured under the seat. I took a surreptitious peek. I didn't need a translation. I saw rifles. A lot of them.

•   •   •

The Maasai tribesmen tried to teach me Kiswahili as we drove toward Masai Mara, but I was too nervous about the drive; we jounced in and out of huge ruts and along rocky washouts with such force I caught myself wishing that we had brought parachutes. I didn't remember much of my vocabulary lesson except that *tembo* was "elephant" and *asante* was "thank you."

•   •   •

The sanctuary was just west of the game reserve, on the border with Tanzania. It was part of the Serengeti Plain, and it was under siege from not only the severe drought but, Tom pointed out, government policies that allowed the Maru River to be plundered by industry and repopulation. We passed wandering Maasai tribesmen herding bony cattle that were looking for something to graze upon. Walking slowly along the sides of the road, too, were small herds of emaciated giraffes. There were very few other wild animals to be seen. Tom explained that the wildebeest had died off in great numbers, and the hippos, zebras, and rhinos were now dying off as well. The drought was exacting a terrible price.

•   •   •

We reached the sanctuary early in the evening. It was a simple place. High fences of wire and wood that swooped and sagged as far as the eye could see, and two large metal gates with a sign hanging from one, announcing we had reached the Ian Pontwynne Elephant Rescue.

Two of the Maasai jumped from the Rover and pulled at the creaking gate until it opened; then we drove through, to follow a long, narrow, dusty path to the main compound. Chief Keeper Joseph Solango greeted us warmly and gave us a quick tour while he brought us to Mrs. Pontwynne.

I was wild with anticipation, but, to my terrible disappointment, there were no ellies to be seen. They were busy playing, Joseph explained, in their favorite nearby watering hole, or perhaps busily engaged in a game of soccer or practicing how to uproot small trees. They would be returning soon, he promised, when he saw my face.

We met Dr. Annabelle Pontwynne, a plump, pleasant widow in her sixties who had spent her life rescuing elephants. In her long, flowing yellow dress, she resembled one of the buttercups that grew in such abundance along the roads.

Her office was little more than a large wooden cabin, with dozens of elephant pictures hanging on the walls, names and dates below, like portraits of students who had graduated. The furniture was comfortable, several brown leather chairs facing a large desk with a computer. In the corner stood a small table with metal chairs, where she served us tea and little honey cakes. She and Tom spoke about elephant formula, and medical care, and rescue protocols, but I was restless. I wanted elephants.

"Family is everything to them," she said more than once. "They must have that security. They are happiest when they are with their families."

I wondered if Tolstoy knew that all happy elephant families were alike, too.

She and Tom were discussing finances now, and my anticipation had gotten unbearable. I finally excused myself.

The preserve was dusty and dotted with acacia trees, and rough outcroppings of red rock, and muddy ponds that were in their last gasps of drying up. Red sand packed hard under my shoes as I wandered aimlessly around the compound. The sky was blue, and still heated, even though it was full evening now, and the few high, white clouds offered no respite from the blazing sun. I wiped my face and sat down on an acacia stump. The air was heavy with dust and humidity, and smelled of elephant and acacia leaves and the profusion of thin, reedy grass that managed to get a toehold in the sand. Everywhere smelled of rock and heat and earth that was nothing like the earth at home. Mostly, it smelled from elephants.

"Mademoiselle Neelie?" Grisha was calling me.

I jumped up.

"Madame Pontwynne recalls you to see ellies now," he said. I followed him back to her cabin, my heart pounding with anticipation. She and Tom were just coming out of her office, and she greeted me again with much warmth.

"It's time for the babies. They're coming in for the night," Mrs. Pontwynne announced, clapping her hands together. "You won't want to miss them."

Chapter Fifty-three

FROM THE distance, a great rumbling rose through the air and rolled toward us. The sound of elephants. My stomach lurched with excitement, and I held my breath and pressed my hand to my mouth and waited. A long line of squealing, trumpeting baby ellies, marching single-file, little trunks grasping the tails in front, ears flapping, were trammeling toward us. A long line of gray, dusty little bodies, of little heads nodding in rhythm with their thumping steps, dozens of them, with all the crazy grace and lumpy good humor they could muster, marching through great puffs of dust that floated above them, giving the impression that they were stepping out of a dream. Some wore blankets—their small bodies draped in pink and green and yellow cloths to protect them from the heat and sun. Since they had no mother to stand under, a blanket would have to do. Suddenly we were surrounded by elephants. All sizes. Some tiny and fragile, and anxiously pressing close to their keepers, nervous about us. Some half grown. They were friendly, examining our faces, going into our pockets, opening our hands, touching our bodies with their trunks, sniffing, rubbing, grasping, grunting with curiosity. Pushing against me. Batting their caramel-brown eyes and thick black eyelashes, trumpeting and squealing and sighing.

"Oh!" I gasped. My heart was full. My heart was breaking. These were all orphans. Babies left by a storm of ivory poaching, of culling, of their mothers' getting caught in wire snares and dying slowly and horribly, victims of human greed and callousness. Babies left behind, ruptured from their family, left to die. Babies rescued in the barest nick of time. But because of this place, they would live. They would live.

Satisfied they had examined us thoroughly, they picked up a trot, urged and guided by their keepers, to move along, not to push, to stay in line, to behave themselves. Like rambunctious grade-school kids at recess, they were herded, one by one, the larger ones into roomy wooden stockade pens to spend their night, two or three together, and the very young and fragile, the newly rescued infants, each put into their individual huts, just small enough for them and one keeper, to get ready for bed. Until they were much older, they would have a keeper always by their side, to feed them and to sleep with them, to be their family.

I would have stayed there forever, watching them. I could have. I felt nothing of the heat, of the dust. I saw nothing but elephants. Tom pulled on my elbow. The red sun was sinking into a cerulean sky, its aching brightness relenting into night.

"Let's go," he said. "It's time for them to sleep. And I could use some sleep myself."

*   *   *

We spent the night in a small hut on the edge of the sanctuary. We lay in bed together, on a single mattress, under a slow, ineffective ceiling fan that barely moved the thick air. Our bodies clung together from the humidity, slick with wetness, sharing secret intimacies, bare skin to bare skin. Tom ran his fingers through my hair, letting the strands fall back against the pillow.

"Are you happy?" he asked me.

"Oh yes," I said, and pulled him close and kissed him, losing myself in his scent and his warmth and the feel of his arms wrapping around me. We made love, his body melting into mine, the heat of the air now no match for his touch.

We fell apart and held hands.

"I'm glad I can make you happy," he said. Then he paused, turning to face me. "I have, haven't I?"

"Yes." I smiled back at him. "I have never felt this way."

His eyes searched my face. "I want you to know that I love you," he said simply.

I caught my breath. A thousand things raced through my mind. I had gotten a glimpse of what I wanted in life. I had dug into the depths of my own heart and knew where I wanted to be, where the pieces of the puzzle lay for me; I just had to pick them up and put them into place.

"Oh, Tom," I said, putting my hand on his arm.

His face fell. "What's wrong?" he said. He pulled his arm away from me and sat up, clearly frustrated.

I sat up, too. "I think I want to stay here," I said.

"To do what?" he asked. He reached over and turned on the battery-operated lamp. His hair was tousled; his eyes squinted against the light. He looked so handsome that I ached to pull him close again. Yet I could almost feel little gray trunks sniffing again at my face, pulling at my pockets. I belonged with them.

"I don't know," I said. "Maybe I could be a keeper?"

Tom laughed. "You have to commit yourself to living with them for ten or twelve years," he said. "You can't do it on a whim and then leave them. You have to be their family. Do you think you could sleep here for ten years?"

"No," I said, feeling stupid.

"But I can offer you something else," he said, his voice quiet. He turned my face to him, gently cupping it with his hands, and looked deep into my eyes.

"What?" I asked.

He grew solemn. "Isn't there anything you want from me, Neelie?" he whispered. "I can give you anything."

I was afraid to answer him. I loved him, I loved him so much, but I couldn't get the words out. He was part of my puzzle. He was the main piece, he fit under my heart, and I couldn't tell him, because I was afraid that fitting him in would not leave room for the other pieces.

"Don't you want to marry me?" he asked softly. "I asked you when we were in Bretagne, but you refused me."

"You asked me to share," I said. "You never said you loved me."

"Ah!" He thought about that. "You're right. I was trying to be so careful with you. You withdraw so easily." He pushed my shoulders down gently on the mattress. "Listen to me," he said, lying down again, next to me, and turning on his side to face me. "I love you. I love you. I can't picture my life without you. I am asking you to marry me."

"Tom," I said.

"But you have to know this," he continued, a shadow crossing his face. "I can give you anything except children. I don't want children at this stage in my life. You understand? I don't want children."

Children. A daughter. If I married him, they would never be mine. I studied the length of his arm for a moment, tracing the hair with the tip of my finger. There was a man waiting for me in New York who could give me at least that. An ellie trumpeted outside.

"Do you mind so much?" he asked.

I reached over and stroked his face, then dropped my arm back to my side. Why did the universe feel so compelled to give and take away with the same hand? I tried to throw the gears in my mind into forward, to picture myself in the future, without children. Every year that I spent with Tom, my clock would tick on, every minute, every day, ticking away the chance of a child, until it was too late. I could hear Tom next to me, his breath catching, then letting go in a soft puff. I loved him. We fit, I knew that. I would love him for the rest of my life. An ellie trumpeted again.

"I'm sorry," he said very softly. I could barely hear him. "I have a son—but it was a different stage in my life then. I just wouldn't make a good father now." He lay back against his pillow.

It was a crossroads, I thought. I was standing at a crossroads, with arrows pointing in two different directions at the same time, like in *The Wizard of Oz*. Here and there. Babies and ellies. I laid myself down and rolled close to him. He put his arms around me.

"You don't have to make a decision right now," he said past my ear, into the dark.

"Tom," I said softly. "Oh, Tom, I love you so much. I don't know what to do."

Chapter Fifty-four

TOM MADE a second proposal over breakfast the next morning. Someone had brought us a tray with hot coffee and fried sweet dough, and fruit, and we were washing up and dressing and eating all at the same time.

"How would you like to help me set up the new sanctuary?" Tom suddenly asked me. "You'll be working with Grisha, maybe Maryse and Gérard, maybe a few others from my organizations."

I gasped. "Do you mean it?"

He nodded and took a great gulp of coffee. "Of course I do," he said. "But it'll mean lots of travel and very hard work. That's why I haven't mentioned it before. You see the conditions. I didn't know if it was something—"

"Yes!" I interrupted him.

"You'll be working with my charities. We'll be sending food and stealing eleph—"

"Yes!" I fairly shouted. "Yes! Yes!"

He pulled me close to him. I pulled away.

"I can do it," I said earnestly, looking up into his face. "I don't care how hard it is."

"Have I finally made you happy?" he said, grinning.

"Yes," I said. "I have everything I want."

* * *

We bade good-bye to Mrs. Pontwynne, and I stood by the nursery with her and Tom to watch dozens of ellies, their breakfasts finished, their little trunks wrapped around little tails, marching along, squealing and grunting excitedly, ready for another day of play.

Mrs. Pontwynne hugged us both and wished us Godspeed. We got back into the Rover with Grisha and the security men and started our journey once again.

Tom was looking for large parcels of land that would be suitable for a new sanctuary, and now we made our way east toward the Rift Valley, Grisha driving, the four Maasai tribesmen sitting, one in each corner of the Rover, holding rifles, like the corners on a four-poster bed.

We followed the road east from Masai Mara, then north along the Great Rift on the "Italian Highway," locally nicknamed for the Italian POWs who built it during World War II. It obviously hadn't seen much repair since. We continued north for three or four hours, through the valley, getting jolted along red dirt roads, bouncing in and out of craters, swerving around boulders that had fallen on the wayside. The valley itself was filled with grasses just turning green from the rains, hazes of pink wildflowers and yellow buttercups rimmed the sides, contrasting sharply with clusters of small tin shacks. To the west was a ridge of brown-red mountains. As we drove along the crest, the huge, majestic sweep of the valley dipped below us, enormous and breathtaking. The Rift cuts across the whole of Kenya, through Africa from Syria to Mozambique, and one very poor road more or less follows it. Our Rover scrabbled up steep ascents, bounced along precipitous plateaux, then hurtled again into the wide valley below.

As we drew toward Lake Turkana, the land became desolate, arid, and far too inhospitable for Tom's purposes. Tom stood on the barren rock-dry soil and shook his head. Though the parcel he had been directed to was very large and relatively inexpensive, it wasn't suitable at all. We would make camp that night and turn around first thing in the morning for the long drive back.

"I didn't want to go south again," Tom said, as I helped him set up the tent for sleeping, "because it makes it hard to get the elephants there, but we may have to consider settling somewhere near Mount Kenya or Kilimanjaro. Maybe even Tanzania." He stopped driving a stake into the ground to look at me. "Are you up for it? It means going back to Nairobi for supplies and then another week or two of driving."

"I need to go home first and make some . . . arrangements," I said. I couldn't be away so long. There were Grace and Alley Cat, being babysat by my mother and no doubt being fed huge amounts of steak by my father. And Conversano to sell. And I had to find another instructor for my riding students.

"Do you mean make decisions?" Tom asked me.

"I already made some," I said.

＊　　＊　　＊

It was a beautiful drive down through the Great Rift the next morning. Mist hung along the rocks; the green vegetation looked smoky; the small river that ran alongside the road gave the impression that it ended in a cloud. The Rover jounced and jolted us nearly senseless; Grisha had to stop several times so that rocks could be cleared away from our path, or the wheels dug out of deep ruts that defeated them every few miles. After two days of hard driving, we were back in Nairobi, driving through the bustling, scrambling city, back to the airport.

"I'll leave you in New York," Tom said as we boarded his plane. "I have some business to take care of in London, and then I will be returning. I can bring you back here with me." Then he added meaningfully, "Only if it's what you want."

I stood in the doorway of the jet, just before the doors were shut, to take a long look at Africa, to take a lingering breath. In the distance were mist and grasses and drought and heartbreak and challenges. In the distance were baby ellies that would need me. But I had to leave. For now.

"*Asante*," I said softly. "*Asante*."

Chapter Fifty-five

THE PROBLEM with yellow brick roads is that they not only take you forward to Oz, they can take you backward, to where you have just been. There are no signposts. Nothing to tell you that if you go one way or the other you are making a big mistake. You just have to make your decision and then follow the road to your destiny. I had Matt standing on one side of the road, asking me to resume a life with him that had a house and children, and Tom standing on the other side, asking me to give that all up for dust and heartbreak and big gray animals.

I felt very sorry for Matt and his new baby. It was going to be very difficult for him to raise a daughter alone and run a busy practice. Not that single moms haven't been doing it for years, but it's always a heroic struggle. I realized that, though I cared about him, I had stopped loving him. There are outer bounds to love; he had stretched ours beyond its limitations. The baby, Holly, the vet practice—this was Matt's life, and I didn't want to share it. I didn't want to raise his child. Perhaps someday he would find a wonderful woman; I hoped so, and hoped that they would make promises to each other, and start a home together, and that he would be happy. I wished that for him. I would be happy for him.

And there was Tom. I was so very much in love with him, but I hadn't wanted to come to him needy and broken. I wanted to repair myself. Make myself strong and whole, come to him with my heart filled with peace, my roadmaps in order. My ducks in a row.

Tom had offered me a great position in his rescue operation, and I accepted it. I would be able to help run a big organization and feed people and rescue animals. That much was settled. As for the marriage part, it would come. I didn't want it right away, and I think Tom understood that. He promised to be patient with me, and I loved him for that, too.

In the meantime, I would be making enough money to support my own home. It was important to me that I have something of wood and brick to call my own. A door to open, walls to touch, a piece of land to stand on. It had to belong to me and me alone. I made a mental note to call Mrs. Hammock, former loving owner of Tony the Pony, and find out if her house and barn were still for sale. I would buy the property, and no matter what happened between Tom and me, it would always be there.

We had gotten back from Kenya early in the morning, and I had declined Tom's offer of a ride home. I needed to think and sort it all out, and be alone for a while.

⁕   ⁕   ⁕

I will have all the elephants I want, I thought, driving back from the airport to my apartment. My life will be filled with ellies. I will never stop riding, of course. Even now, holding the steering wheel, I could still feel the reins in my hands; the motion of a horse was still part of my body. The way I made small adjustments to the curve of the road as I passed a slow car in front of me, a little tweak to the left, an acceleration, a small swerve back to the right—the feel was always there, so vivid that I actually caught myself pressing my calf muscles against the seat to keep the car moving forward. The rest of the traffic raced past me like a wolf pack, and I pushed the car forward, to ride through it.

A car behind me honked, and I found myself stretching my shoulders upright in response. I sat deeply in the saddle, waiting for my car to spook at the sudden blast of sound. Then I caught myself and laughed out loud.

What Matt had offered me wasn't enough. Maybe it had never been enough, and maybe he knew it, and that's why he reached out when Holly called to him. Maybe I had always been restless and in pieces. An incomplete puzzle. Maybe he sensed that, too.

And I was hungry to rescue. This is why I rescue, I thought. And because there would always be elephants waiting for me, needing to be rescued.

A lot of elephants.

I wouldn't have to listen to words. I knew I would never be good with words, but that was all right. I was putting the pieces back together, and I knew where I was going and where I had to be and who would be by my side.

In the end, in the end, the call was very clear.